Dearest

Sparrow

& Other Stories of Altered Lives

Joanne Johnston Francis

Published by:
    Last Dance Press
    Tacoma, Washington

ISBN: 978-1974645893
First Edition

Printed in the United States of America

Cover illustration by Joan Stiles Bell
www.joanbell.com

Author photo by Wendy Stephens Firth

Contents

Dedication

for
Mary Ann Fitzgerald

Since 1962 and Woman's College days in
Greensboro, North Carolina, Mary Ann has been
my trusted friend. Without question the quality of
logic she brings to her role as first reader and critic
serves me well. But more essential are those
moments that I always sense are coming when I
know she's been listening in on my conversations
with myself.

The Last El Paso Cattle Drive

EL PASO, TEXAS — AUGUST 1955

THE END OF FIFTH GRADE was the last time Jane moved back to Texas. Her stint in Tucson began in the middle of fourth grade when she kissed Ruben Baker good-bye and parked her rodent skulls and prized Oregon thunder eggs in a cardboard box under his bed. Ruben Baker was the one friend she could count on to stay in the same place — either on Montana Street at the Texaco station chugging down a brown cow soda, or at home in The Bunker doing another original comic strip of the "True Life Adventures of Ruben and Jane".

In a matter of days, Jane would have to leave El Paso for the fourth time in as many years, this time kissing Texas good-bye for good. Her stepfather had finished following the oil. He was done with surveying and with flogging vacation lots in paradises yet to come and with all the other jinxes on his luck. He'd be his own man again. Maybe they wouldn't be in the money, but neither would Skip Rankin be left in some other guy's dust. Jane knew something about that just from being the new kid in town nobody ever gets to know all that well.

The temperatures were brutal those last days — sidewalks blazing hot before noon, bright squares of lawn toasting further in bake-oven heat, the stockyard stink so close and present it seemed that as far as the eye could see, cattle would round into view and thunder down busy Montana Street.

Meanwhile, Jane watched for their dinette set to vanish, followed by their royal blue davenport, and last of all their nice comfy beds — all out the door in an afternoon. Now at least she knew what to expect. As Skip liked to say, "When the time comes for a man to move on, not every damn piece of family flotsam gets to move on too." Her mother as well seemed to embrace this pared down existence well enough, being the sort to stand back in her oxfords and year-old Toni to praise what she could never change that much anyway.

By the end of July though, Jane had begun to wonder what strange new twist in the road lay before them. Long past time when they should be settled in for the night, she'd hear Skip rumble around the duplex, hear her mother's plea they not quit Texas before sounding Marshall out one last time. Something about the name, or maybe just the rare urgency in her mother's tone fanned Jane's hope this Marshall was the trusted old friend of the family that other families always seemed to have in reserve. But too soon time ran out on this last remaining hope, the day dawning for going in for her school transcripts for whatever school came next. Surely this principal would say what they all said: how much her old school would miss her, making her school sound as bereft as the lonely student moving away.

Still, she had to admit that her friend Ruben, so close to repeating sixth grade, was in a tough spot too. He was smart in his own way, but had to struggle to get his thoughts out. Not to mention that while she'd been stranded in too many Panhandle cow towns, he'd got himself crossways with the boss up at the drug store. Did sneaking a peek at some of their comic books for free make her friend Ruben a criminal? And why wasn't Ruben's father standing up for his son? Back when Ruben's mother was alive, Ruben was the one out in front leading the whole parade at Crockett Elementary. Then all the kids were in awe of him, and no one more than bespectacled Jane Hope Rankin marching along with him.

The year at Crockett Elementary was the year they lived just two doors down from each other on Nashville Street. It was the year of El Paso's big snow, the year Ruben's mother Lil took them to Deming with her, where they warbled hit parade songs the whole way up and napped like cats all the way back. It was the year Jane was introduced to satin hair ribbons and black ballet slippers, to ice-cold drinks on the patio, to feel life under the pale pink gathers of Lil's maternity smock. It was a time when she would have traded her own mother for just one more afternoon with Ruben's.

But all that was before Ruben's happy home on Nashville Street burned to cinders, before his carefree mother and unborn baby brother or sister were laid to eternal rest in a single Deming grave, before Jane had to rally all her pixie strength to keep her poor friend Ruben going to school just one day more.

Now it was his turn, time for Ruben to do all in his power to help cheer his friend. There was nothing he wouldn't do, limited only to what a boy of twelve could do. But as their days wound down, he settled on drawing more Ruben and Jane cartoons, Ruben sliding off a burro's hind-end, Jane with a banjo on her knee, him in a pith helmet, her driving a jeep, him beneath the Texaco sign watching her fling her three stone of sheer girl-grit over the back of a steel dust mustang and fly off the Sugar Loaf into the sun, not that his drawings fixed anything. Still, they were his token, something she could take with her wherever she'd go.

Ever since the fire, Ruben and his father had set up housekeeping in a concrete-block, two-car garage Ruben named The Bunker. Built in the open and not in the side of a hill like a real bunker, the inside did have a bare-bones feel to it, with metal bedsteads, metal chairs, and a sheet metal table made to drop down from the wall on metal chains.

Austere as it was, The Bunker was where Ruben and Jane went each day for their after-school snack, where they did homework and read aloud from books on loan from the big public library downtown. Over summer vacation, The Bunker was where they went about transforming the interior, one wall at a time, with their mural of the last El Paso cattle drive, of long-gone Texas longhorns stampeding past the Poplar Dry Goods Department Store and around the downtown plaza through Five Points to busy Montana Street and out past the new motels and airport into the open range.

Still, ever since they started it, Jane had sensed their last El Paso cattle drive mural would fade from memory. The cattle would fade… and Montana Street… as would the busy downtown plaza. Eventually, even the brilliant mind-pictures of her time with Ruben would pale into creams and tans. Some days just thinking about it made her want to hurry and get the whole mural deal over with. And once they'd cleaned the brushes and put away the last of their paints, all she wanted was to be out in the clear Texas air riding their bikes to Ysleta and to the zoo and up past the Sugar Loaf on Scenic Drive.

Yet, it was almost the last day before she came up with the idea of making a pilgrimage over to Memphis Street and Stephen F. Austin High School, which to her was a place holier than any church since it stood at the center of the one prayer she'd prayed since leaving the house two doors down from the Baker's old house on Nashville Street. Almost the minute she got to Ruben's that day, she began laying the groundwork, alerting him to the fact there was one place left to go. She wouldn't say where, not till after he had said not today for the second time and made some excuse about the heat and she'd insisted it was no hotter than it had been all week, which was the truth. And not till she said she'd already had a sandwich when he asked if she'd had anything to eat yet, and he'd said his usual about putting some meat on her poor little sparrow bones if it was the last thing he did.

She didn't say where they were going till he'd finished his lecture about getting up some courage to stand up to her stepfather, and her trying to even picture such a thing, when what was important had nothing to do with courage or standing up to anyone, least of all to Skip. More important was going to the old neighborhood and sitting out on the steps of Stephen F. Austin High School, the school with the beautiful tower, the school where she still held out some hope of graduating one day. But if he was going to let a little heat stand in the way, she told him, determined not to concede more ground to lame excuses, then they'd just go in the morning.

In the end, it was the look Ruben gave her. And the way he said, "If you'd just shut up and listen for a change," then adding, "But you never do, do you?" not saying it once but twice. It was down in the old cemetery below his house that her legs caved in under her and sand burrs bit her cheek and hot tears ringed her neck. It was some time before she brushed herself off to go home, trying her best to remember how it felt when she and Ruben were young and would curl up like cats in the back seat of Lil's convertible when Lil was still alive.

Naturally, Skip and her mother were in the kitchen when she came in the door. For a minute it seemed neither one heard her, but then her mother called, "That you, Janie?" and her comeback, "No, it's the Marines!" came out sour, not funny like it was supposed to. Alone in her room, she pulled the shade down and dropped to her knees, feeling around under her bed for her box of Oregon thunder eggs and rodent skulls and the spiral notebook where she wrote down her thoughts.

She'd just finished writing when Skip rapped on the door. "Anybody home in there?"

"Nope, we all left town."

"Now isn't that a gosh darn shame seeing as how the rank and file need to talk turkey tonight."

"Tell them I'm busy; they have to wait." Did Skip really think she didn't already know there was something in the pipeline? Did he not understand that when they lowered their voices, it was as good as an announcement that might not tell her where and might not tell her when, but did tell her soon? And her report card lay there on the kitchen table for all to see. Was he blind?

Once Skip went back to the kitchen, she looked over what she'd written, and crossed out disloyal. She crossed it out because it was the one thing she could never bear to think about the kind of friend Ruben had always been to her. She replaced it with *complex* because him taking the chance on her thinking he'd called her chicken when he must know she wasn't chicken might just mean there was more to it than she thought. Besides, how could he think that, when he had no idea just how much courage it took to stand up to a man like Skip? And if *complex* didn't fit Ruben, what did? Still, why should getting the right word matter so much when her vocabulary got her criticized anyway by kids at school?

She was busy mulling this over when her nose started to bleed. She let it bleed down her front and down onto the white swan throw rug before she got up to go bleed in the bathroom sink. To her it always seemed like watching someone else bleed, because nothing ever hurt like when she ran into something going around without her glasses on, or like just that afternoon at Ruben's. But surely someone could do better than explain away her nosebleeds like Skip did with that thing he'd say about throwing wet Levis over the line at eleven and putting them on dry at noon, and that should tell her something.

Still, her nosebleeds did come in handy, this time excusing her from going out to the kitchen to watch Skip trace yet another route across their map of the west to another lonesome cow town. She knew before long her mother would find the trail of blood and ask through the door if she had her head tipped back the same as the teachers had her do at school. She'd been pressing more firmly on the wash cloth, sliding slowly down to the cool tile floor, listening for footsteps, thinking about Ruben and the nice thick Velveeta cheese sandwich he made for her just before he bit her head off.

The next morning she slept in too late to sit down with her mother for their usual breakfast. But even she must have started late, for her mother's closet-size office off the kitchen remained quiet. No typing going on in there. For six days a week that's where her mother typed until she came out for a quick sandwich and glass of buttermilk, all her fingers carbon-stained. On Saturdays, Jane's savings-minded mother got up even earlier and baked loaves of bread for the family. Good hearty whole wheat bread, even if Ruben liked to make fun of it. But she wasn't going to think about Ruben, not with that look on his face making her want never to see him again, even if soon she'd have to head back over to his place for her bike.

"I thought I heard you out here. How's that nose of yours this morning? Skip said he found you asleep on the bathroom floor. But before I forget, I had your friend Sonny put your bike in the backyard. He looked very handsome all dressed up in his coat and tie."

Jane poured milk over her cereal and carefully set the milk bottle back down on the table. "You mean Ruben?" she said. "Ruben was here?"

"Now why will I still call that boy Sonny? But yes, he came maybe an hour ago, just after Skip left for work."

"Did he say for you to tell me anything?"

"Just that you went off and left your bike."

"Not anything about why he was dressed up?"

"He did say something about a trip up to Deming with his father. You were still sleeping, and I thought, why not let you sleep? He called last night and told Skip he'd bring your bike in the morning. Well, my Underwood calls. I'll put a quarter out if you'll trim the walk and weed the flowers. It's getting so we can't see the flowers for the weeds. Oh, Ruben said he'd leave your glasses in the usual place. Right, we'll catch up with each other later on."

Throughout that whole morning, thoughts of Ruben wafted up from thick clumps of red carnations, slowing her advance on the mean pyracantha along the back wall. She wondered if he was in Deming yet as she bowed her head to sniff the roses he was sure to lay on his mother's grave, certain the one reason for Ruben to dress up would be for Lil, and yellow roses were still Lil's favorite. She wondered if he prayed for his mother who'd been praying for a baby sister for her wonderful Sonny when she died, as if anyone called him Sonny anymore. And she wondered if he was *wonderful* when he showed a temper that could blow up quicker than a Texas sand storm, making it feel as dark as midnight when it was still only afternoon.

She'd nearly finished edging the front lawn when Skip came home and started the third degree. Who was this Ruben Baker fellow anyway? How old a boy was he? Where did he live? She'd been expecting Skip to ask questions about Ruben, but nothing quite like this. Still, she'd picked up on a few things from observing her mother. She knew, as with a dog looking for a fight, never look him in the eye. So she kept on edging and told him Ruben was her friend who was a very good artist who won prizes. The only other thing she told him about Ruben was he stammered sometimes, but that was mostly just at school.

"By golly, he sure didn't stammer with me last night. He got right to the point. He said there were jobs right here. Good jobs."

"Ruben did?"

"He seemed to think I was out of a job. I told him I had a job."

"Is that what he called about?"

"You tell me."

Jane concentrated on not looking up at her stepfather, trying to remember the exact words Ruben might have said about courage and standing up to Skip. "I don't know what he called about, and he's gone to Deming," she said finally.

"He says his father works for the railroad. He tells me that's where the jobs are."

"Ruben's really nice, Skip."

"By any chance, you didn't tell your friend I was out of a job?"

"No sir. Only we're moving again."

"Because you know the rules, Jane. You read me?"

"I read you. No talking out of school. But I better get going. I better get my glasses before it gets any later than it already is."

"I don't get it. Do I have to glue those god-damn glasses on you or what? And since you were too busy to bother with anything important last night, I'll tell you now, so you know. We leave at daybreak day after tomorrow."

"For where?"

"For California. A place called Modesto. I'll be going into small appliance repair. It's good country out there. Lots of sun. Hope likes it out that way and you will too. It will be my own business this time around. Oh, and we go to get the travel trailer and the pick-up tomorrow. Didn't Hope tell you? It's a doozey of a trailer too. Your mother says it's going to be way nicer than any house."

Jane stopped edging. Had he said they leave in the morning? "When? When did you say we leave?"

He shook his head. "What I said was tomorrow we pick up our trailer and Thursday we take off at daybreak. And you can tell that boyfriend of yours that where we come from, we show a little respect. But I guess you'd have to be raised that way to understand something like that."

She took the long way — up to Montana Street past the grocery store, past the drug store to the rock wall, the same route they took home from school. In the fall and spring they'd just sit on the wall and watch the cars go by. In winter she'd walk Ruben to his house and, before it got dark, take the shortcut home through the old cemetery. It was always quiet down where the pavement stopped, just the occasional breeze stirring in the Baker's lone tree. His note was tucked in the top of the milk bottle under the stoop.

> *I was wrong about your stepfather. I didn't mean to but I think I made things worse. Just don't go anywhere before I get back from Deming. I have this idea and this one should work. Remember my moms friend Patty you like so much? Well, I called her and told her you need help. See you Friday. Theres cheese in the icebox just in case your hungry. Your loyal and true servant, RRB.*

Jane reached into the hole of the poplar tree for her glasses and got out the key to Ruben's house. Soon it would get dark; but before night fell, Ruben's rampaging longhorns would turn into the ripe plum red of a Texas sunset as they fanned into the flat scrubland painted on the east wall mural. And yes, she could remember his mom's friend Patty and her airline pilot husband on Nashville Street. She pictured Patty being so nervous when her husband was away on trips, and going over with Ruben to sprinkle fish food in her fish tank and stay to keep her company. Something she couldn't quite picture was her mother's face when she'd break the news she'd be staying in El Paso with Patty on Nashville Street. That picture came out blank.

When she got back home both Skip and the car were gone; her mother perched on the bed in her bedroom staring down at the floor. She motioned for Jane to come in. "I'm probably just overtired," she said, "but this time I just don't know."

"Where is he? Where's the car?"

"He went to gas up. He's a little upset I guess. I told him I'd want to keep the car and now he thinks everyone's against him. I told him nobody's against him. Just he'll be using the pick-up, and you and I won't want to be stuck at Marshall's without a way to get to the places we need to get to. But I honestly don't know how much more of this I can take. You're much better at this than I am."

"What makes you think that? And who's Marshall? Marshall who?"

"Marshall's his cousin. I've never met him, so let's just keep our fingers crossed. But to me you always seem cheerful. I like the way you can turn something sad around into something nice. I used to be able to do that, but not anymore. But if I were you, I'd hide that last drawing your friend Ruben drew. Skip won't like it, not in the mood he's in. Anyway, I finished your skirt, and I think I got it the way you want. It's on your bed. In the morning we'll make some time to take up the hem."

Back in her room she stepped out of her boxers and into her orange and yellow squaw skirt. She wrote to Ruben, saying she'd be gone by the time he got to read her note. She told him she would never ever forget him going to bat for her and never ever have a truer friend. This time around he'd better just answer every one of her letters and look Modesto up on the map so he'd know where in California she'd gone. Then she added a P.S. thanking him for bringing back her bike and for finding her glasses down in the cemetery. She told him she'd thought about him all day and never could smell a rose and not be reminded of Lil.

In the morning she'd go to Ruben's for the last time. In the meantime, she decided against taking any chances and tore up the last cartoon Ruben made for her, one of a highway billboard advertising Skip's Bomb Shelter Kits:

SKIP'S BOMB SHELTER KITS & RADIO REPAIR
Truth or Consequences, New Mexico
Same Day Service, Ice Cold Soft Drinks While U Wait
See Jane's Amazing Thunder Egg Display
Next Left
26 Miles

Her mother was right. Skip couldn't always take a joke, especially not the ones about bomb shelter kits or the Army Surplus / Rock Museum / Trading Post / Barber Shop set-up before that. The best thing about Skip was he had this huge interest in small desert animals — the round-tailed ground squirrel, the flat-tailed horned lizard, the cottontail rabbit, the prairie dog, even the sidewinder and the black widow spider. And he knew about rocks. But probably the best thing about him was that he was a panther: Stephen F. Austin High School, Class of '38. He was proud of being a panther and a high school graduate. Maybe there was some hope even now she'd make it back and graduate from Stephen F. Austin High School someday herself.

Starry Nights

ADIRONDACK MOUNTAINS IN UPSTATE NEW YORK;
NORTHERN NEW JERSEY —1962-1963

A HIGH SCHOOL DIPLOMA was never worth the trouble in Jane's
book. All that counted was making it to legal age and after that
finding a way to put some distance between her and her
stepfather. Any kind of paid work would do — stoop work,
assembly line work, anything but school work. She'd happily pick
brush like last summer when all she had to do was turn in a day's
work to pick up a day's pay. The worst you could say about
brush-picking was how lonesome it gets in the woods, but better
than high school. High school was all about joining in. "Jane, be
a Viking." "Jane, be a Tiger." At Lincoln, "Jane, be an Abe." An
Abe? She was really going to be an Abe.

But everything had been going along. Spring semester she
took crib courses and never cracked a book. Her mother was
happy since landing her dream job typing at the college. Only
Skip hadn't settled into a routine. Always some place cutting him
loose, followed by another long wait for something better to turn
up; never satisfied, not even pulling down some pretty fair pay
swamping box cars. Had anyone asked her, Jane could have told
them their quiet little life was past due to go off the rails. For
them, anything approaching normal usually did. And this time all
because of a wager that ended up with the other guy a bloody

corpse — a fight that could easily have left Skip dead as well. Likely he tricked the sucker, being the lousy loser he was, always looking to get the edge. That was him all over, that and playing the innocent. And then the incident report had to come back *inconclusive*. For Skip and possibly for her mother too, the *inconclusive* read as it always did — "Skip wins again".

Here they were at the old familiar junction with their same old song playing. Jane told her school they were due in the Big Apple by the end of the week, that they had a gig waiting, when all they had was a phone number of a friend of a friend in New Jersey who maybe would help them out. Her poor mother, poor Hope. Jane had to think even Skip might just be sorry this go-round, not that he'd ever stick it out anywhere for Hope's sake. Never happened yet, never would either. Not till somebody someday did something different that got Skip turned around.

They took turns driving; Jane behind the wheel when the trouble started early their third day on the road. With the sun streaming through the windshield, both Hope and Skip had dozed off. When she pulled over and raised the hood, she smelled heat and saw oil. And not just some oil, oil all over the place.

"What the hell kind of mess you got us into now?"

"We're losing power."

"The hell we are. Here, give me the key. That sonofabitching Baker City baboon! Give me the key godammit."

"It's there," Jane said pointing, knowing what was coming. "In the ignition."

"How many times you hear me say it? You don't leave the key in the ignition. You take the key out when you take it out of gear."

"I only went to check under the hood."

"Oh, you did, did you? You some kind of whiz kid mechanic or something now you got a license?"

"Only using what I know."

"Don't get smart with me, Jane."

"This exact thing happened to Tubby. We were heading into the brush shed to cash out and we couldn't pull the hills. Old Tubby had to go a bundle to get his short block done. Took a week out of his pay."

"You ever think maybe a hundred degrees in the shade might be the problem here? Now get in and try not to be such a big shot for once, will you? We need to make time. If we're ever going to get where we're going, we don't need you looking for trouble every time it's your turn at the wheel."

It was one of those times when Jane would give anything to be wrong. "'Fraid so," said the man with *Pete & Shirley* tattooed on his right forearm, twelve miserable miles farther along. "The wonder is she made it this far. Good thing your little gal here had the good sense not to push her. I'll call around for you though. Maybe take a day or three, but we'll get you folks back on the trail again."

It took a week to get them back on the trail again. That week at the High Road Garage in High Road, Nebraska, in no way was wasted, however. For one, Jane picked up on some things from Pete and Shirley's youngest kid Sophie. Every day after breakfast Sophie turned up at the High Road Tourist Court's single kitchenette unit. "You 'bout ready to bust out of here?" she'd call from the stoop.

Sophie was eighteen, younger by a year short a month than Jane. Her next sister Goldie was already nineteen, oldest sister Harriet nearly twenty-one. Most days when Jane had just sat down to her bowl of cold cereal, she'd see their *School of Twirlette* station wagon already parked at the High Road Garage. Harriet and Goldie had a place in town where they taught baton twirling to aspiring drum majorettes. If Sophie ever made it through High

Road High School, she might even join Springer Sisters Enterprises someday herself.

By the end of the week, afternoon temperatures in High Road were closing in on a hundred degrees again. "There's this lake," Sophie said peering through the screen door. "It's not far. We can go in swimming."

"Okay," Jane agreed, "only I don't have a swimsuit, just these." By *just these* Jane meant shorts. She lived in shorts, though the last thing she thought about was how she looked. She didn't think about clothes. She didn't think about hair, though she had *good hair* according to Hope — thick straight biscuit-colored hair that Hope said she got from her cowboy daddy — hair she whacked off at the ears when it got this hot. Over all though, Jane didn't look backwards and didn't look forwards and didn't look in the mirror much.

"Great. Give me an hour."

"Your sisters, they coming?"

"Harry's at Auntie Ems and Goldie's in Alliance. Ask your mom. Your mom sure looks like she could stand a change of scenery."

Jane shook her head. "She won't come."

"Maybe she will. You want me to ask her?"

"I know her. Anything Skip won't like her doing, she won't do."

"Up to you. I'll fix us a picnic. I make super chicken salad and I baked a fudge cake last night after the house cooled off. And you can bring the pop. Any pop but orange."

They had to hang on for dear life getting to Sophie's lake, the lake that really was only a big pond enclosed in swamp willows. "We'll just go in our birthday suits," Sophie said pulling her peasant blouse over her head. Jane was game if Sophie was.

They swam to the raft and hauled themselves out. "Pretty nifty, huh?"

"Very," Jane had to agree.

"The one place around we can do this," Sophie said. "Someday I'll probably live in a nudist colony. My sisters though, they won't go in their birthday suits — not till after its dark. It's not like anybody's around though; nobody here but us chickens. Teddy's the only one who goes in skinny besides me."

"Your boyfriend?"

Sophie nodded. "Unfortunately, we'll be getting engaged if I don't say something. He's in the service now, but he gets out in two months. I'm going to have to tell him 'cause no way is this girl ready to get hitched. I want to see the world. Goldie and Harriet think I'm out of my mind, but do I care his class voted him most likely to succeed."

Jane was out of her depth. She didn't know about these things. Still, why would any sane person forsake the good life in a steady sleepy place like High Road, Nebraska, with or without the boyfriend if she didn't have to? Here everyone knew everyone. Here everyone knew everything they'd need to know even before the local news came on, the radio announcer only reminding them of funerals, revivals, class reunions, births, deaths, shut-ins, white sales, appliance sales, cattle sales and what was up and what was down on the Chicago Board of Trade.

"What would you do in my shoes?"

"Beats me. I don't have the problem."

"But say you did?"

"I've already seen more of the world than I want to."

"What about the love part?"

"Don't know much about it. Haven't been there, or I slept through it and missed out if I was."

"Seriously though. You make it sound like love is some wide place in the road you only have to slow down for. My sister Harriet sees it like that. All I know is love finds us. Whether we're looking for love or not, love finds us and then love's in charge. And maybe it's already waiting to complicate your life back where you're going. Who can say what lies ahead? Ready? Last one to shore gets the broken bed!"

Later Jane couldn't remember whether it was that same night she dreamed that Skip and Hope took off without her, or the next night, their last night in High Road. All she could remember was waking up in her dream and them both being gone, the dream ending with simply rolling over and falling back to sleep again. The whole thing was that easy; Skip and Hope on their way, Jane finding her own way, the way she hoped it would be in real life one day real soon.

The remainder of their trip east went without incident. For their birthday, Hope had selected a mountain lake in the Adirondacks, arriving there just at dark by driving a hundred miles farther than they usually drove. From their room they could hear carousel music and look out on a beautiful white-painted dance pavilion. At supper the eve of their birthday, Hope asked who wanted to go for a ride on the Ferris wheel. All Skip wanted was to go to bed, but Jane said she'd like to go.

Hope paid for three rides each on the Ferris wheel. After their rides on the Ferris wheel, they crossed to the tavern where Jane drank a beer and Hope had a Coke and opened to her place partway through a romance novel. At the next table two young guys in work shirts shared a pitcher, the lanky one with smoky eyes looking Jane's way as his friend got up and put a coin in the jukebox. "I Can't Stop Loving You" was her mother's favorite song, something Jane would never know if not for Hope turning the volume up each time it came on the radio. Jane glanced across at her mother, thinking how they were almost like normal people

— just your normal mother and daughter out for a good time doing what normal people out for a good time do.

But this kind of thinking made Jane nervous and, sure enough, when they got back to their motel room, the family pick-up was nowhere in sight. Still, her mother didn't act bothered, saying only another room key would come in handy, and while she took care of that she'd find out where they could rent a boat for the next day. In the morning they'd rent a boat and go out on the lake. That would be something different to do for their birthday, didn't Jane think?

She was nearly asleep when Hope returned with the room key and directions to Crist's Canoes. Always the one on the outside looking in, Jane knew from experience it would be morning before she'd find out what the motel lady told her mother. Meanwhile she'd keep her peepers open. The next clue would be Hope laying down a solitaire hand. After that came some long-buried story from the past softly sending ripples through the wee hours of waiting — a story about coyotes or a story about drought or wildfire or about moving their sheep camp out of the way of a gully-washer with mere minutes to spare. Over the years, they'd waited for three days, four days, once for a week. But when Skip showed up, they'd get right back in with him, relieved all was well.

Next morning, Jane bought a postcard with a picture of their beautiful mountain lake on the front. She wrote "home sweet home" on the back and addressed it to Sophie Springer, High Road Garage, High Road, Neb. Then the day after their birthday paddle on the lake, Hope opened the local paper to the classifieds. "Girl's camp seeks assistant cook," she read. "Some experience required."

"But you don't even like cooking."

"I was thinking of you, Janie. You did some of that out in the valley once, right?"

"I only washed dishes. I never cooked."

"Let's call. It might be fun. It's nice here, and Skip won't mind you settling in here making some money while we look for work and some place to live down in New Jersey."

Jane stared at her mother. "You don't really believe that."

Hope shrugged. "One day Skip will have to cut you loose. Here you are, all grown, and he's still got you snubbed up. It's time. I'll be fine. And you shouldn't have to worry all the time about what's going on in that busy mind of his."

"I know. But each time he says I'll pay for all the grief I give him, I worry just what does he have in mind. How can I not worry when he's always shooting his mouth off? Now at least he takes his bad moods out on me, but what's going to happen to you once I leave? Then what? Won't he just think up some new hell to put you through? Someday someone is going to have to shoot him to get him to quit."

"He just gets upset. He gets wound up. You know Skip would never hurt us. You know that, Janie. And he doesn't mean all those things he says. He wants only the best for us. That's why he took off like he did, so we could have some time to celebrate. Have our birthday on the lake."

Jane asked to use the phone in the motel office. By then Bertha the motel lady was their friend. She'd brought them supper their second night and Jane was certain at some time Hope had filled her in about Skip. She got the head cook Geneva on the phone, Geneva giving Jane to understand she'd been cooking for camps since the beginning of time and her assistant cook Mike for more than a dozen years. Still, if Jane was ready to learn, they were ready to teach. The cooks' cabin was behind the big camp kitchen to the rear of the main lodge, with Jane's room on the second floor of the staff house. Staff was due that day, campers Sunday afternoon.

From the dining hall porch, she looked out on five low cabins with pitched roofs hunkered in a semi-circle in a large mowed meadow. Behind the cabins, trail signs pointed in three directions to more cabins. In the opposite direction, men's voices floated up on the morning mist over what she thought must surely be another lake. Everything serene, even the men's voices in the distance was sweet music to her ears. What if Geneva was on the gruff side; she didn't mind people speaking their minds. For two months she'd be out of the fray, assisting cooks in a camp kitchen while salting away her money, no Skip after his cut. But would this be the time and place to make the split, finally take matters in hand? That was the work she had cut out for her, the truly serious work she had to get done no matter what.

At the staff house she knocked once on the screen door and went in. She could smell cold ashes in the fire grate and hear someone moving about on the second floor. "I'm the new cook's assistant. Mind if I come up?" she called up the stairs.

"So they found one at last! Bully for us! Yes, come up. However did they find you?"

"My mother reads the Classifieds. But don't ask me my camp name. I still have to think of one."

"You can call me Badger. I teach crafts here and will likely teach crafts here till I die. I started here when I was ten and I just turned thirty a month ago."

"I never went to camp," Jane told the young woman in horn-rimmed glasses, a thick brown braid falling down her back. "But I worked at a boy's camp once."

"Not the same animal at all," Badger informed her as she re-plumped her pillow. "Boys camps are for learning how to sail using celestial navigation and for learning that most important lesson in a boy's life: never have to ask the score. "Girl's camps are different," she went on, warming to her subject, down on one knee by then pairing shoes under her bed. "Because girls routinely beg to stay at camp and would gladly stay all year. Why? For the simple reason girl camp counselors are college girls and college girls are fun. Of course they're no more fun than any other girls. But together, as they are at camp, they're stars shining in the firmament. They're their own constellation and, with younger girls dancing attendance, make up their own Milky Way."

This was only Badger's opening gambit, Jane was to find out. Meanwhile she had to come up with a camp name. She'd been introduced to a Shorty, a Chip, a Woody and a Pepper, a Parky, Pinky, Bitsy, Rocky, and Birch, and decided she'd like to be *Sparrow*. Her old friend Ruben had once likened her spare stature to a sparrow's.

Over the summer, she would see with her own eyes what Badger had gone to such lengths to explain — clutches of excited young campers revolving up through the mowed meadow and into the dining hall, always a sunny young college girl counselor at their center.

And before long she herself had Elizabeth, who lived up the road in a trailer home with her mother, brother, and aging beagle Ranger. Elizabeth, who would bring her pretty stones and snail shells and write her verses and claim her for her best friend. Still, at the boy's camp where she'd worked, the boys were never trained in celestial navigation. There the boys did push-ups, shinnied up ropes, marched in terrible heat, swore, farted, and hocked up amazing phlegm.

Kitchen prep kept Sparrow occupied well after supper clean-up each night, the advantage being to put her right where she wanted to be during the quiet time after taps. Taps was at nine and off-duty counselors drifted into the dining hall soon afterwards. If the evening turned cool, she'd get a fire going in the fireplace. From the back of the kitchen, she could hear one of the counselors start the singing, often a sad song about love... maybe all of them sad songs about love. *Dumbarton drums, they sound so bonnie, when they remind me of my Johnnie, what fond delights will steal upon me, when Johnnie kneels and kisses me.*

By the end of camp, Sparrow would know certain songs beginning to end. She'd know most of the words to "I know Where I'm Going" which, of course, she didn't know. She didn't know where she was going, and unlike the person in the song, didn't know who was going with her, who she loved or who she'd marry.

Over the summer, Sparrow had heard the name Dan many times. She knew him to be Elizabeth's cousin who grew blueberries and rented out canoes. All Camp New Hope's blueberries came from Dan's Berries, and all its canoes were leased from Dan Crist. Just after the Fourth, Dan's blueberries had arrived in a blue flood, with Geneva's crew cooking up blueberry desserts for lunch and supper for weeks on end. Still, even with his daily deliveries, Sparrow never saw Dan once. His berries just appeared each morning till the end of the second week of August when they finally tailed off. Only then did she meet him, three short days before the end of the camp season when she and Badger and some of the other staff went to the tavern across from the lake to dance and drink beer.

"We've seen each other before. You sat right here," Dan told her as he pulled out the chair next to hers. "Your sister was reading a book."

"My mother," she corrected, adding that she remembered him too.

"Close then. We were close. My friend and I decided you had to be related. So, you're Sparrow."

"Not for much longer. For only three days more. Then I'm back to being Jane."

"Nothing wrong with being Jane, is there?"

"Nothing wrong with it," she told him. "Just I like being Sparrow. After camp closes, I go down to New Jersey and finish high school. I'm nineteen now, but I still have a year left to go. Geneva made me swear I'd stick with it and get my diploma."

"And she's right too. Whereabouts in New Jersey?"

"Some little town I've never been."

The jukebox was playing again and everyone getting up to dance, Badger with a partner who spun her around the dance floor in a practiced way. In her own life, Jane didn't go to school dances, and no one had ever spun her around a dance floor even once. But she'd always liked dancing and liked dancing with Dan.

She liked his saying he knew what she meant about being sad everyone was leaving. He knew about that. This same time of year about everyone he went to school with packed off for some college. It would be Thanksgiving before he'd see them again, and that included about everyone out on the dance floor except Badger and Paul. Badger and Paul had been sent away to boarding school, Badger to a private girl's school in southern Virginia, Paul to a military academy nearby. No being sent away to more school for either of them.

Dan promised Badger he'd get Sparrow back to camp, but before that he'd like some time to enjoy a slow dance with her and a chance for them to get better acquainted.

"You said you remembered seeing me. I'd wanted to ask you to dance that night, but there was something about you I couldn't take my eyes off. You looked so peaceful sitting there with your mother while your mother read her book. It felt like I'd be breaking in on something, on something really nice."

"Just our birthday; well, almost my birthday, but really not till the next day. We call the twelfth of June *our* birthday. I know it sounds strange, but that's what we call it. I can't explain. It's just the way it's always been."

"No need to explain. Well, how about this one, shall we? The slow number I've been waiting for since I first saw you in June."

"I don't know what to say to that," she told him.

He took her hand. "Don't say anything then. You're shivering. You cold, Sparrow?"

"I'm shivering, but not because I'm cold."

Still holding her after the music stopped, he asked would she save all the nights she had left for him. She told him she'd save two, that she'd like it if they could see more of each other as well. Later he put the top down on his *new* convertible and turned the radio on so they could sit under a mid-summer sky with only stars for company. They had three nights, then they had two nights, then they had one.

Dan was all for driving her down, but she was against it. Still, she said she'd write to him, not really expecting she'd get letters back. People didn't answer letters in her experience. Only Sophie in Nebraska ever wrote more than once, and her friend Ruben never answered at all. It can break your heart each time no letter comes. Maybe this time would be different. Still, if he did write, what would that be like with two hundred miles between them? Distance will put an end to this in a hurry, she told herself, hoping she'd be both right and wrong at the same time. It made her dizzy, all this back and forth inside her own head, but at least it didn't make her sad.

She said her good-byes to Geneva and Mike, holding back tears as they walked for the last time from their homey cooks' cabin to their two weighted down and waiting station wagons. Geneva was returning to Troy and her husband, warning it would be Christmas before she'd get a letter off but not to give up, and Mike just down the pike in Gloversville saying she'd get one off within the week. Badger was next to leave. She'd write Sparrow from France and expect Sparrow to write too.

Elizabeth was last. Jane gave Elizabeth stamped envelopes and a Big Chief tablet. Elizabeth gave her a bracelet woven of grass. Stretched out on her friend Sparrow's bare bedsprings, Elizabeth wished camp ran all winter and they could go skating on the lake.

In Hope's story, was it a frozen lake the time they waited out a blue norther, certain Skip would never make it back alive... or was it a frozen *river* in her story and not a lake at all? A bright braided rope of river dividing again and again, throngs of happy children skating into the sun. She, the same age as Elizabeth now? Was that the winter her mother's pretty diversions first began to pall?

Jane back-pedaled in her early letters, writing her first one over so she didn't say too much. Dan wrote her back, saying how pleasantly surprised he'd been at getting her letter. Pleased that he remembered she liked being *Sparrow* better than she liked being *Jane*, she wrote back saying, after all she did say she'd write and she mostly did what she said. For the rest of August each kept the letters flowing, Dan regretting again not asking her to dance when he should have the first time he saw her, and Jane regretting she turned down his offer to drive her down to New Jersey... if only for the few precious hours more of the little time they had left.

The weekend before school started, Dan did drive down to see her. Hope was nice enough once Jane explained they'd gone canoeing in one of his canoes. Skip's attitude? *So what's he doing here?* All that saved the day was Dan agreeing to go on Skip's tour of the town — not much of a town really, only the one street with a grammar school, a post office, insurance adjuster's office and grocery mart. Even Jane's big consolidated high school was three towns a way. For two days, all either could think was how much better off they'd be had she stayed put in New York where they could talk on the phone and go out in the evening and dance the night away.

All September each wrote the other letters filled with longing. In October, Dan made a trip down to see his dying uncle in the city. In his next letter he reflected on how few hours he'd been able to spend with her, and realized then he was in deep. He wrote, "When together our love growing stronger; when apart only poor paper words filling in." She couldn't possibly know how hard leaving her was, followed by another lonely drive home, a battle fought within for the first fifty miles if not for the next fifty after those. Should he turn around or keep going? Was it just him or did she feel it too?

A week later he wrote that her summer camp had asked him to be their off-season caretaker, an idea he was giving serious thought. What did she think? She asked what did his folks think? He told her what they thought didn't concern him — her first hint that Dan's family had problems too. Soon after, he wrote to say he was all moved in, that Elizabeth showed him Badger's room and a settee Sparrow made with her own hands. And just how had she come up with a table that dropped down from the wall? Pleased at Dan's praise, she was reminded as well of the coward she remained even after the past summer, of all the things she still couldn't talk about, all the things she still couldn't say.

Meanwhile, she felt too old to be in high school, her new high school too huge. Dan wrote her to hang on; he'd be down to see her over the Thanksgiving holiday. Could she hang on till then? Naturally more separation would be hard, but Dan in the house with them for the Thanksgiving holiday wasn't even thinkable. The Rankins didn't celebrate holidays, not since New Mexico and the mountain cabin when she was thirteen, not since Skip made her mother join in on his holiday benders if only to remind her he wrote the rules.

She wanted to write Dan and ask if he could make it earlier. She'd sit on her bed to write him, but when she'd pick up her pen, the pen would stop at *Dear Dan*. Days went by without writing to him, a week, and then two weeks. She got letters asking was she ill, why hadn't he heard from her? Then she got the one beginning *Dearest Sparrow*, nineteen days without a letter! Nineteen days! *Do you not know by now what you mean to me?* Yes, she meant as much to him as he meant to her and her desire to be near him ever stronger with every *longing-for-her* letter he sent. But there were things she never could tell him, because how could she tell him she's not the girl he thinks she is, not the nice girl he'd been so taken with since that June evening sitting quietly the next table over with her mother who was reading a book.

The week before Thanksgiving her big high school became her one refuge. Each morning she left earlier and earlier to wait at the bus stop, and afternoons she took the last bus home. Still Dan didn't give up on her, another letter from him in the mail every day. Could his plans for Thanksgiving be what was troubling her? Families can be funny. Holidays can bring out the worst. Just tell him. Please, please, tell him. He would understand.

Why was love this hard? She wanted to be with him, more than ever — ride in his *chariot* as he liked to call his car, relive the August night they thought they'd burned the car radio up playing it till dawn, say how anything gone wrong between them was her fault to keep him from ever thinking it was his. She wrote a letter to Sophie in High Road. She wrote one to Badger in France. She wrote to Mike in Gloversville and Geneva in Troy. She wrote everyone but the one who called her *sweetheart*, the one she loved most.

Then Monday before Thanksgiving she was dying. She knew she was dying because she could no longer get food down, and Hope was at her every minute to ask what was wrong. "Is it your school, Janie? Why won't you talk to me? Do you hurt somewhere? Tell me where you hurt."

"I hurt right here," she told her mother, palms crossing her heart. But Wednesday afternoon their Thanksgiving celebration began right on schedule. There were five fifths, and Skip was all smiles. By golly they had the world by the tail this time, didn't they? Didn't Hope look prettier every day? Wasn't Hope his pretty chicken? Wasn't Jane the smartest and best kid ever, bar none?

When Skip and Hope both passed out, Jane went up to take a bath. She felt the need of a good long soak in the tub. She didn't want to smell like a gin mill or have to explain what had her close to tears, because Jane didn't cry, not even on the twelfth of June, regretting every year how only two people in the world knew her birthday, and their names were Hope and Skip. It's now or never, she told the mirror as she pulled on her sweater and put in contact lenses, hoping the nice lady next door wouldn't notice the dark circles under her eyes. Let them booze away on their own. If they were determined to be boozers, she told her mirror self, they didn't need her.

She'd filled out the change of address form at the post office. She'd bought her one-way bus ticket. She'd mailed her letter to Sophie and hidden her suitcase under the stoop. Now all she had to do was go to the house next door and tell the lady who gave her the friendly wave every morning that any letters for Jane Rankin would be left with her. As soon as she got to Sophie's she'd be in touch, and she hoped it wasn't too inconvenient, all she was going to say.

The night, starry and clear, the moon a full moon, reminded Jane of the first time she met Badger when Badger told her how it was that counselors at girls' camps shone like stars in the firmament and how the girls danced attendance as they made their own Milky Way. Good old Badger. What would her summer have been without Badger there to light the way! Badger, prickly and opinionated, but with a sixth sense about people too. A sixth sense similar to Dan's sense about what was going on in someone's heart. Dan! What would life be without Dan slowly and gently pulling her into his orbit, into the cup of his own constellation?

Her hands balled in fists in her coat pockets, she stood in moon shadow on her neighbor's porch waiting for the porch light to come on. "I live over there," she began, "in the little house next door."

"Yes?"

"And I know you're busy, but I left a change of address at the post office. I asked them to leave my mail here. It's an emergency or I wouldn't bother you."

"You're having your mail left here? Come in. Please. Come in out of the cold. It's very cold. We may even be in for some of that snow they've been predicting. Now tell me again. Here, sit down by the fire and warm up a bit. Why, you're... you're having a bad time of it, aren't you? Now tell me, please, what I can do?"

"There's nothing. Nothing you can do. They're drunk out of their minds. They've been hitting the bottle all afternoon."

"Your mother and father?"

"My mother and stepfather."

"I see. And she's drinking too? What I mean to ask is, your mother is as inebriated as he is, is she? He didn't try anything out of line with you I hope."

Jane shook her head. "He goes in my room and reads my mail. But I don't want him angry with me so I don't let on. And he didn't try anything like that — not like you mean, and when he's smashed he's nicer. For a little while anyway."

"And that's a problem too. Now tell me your name again?"

"I'm Jane."

"And I'm Millicent. And I do know something of what you speak. I'll just go in the kitchen and put the kettle on. Have you eaten anything, Jane? You look like you could stand a bite to eat."

She spent the night on Millicent's sofa, knowing she had to be home before dawn or *bad* would turn into *worse*. When Skip came to, he'd be turning the corner from nice to nasty; Hope would be throwing up, having tried the door to her daughter's room and discovering her empty closet. She would be frantic, but were she to tell Skip that Jane was gone, he'd be in a fury, righteous fury being his stock in trade. Yes, he knew goddamn well what was going on. Hadn't he always suspected that Dan guy from some damn place in New York? And just what had Hope been thinking leaving Jane alone with him last summer?

Dan's letter arrived the Monday after Thanksgiving. It broke her heart.

Dearest Sparrow,

It is Sunday nite and Thanksgiving has ended for another year. I'm glad to say good-bye to it as it was just a big mess. Nothing went right – mostly the plans I had to see you. I waited to hear from you — Wednesday, then Friday, but nothing came. I was very sad to think that after our plans, here I was in New York and just where you might be I didn't know. Then Saturday I began to have a horrible feeling that possibly you were home and that for some reason you didn't inform me of this. This grew and grew through the day until at 8:00 pm, I finally picked up the phone to call New Jersey. The phone was busy and I never called back. Now I don't know. If I find you were home and I missed you just because of my blundering, I'll die.

I now know how much I really miss you — being alone when I planned to be with you. Oh well, I guess the only thing to do is start counting the days till Christmas. Tonight is one of those nights when I feel the only way to send a letter to you is by personal delivery. I'd like nothing better than to start out in your direction. Will you meet me in the middle?

I still miss you, Sparrow – more than anything – I still love you. Dan

She answered yes, she had been home. She would have liked to say she wasn't home over Thanksgiving but couldn't lie. Not to him. There were reasons though which she'd be able to tell him about someday she hoped, just not yet. Now was not the time. If she wanted her diploma, now was not the time to upset things at home. She hoped he'd forgive her, but if he chose not to, she wouldn't blame him. Who in his right mind wants to trust a liar and she was a liar in a way. Still, just reading his letter had made her realize many things about him, about the two of them. She still loved him too.

Dan's answered her letter the day he got it. She wasn't surprised to hear back from him so soon.

Dearest Sparrow,

I got your letter and must admit it did leave me rather confused. I think it was written by both persons at the same time — Sparrow #1 & Sparrow #2. I wish I knew which traits went with which Sparrow so I could decide which one I want. I do, by the way, want one of them — that is if I can have one. But I think it best to can this subject for the present as I'm hoping things may be clearer the next time I hear from you.

I understand your family problems make you lose interest in other things and therefore would not have made a T.G. meeting all we may have expected. However, it isn't too far till Christmas and similar plans could probably be arranged if both parties were to be in agreement. I can only speak for myself — how about you?

It's now Tuesday — I fell asleep last nite while writing to you — not because of lack of interest, but because every few words I'd have to stop and think about you. That's what I'm doing right now, thinking about how nice it would be to spend part of the coming holiday with you. You give it some thought and let me know what you think.

Always, Dan

She wrote to him that just before New Year's would be best. She'd arrange for him to stay with a neighbor rather than have him sleep on the couch at her house again. And this meant he could stay longer. She hoped three days. Any time from the twenty-ninth of December she told him, calculating Skip and Hope would recover by then from their Christmas hangovers. She didn't have to worry about them celebrating on New Year's Eve. They never celebrated on New Year's Eve. When the whole world was tipsy on New Year's Eve, Skip and Hope were sober, some strange point of honor with them. Still, there was no need for Dan to be in on any of that.

Dan's answer was ecstatic. He would arrive late on the twenty-ninth and leave on the second. The rest of his letter described a spruce tree he and Elizabeth had been decorating down by the lake. Maybe they'd find a way to get her up to New York so she could see the tree. And then maybe when she did come, she'd stay and all their problems would go away.

For the first time since Dan's letter telling of his bleak Thanksgiving waiting for word from her, she felt close to being his Sparrow again, the one he believed loved him with all her heart, the one she truly wanted to be if only she could bring back that same girl of a summer ago, make it through three more weeks till they were together. But at least she could bear the radio playing their songs again and feel much better off in the friend department than she'd ever been before with Sophie in High Road now and Millicent next door, Millicent offering a key to her house that she could drop by for at any time.

"Just feel free, dear, and make yourself at home," Millicent urged. "That goes for anything in the fridge too. But while I have you with me, I'd like to hear a little something about your young man. His name is Dan. I know that much."

"Dan Crist," she began. "I was cooks' assistant at a summer camp near where he lives. But we never did meet till the end. We almost missed each other. We could easily have missed each other."

"And what does Dan do?"

"He grows blueberries on acreage he leases near the camp."

"He's a berry farmer then."

"Since he was a kid. He has another business too. Crist's Canoes. He rents out canoes on the lake and leases canoes to summer camps."

"You could say he's a Dan-of-all-trades — blueberries, canoes. What else?"

"He loves music. He's a good dancer. He's smart and kind-hearted and he makes me laugh. He writes beautiful love letters. I only wish mine to him were half as good as his to me."

"Older than you?"

"Six months older, but much wiser than his years."

"Well, I know I'm going to like him. I look forward to meeting him. And you can trust me, Jane. Anything you've said to me is between us. I'm just glad I can help out."

Millicent was helpful, or at least everything Millicent did for her felt helpful to Jane, just her warm welcomes and interest alone. And the sleeping arrangements she made for Dan were sure to be an improvement. He wouldn't be so exposed at Millicent's house, although he'd still be sleeping on a sofa. And when he got to her folks' house, they wouldn't have to stay long, just long enough. It would be cold out, but they wouldn't feel the cold. When did they ever feel the cold?

Finally! They would say to each other, *Letters are good, but not as good as this. Nothing was this good.* And this time they'd have three days. What would they do with that much time? If he brought skates, maybe they'd go ice skating on Burnham Pond. Or maybe they'd just make the world beyond the two of them disappear as they'd done before. Meanwhile, she wouldn't worry about Christmas. Soon Christmas would be behind her. Soon she'd be counting down the days to December twenty-ninth.

Only Jane was still up when Dan arrived. There'd been traffic and he'd had to stop for coffee. It had been a slow trip. They sat out in his chariot rather than go inside. "I ever tell you what Skip said about you that time he took me on his famous tour of the town?"

"You never did. But whatever it was I don't think I want to know."

"Even praise? I'd asked him where you learned your way around a mallet and chisel and he asked where did I think you learned it. Of course, he meant from him. He said you were the quickest to learn something new he ever saw. He was telling me about New Mexico when you were... how old, thirteen? He said you learned more that year and a half in the mountains than you could ever have learned any place else."

"Is that all he told you?"

"And he kept you out of school. He said he had to keep you out of school."

"I used to love school. I used to be good at school. School's where I had friends."

She tried not giving too much away, knowing this was not the time for true confessions. What's more, it was plain Dan regretted even bringing up Skip. But since then, he'd seen more of her handiwork. Halved corners pegged with hand-made dowels? Maybe her missing time in school was worth it after all if only to learn many useful skills

"Only if you think I like being stuck down here in the New Jersey boondocks desperately missing you! And you're buying what he sells. He'll sell you anything. He's not who you think he is. Skip's a low-life, a sneaky nasty boozing abusing low-life! And for years now he has my mother boozing right along with him! The two of them binge on holidays. That's why you couldn't come Thanksgiving, why you couldn't come Christmas."

Dan was nice about it, pulling her closer, silently taking in all she'd uncorked, though maybe his long silence afterwards said it all. She didn't know. All she knew was she wanted to take it back, say that anything she might have just implied wasn't true. "But sweetie, the two of us together, we'll make it through all this, don't you see?" he said when he finally did say something. And then he said he wanted to know what she'd been up to lately, who she'd heard from over Christmas, and all about her friend Millicent. All she'd told him about Millicent was she lived in the house next door.

She told him Millicent was her next-door neighbor. That they'd met almost by accident. That she lived alone and she thought Millicent was very lonely. And that was probably the reason she was eager to help out. But even so, that was nice of her, wasn't it nice, her offering her sofa? So many words over the dam, as if with enough words and what she'd come very close to spelling out for him would disappear without a trace. But yes, she was doing well in all her subjects. And Badger wrote often from France. She'd told Badger about him coming down over New Years and got a card back saying how much she'd always liked him. How she'd known Dan a long time.

They drove around till ten-thirty, and when they arrived at Millicent's door she was ready for them — a blazing fire in the den, hot spiced rum warming, and a plate of fresh-baked cookies out on the sideboard. Jane had never been in Millicent's den, a cozy room with bow window and window seats. Three of the four walls were covered in likenesses of the founding families she was descended from, Millicent all dressed up in a wool suit fresh from the hairdresser's looking expensive, something she'd never really noticed before that night. Still, she and Dan might have been high society too, as Millicent refreshed their drinks and asked

Dan had his trip down gone smoothly and asked after her parents as if they were friends.

For Jane, born to a teenage mother in a Southeast Idaho sheep camp where neither mother nor child would likely survive if not for Skip happening along, life was black and white. White was Dan in her life to love; black was no Dan. Were she to tell Dan more about that terrible time in the mountains of New Mexico when she was thirteen he would stop loving her. Of that she had no doubt. But then if she didn't tell him, how long could they go on when history would keep repeating itself, Dan always at a loss as to why she couldn't simply kiss off two people who brought her such grief.

In all, Dan wrote her twenty-seven letters, letters never expressing doubt they truly did love one another even during the long dry spell when he'd had no letters from her, letters recalling a lost time when all she'd say was there were certain things she couldn't tell him, a time when he believed enough love from him would bring her back. But now, with all the many miles between them and the many weeks and months between visits, even the least time away from each other would become unbearable after three days in each other's arms. With each passing hour of those three days, each must have hoped the other would feel this same way too, and not because the force of their attraction was fading or the pull of that all-powerful thing called love less potent, but because even a true love story like theirs must end.

Ever since she kissed him good-bye the second day of January and he left on his long lonely 200-mile drive home, promising the next time they'd never let each other go, she'd been hunting a way out. What she wanted always to believe was neither of them broke it off; they simply had to give up. At age nineteen-and-a-half, she was only starting to understand what her friend Sophie forewarned of that hot day at the lake. When love finds us, we have no choice; and once love finds us, there's heartache.

Over long winter nights, her resolve came up short many times: on nights she'd begin a letter to Dan, on nights she'd write to Geneva asking for her old job back at camp, nights she'd be sure she was less well off than before, those loneliest nights of all when she'd open old love letters thinking if what Dan wrote was true the day he wrote it, then that was good enough for her. Still she had that much left; what they once had together no one could take away. In his last letter, he wrote of a place where only people in love can go and no one can interfere, a place they would never leave. Even with snow frosting the ground in April, in her heart Dan's *place* kept the promise of spring.

Soon, she'd remind herself, soon she'd have her high school diploma in hand. After that, well she didn't know. One step at a time was all she knew how to do, that and keep her peepers open, important to keep her peepers open. And then, predictably, Skip and Hope flew the coop and missed her graduation, her mother's thirty-sixth birthday coming first, the critical celebration for the two of them if not for her.

But Badger was there in the front row on graduation day. And Millicent, one aisle over, was pleased to finally meet Jane's dear friend Badger from camp. Following the ceremony, they toasted the graduate and drank champagne on Millicent's porch. Very likely over champagne was when Badger came to certain mistaken conclusions about Millicent's helpful hospitality.

"But Millicent never said anything," Jane told her once they were back in Badger's brother's apartment in the city, trying again to explain. "I know she didn't because I never told her all I told you, and that's not how Dan found out the truth about me anyway; I told him myself."

"What truth about you? That your step-father's an abuser and your mother's pathetic! That's not about you, Sparrow. That's about them."

"I see that. I see that now. But what if I'm just not ready for Dan? I mean when you don't know where you're from, how can you know who you are? When you never stay in one place, how do you know you're home when you get there? In my life only one place ever felt like home and that one place was camp. Dan says I'm like two Sparrows who can't agree on which one I really am: Sparrow #1 from last summer at camp or Sparrow #2 from the rest. He used to want one of them if he could have one, but I doubt he wants one anymore. I'm too much trouble. He deserves a girl who's not trouble."

"And maybe he just wants the one named Jane. At any rate time will tell and that's between the two of you. Meanwhile, I need help. What I've got in mind is work, just not a real job. In other words, I can't pay you. But the simple fact is I can't do the work on our poor old family camp without someone handy to help me... like you. You... you need to get away from that stepfather of yours. And then once you're gone, your mother will have to open her eyes. Trust me, Sparrow. She will."

Never could Jane have foreseen such good fortune. Another summer to work alongside her friend Badger on a clear mountain lake in upstate New York. She never could have imagined her twentieth birthday and a birthday party given just for her, Badger bringing Geneva and Mike out from camp, as well as two of last season's camp staff, and inviting little Elizabeth — this year a taller sassier age thirteen, inviting Sophie out from High Road, Nebraska, and Sophie coming from halfway across the country!

And then swimming in a cold clear mountain lake in their birthday suits on her birthday till three in the morning when they finally gave up the ghost, the clear mountain lake returning the stars to the firmament, the moon in its cradle, the perfect day just done. But for the Jane-who-never-cries, were the tears that came in the night tears of joy or tears for joys she had missed? In the morning when she woke to friends who had come to celebrate with her, would yesterday's song still be in the air? Would she still be able to hear it, sing it herself? Could the song go on? Could it last?

As she drifted awake that bright morning, a familiar voice broke through as she swatted at what she'd thought was a big mosquito but was only a harmless speedboat towing a skier out on the lake. *You about ready to bust out of there?* It was Sophie... Sophie out on the dock waving at her to come down. Then she remembered she was twenty and even at twenty still young.

Last Dance at Badger Point

ADIRONDACKS — JULY 1982

BADGER'S MORNING MESSAGE WAS SHORTER than her usual: *'You'll never guess who I heard from!'* Dan knew Badger could mean only one person and that person was Sparrow. How many years since any news of her? With Sparrow, there'd been times when the best news was no news at all. Too often in a jam, too often down to her last nickel, but was he being fair? How many breaks did she ever get in life? Poor Badger though, always the one to keep the faith even knowing she stood to lose both friend and friendship after too many years with no word at all. As for Dan's take on Sparrow, he'd be the first to admit that while the old embers still burned, they'd been slowly burning out for years.

Still, should a visit from Sparrow be in the offing, he knew better than to waste even a minute. Past experience told him she could be here and gone again in less than a day's time. But first there were certain logistics to consider with the family station wagon in the shop — how to fit four little girls in the front seat of a pick-up.

"Okay, sneakers on everybody. Get your play things up here on the porch. Donna, you and Daphne ride in front with me. Sarah, Becky, I didn't mean when it suits you. I meant get cracking right this minute. Then get your hinders up in the truck bed and we'll be on our way."

"But we're playing, Daddy."

"And you can play at Auntie Badger's as well as here. Just find some place to play away from the water. You know the rules."

He had no idea what to expect, though to his ears Badger's tone had been calm enough. In twenty years he'd seen Sparrow exactly twice. Ten years since the last time when everything was coming up roses for her after graduation from some kind of training program. And while he liked to think of himself as Sparrow's loyal defender, as loyal as Badger, he knew the truth to be otherwise — too many of his own expectations weighing her down those dog days of August 1972, the last time they saw each other.

That time she'd been too slender, dark shadows under her eyes, once again resolve failing, allowing old fires to rekindle from their one short season together and that one so long ago. He stepped on it. Better to get the news and get the worst over with, better to know than not know. And poor Sparrow, no way of preparing herself for who he was now — husband to Cindy with two little girls to show for it already in school. No way of preparing her, and only because the old songs played on in his heart, those same sad slow numbers.

But no amount of warning could prepare him for Sparrow just inside Badger's gate, one leg tucked under her as if she'd been waiting there all the years she'd been gone. As in his dreams, there on the same bench by the same gate, then on her feet and moving toward him, bringing that same glad feeling knowing she was near. Even now, even after all the years moving him with the merest glimpse of her, her hair still bright as clover honey shining in the sun.

"Hi there! You guys on some kind of camp outing?"

"So it *was* you. I knew it was. Kids, this is Sparrow, Badger's and my old friend Sparrow. The big girls riding in back are mine, Becky and Sarah, my twins. The little ones up here in front are my nieces, Donna and Daphne. What's the problem now, Becky? Why the long face?"

"'Cause you made us hurry up and you didn't even give us a chance to put our shoes on. And now we don't have our shoes on."

"Then you'll just have to watch where you walk, won't you? All you kids, scoot on up to the house and tell Auntie Badger she's got company. Pronto! Vamos! Jesus, Sparrow, I don't know what to say."

"Two kids, Dan? Who's the lucky lady?"

"Don't know about the lucky part, but I'm speechless. I'd given up on you. I'd been thinking of writing that friend of yours."

"I take it you mean Sophie. She was three months gone last I heard anything from her and not very happy about it. And your cousin Elizabeth had two stepsons my last letter from her. I've wondered why she stopped writing. It was sudden — Elizabeth always such a tender flower."

"I've not seen hide nor hair of Elizabeth, not for a long time."

"And you, Dan, a famous writer. I buy your books to get all the latest. I'll be reading along and it's as if you're saying, 'Sparrow, be careful. Sparrow, don't take so many chances. Sparrow, don't be like the poor kid in my book who gets killed his first day on the job.' That's the way I read it anyway. But tell me, why didn't Badger get in touch with me? Wasn't she supposed to pass on all our news? Wasn't that the way we left it — up to each of us to pass our news on to her?"

"Why didn't she? Because you don't stay in touch. You know you don't. You used to write to us once in a while. Now you never do."

There he'd said it, and nothing about saying it felt redeeming. He still wasn't going to talk about Cindy, not with Sparrow, and not because there was anything wrong with Cindy; Cindy was fine.

The book was more difficult yet to talk about because the story wasn't made up. The kid in the book was James, Elizabeth's little brother James, the reason the letters to Sparrow from Elizabeth had come to such an abrupt end. And apparently since the judgment he won in court and his book about James, he was the one his cousin Elizabeth held responsible for James's death.

"So, you here to stay or just passing through again? You look good. In fact, I'd have to say you're looking pretty wonderful."

"Am I? Am I really? You're looking wonderful yourself. Ten years since we last saw each other. All I can remember is life throwing us curve balls. Does the name Ruben ring any bells? Does El Paso? You probably don't remember this, but I grew part way up in Texas. No reason for you to remember all the different places I grew up in. But before I met you, the only person I was ever close to was Ruben. We were always together. Ruben would go to bat for me, and I'd do the same for him. We made it through all kinds of terrible times, the worst being the year Lil died."

"Lil?"

"Ruben's mother, his beautiful mother, and I loved her as much as Ruben did. She was completely opposite everything my mother was, very free with us, so totally free. You remember my mother and my step-father? How could you forget! Skip and Hope finally split up and she went back to Texas. She found a job and a place to live. Then she found Ruben in the phone book.

He's been married twice, but I'm the one he's been waiting for, or at least that's the way he tells it."

That Cindy was away worked out well, as it meant they could all stay without the usual objections about overnights at Badger Point. The hard part was getting four little girls to settle down; past nine before they went up to bed, after ten before the last hold-out won one minute more in Sparrow's lap, all four girls gaga over her. He watched her let Becky brush her hair, watched Sarah's questions get her total attention, watched his nieces hang on her every word telling about how tow-headed little Hope rode her pony to her one-room country school. How long since he'd seen her so at ease, so at home. He couldn't get over the change in her — a return to the old Sparrow he met long ago.

At midnight Badger excused herself. She'd had a busy day and an early morning. There were two sleeping bags under the stairs if they were interested. No need to get up with her and the birds; she'd see to the girls. No need to concern themselves with anything; this was their time, Dan's and Sparrow's time. They must have much to catch up on after all the years. She'd make sure no one interfered.

"Dan, this is my life. Up at six, at my nurse's station by seven, and back home again by three. After which I fix my supper, see some shows on television, then lights out at the end of another day. Of course, now I have Ruben. But you've hardly said a word. Are you happy? Are you satisfied? Tell me how you are."

"Happy? Happy enough I guess. I have my family, my work. I have Badger and good friends and a canoe I'm restoring. You told me about the Willits canoes, remember? We were dancing and you told me just how they're made. You knew all about them and I'd never heard of them before. It was perfect. I mean then it was perfect, perfect back then."

"You found an honest-to-God Willits in the east? I can't believe you even remember. The Willits brothers used to make them near where I lived on Puget Sound."

"I know, I remember. But I found mine in New Brunswick. We go back to the same place every year. Her folks get the house and everybody comes — three sisters, two brothers and their two to four kids apiece. It's a madhouse all week but everybody has a great time. That's where she is now. They kept the place another week to plan the big fiftieth anniversary extravaganza coming up a year from now. No less than a couple hundred guests. She's the youngest, but she's in charge, the one who loves a party."

"Your wife?"

"My wife. But if it was mine to do, I'd have it here. And not that many people. Too many and you forget who's important. But that's where I found my Willits."

"By *here* you mean at Badger Point?"

"Just a pipedream. Cindy and Badger aren't exactly soul mates. I'll get an earful when she gets back home. She likes Badger's brother Paul all right, but she just doesn't get Badger. Never did. Never will. Some of that probably has to do with you."

"But why when she's never met me?"

"Why? Why do you think? You still like Ray Charles, don't you? What do you want to hear? Let's put some music on and dance. We can still talk. If I thought I could, I'd try to talk you out of this Ruben fellow. What's he got that I don't?"

"You'll get along fine with Ruben. And the answer is yes, I still like Ray Charles, and I like Sinatra and Sam Cooke. And I like Linda Ronstadt and Nina Simone and I adore George Jones and Tammy Wynette. Anything sultry, anything sad and nothing too fast. You probably think I've changed, but if I have, I haven't changed much. Still the same Sparrow as I was before. Just older and wiser and one who knows not to go too crazy, not to make everyone sorry they ever knew her. But I don't mind you saying what you said. I'm glad you did."

"About me and you?"

"About us dancing. About wanting me to stay."

"It's true. I dream about it, about us dancing."

Of course, he had to avoid saying anything in front of the girls about showing Sparrow the camp because the old Camp New Hope staff house was now their family home. And he couldn't say anything to Sparrow about buying her old camp, because he'd only been able to buy it having won the judgment in the lawsuit involving his cousin Elizabeth's little brother James. And whether to even mention the lawsuit he hadn't had time to think about. Such a sad story she maybe didn't need to hear except for justice being done in the end for his aunt's sake and his cousin's sake. He closed his eyes and turned on his side. Time he got some sleep.

"Wake up! Wake up! Come and look!"

"It's too early. I'm sleeping. You girls go and play. And don't go waking everyone."

"Your friend is swimming. She doesn't have her swimsuit on. That's her in the water."

"And don't go waking Auntie Badger."

"She's up already. She's been up for hours. She said, don't wake you up, but everybody's up but you. You're the only one still sleeping. Doesn't your friend Sparrow have a swimsuit? She's not wearing one. She's not wearing anything."

"Let's not worry about it. Okay?"

"Okay, but Auntie Badger's baking muffins now. And Becky's frying bacon. And Donna's helping set the table. And Daphne's counting places. You want us to bring you a cup of coffee, so you can wake up? No, we didn't think you did, because you're too tired, aren't you, Daddy."

It was later, how much later? He could hear them down in the kitchen. Hear Sparrow, hear the girls, hear Badger offering more bacon, and Becky saying, "But why, we want you to stay with us forever, even Daddy does. We don't want you to ever-ever-ever leave. Please, stay one more day. Tell her, Auntie Badger, Daddy wants her to. What he wants we can tell." He checked his watch again. Ten minutes before eight. Was there time? He'd wasted all that time sleeping, wasted too much precious time.

First he'd show her the old Camp New Hope dining hall where his Willits canoe and two Canadian Chestnuts were cradled, one sold, the other awaiting a prospective buyer due some time the coming week. He'd save his new book till last, maybe not even mention it. It's hard describing a book not quite halfway finished. Besides, Sparrow would want to see the old kitchen, the one she'd worked in that long-ago summer of 1962, the same kitchen Cindy recently had a contractor remodel and bring up to date.

But it was the cooks' cabin she made a beeline for, where she'd spent much of her free time making useful things out of wood twenty years earlier. Now twenty years later the cooks' cabin looked much the same — the same bedsprings, same rough wood shelves, same broom handle trapezes where the cooks hung up their clothes. But it was at the cook's bench just outside the cabin door where the tears started. She'd no more than sat down when her eyes brimmed over, the last thing he expected.

"It's nothing. Just I miss all this. I don't know why. All so long ago, more than twenty years."

"Is this what's making you sad then? Last night you felt so good."

"Oh, Dan. My whole life I've been afraid of the truth, the truth about me. You remember the day I told you? It was when you told me what Skip told you the day he took you on that tour. I wasn't ever going to tell you. But I couldn't stop myself, because I thought you knew already because you said he'd told you he'd taught me everything a girl would ever need to know about, you know, about men, about men and what they want. All I remember now is shaking, All I remember now is I couldn't stop shaking."

"But don't you remember what I told you? I told you we'd get through it. I said somehow we'd get through it all together no matter what."

"You were kind to me. But I was too ashamed, because I would take all my clothes off and go around with no clothes on, and I knew what I was doing too. I knew what I was up to."

"How could you? You were thirteen? It wasn't up to you."

"But I did know, and it *was* up to me. Not too long ago Hope told me it was her fault she'd allowed it to go on. I said I didn't know what she was talking about and she said she was talking about leaving Skip alone with me that year we lived in New Mexico. If she'd been home where she was supposed to be, he wouldn't have done what he did to me. But now at last she knew why he'd always act as if he hated me, and that was because of what he'd been up to while she was gone.

"I tried telling her. I said nothing that happened to me happened because of her being gone. I really tried, Dan, but how can you tell your own mother you wanted to be everything she wasn't. How can you tell her you wanted to feel free and you wanted to feel unafraid and you wanted to feel everything you're not allowed to feel when you're only thirteen. All you can tell her is you're sorry, you're so sorry, you're so very sorry, but you can't tell her in time to keep her from doing the terrible thing she means to do, and so she shoots him and she kills him. 'You raped my Janie. You raped my daughter. You had no right, no right at all.'"

"She killed him? You saw her do it? You were there?"

"He didn't have a chance."

"And then what happened?"

"She went to prison. Now you know why I'll never have children. I'm bad news, Dan, I'm no good. Not for anyone. You need to accept that. Just forget me. Don't think about me. You have a lot going for you. I know you don't want to give me up, but you have to. For my sake and your sake and everyone's sakes, you have to. You have to say you will. You have to say it. Say, *I give you up forever.* Say, *I give you up.*"

Had he dreamed it? Had they danced till dawn, one dance after another, danced their way down to the boat dock and all the way back up to the porch? Had she asked him to kiss her? Had he kissed her? Had she told the girls at breakfast she had to leave them all for the love of a man in Texas? And then one after the other, had the girls begun to cry, first the big girls and then the little ones, already missing Sparrow as she'd missed Ruben's mother Lil all those years before? That same day after saying their last good-byes at the airport, had their tears met and made a river together, their two hearts breaking all over again knowing it all should have been very different; it all should have been so good.

Eighty Trips
around the Sun

ADIRONDACKS — SUMMER 1982

ELIZABETH LIKED HAVING PEOPLE AROUND; the happiest day of
her young life was the day the Donlons moved from the loneliest
address on the planet to rented rooms over Benz Men's Wear, a
block from the school. Sure, with camp in session, life on the
camp road was ideal, ideal as far as she was concerned if not that
great for her brother James. One year she had all that a shy and
self-conscious girl could want — her handsome cousin Dan
within whistling distance as the camp's hired hand. She'd been
thirteen that year, her brother James seven, the two of them
getting off the school bus at Bob's Tourist Court, by then closed
for the season almost a dozen years.

Now thirty-three, Elizabeth had notched two decades more
since that happiest of years. Still, forever lodged in memory was
the dreary night Dan drove her all around town hunting down
James, her pint-sized hero of a little brother out in the cold
searching the bars for his mom hoping to save her from the bottle
and from her ex stealing them blind, to save her from herself.
Was it coincidence Dan calling her when he'd been so present in
her thoughts? Still calling her "cousin" as in the old days, as if all
were the same between them when nothing was the same at all.

She played Dan's message over, his low voice pleasing to her ears. How would Friday work? He'd come by for her, say a little after five, drinks and dinner on the lake somewhere. After dinner, maybe a drive in the country? Following Dan's message was one from Juliet saying she was on her way with a bushel basket of beans and ripe tomatoes, that she and Jason were off on a fishing trip first thing in the morning. Elizabeth shrugged out of her work clothes. If she hurried, there was still time for a shower.

Such a crush she'd had that summer, at thirteen going quickly from hauling poor Ranger around in her brother James's old metal wagon to pining for Dan on the porch step. Each morning Dan arriving in his blue-and-white-checkered delivery van, she sitting across from him in the jump seat, aglow with sublime stirrings, delirious with sensation, and falling a little more in love every day.

The water barely warm, her head felt much lighter minus a good foot of heavy hair. Was there anything like a new hair style to lift a girl's spirits? She sat at her vanity still wet from her shower. Tucked into the mirror in front of her was Felix's birthday remembrance from his son Michael, coming the day before Felix died, a week late but in time. Michael happy to report landing yet another underpaid he-man job west of the Mississippi, omitting his customary 'miss you guys' scribbled over his initials, making no mention at all of a visit.

Felix's twenty-year-old son Michael was two years younger than his brother Jason and opposite in every way. Michael lacked direction; Jason just like his father, dependable, affectionate, hard-working. Felix was married at eighteen to Oralee; Jason married to his adoring high school sweetheart Juliet the week after graduation.

Would today be the day? She was desperate, and who better to talk to than Juliet who would cross her heart and hope to die, any secret safe with her. She stirred pimiento into grated cheese; first sandwiches and lemonade. After ice cream sundaes on the porch glider, she'd begin: I hope you won't hold this against me, Juliet. It's just ever since Felix passed I need to get this said...

She'd sprayed the porch down, dropped the bamboo curtains, swatted the cat hair off Grandpa Crumb's porch glider. All the times she'd rocked herself to sleep on this same porch glider, Felix left to sleep alone almost from the time she first moved in, when she was twenty-three, he forty-three, his boys twelve and ten. But where were her pictures? The ones they took of a blue-and-white delivery van with the cook's camera? The ones they took of each other down by the camp lake at Christmas time, two rolls of twelve exposures, a roll of twelve pictures each.

"I wasn't ever a camper, but I worked at a camp the year I lived in a trailer on the camp road off the old highway. The head cook took a shine to me. She put me in charge of her berries and fruits. Aside from that, she gave me my own little cot in the cook's cabin with my own pillow and my own spread. How I wish I could remember her name. Funny, I still can remember all the words to all the camp songs."

"You have some pictures?"

"I did have, but now I don't know where I put them. I was such a dreamer, my head up in the clouds. If you can believe it, I had this crazy idea I'd be like the camp counselors. I'd go to college like they did. Isn't that the craziest thing from a girl who just barely graduated high school, from a girl whose mom ended up keeping her baby when all the other moms there at the home gave up their babies?"

"At the home?"

"Nobody was supposed to know that's what it was. And it's closed now, but you look in the windows and it's all still there: the beds in a row, the school desks, that long table they ate at. It's out on the dairy road. You can see it from the cemetery. I see it every time I visit my mom's grave. But what happened to me was I had this huge enormous crush. Of course, he never knew. For one thing, I was younger, and for another we were kin sort of. I mean, if his mom and my mom were first cousins on the Donlon side, then that had to make me and Dan cousins too."

"So this crush of yours — not Jason's dad?"

"How I wish it was. Felix loved me. But that's the luck of the draw. Not for you and Jason maybe, but for me, for me and more people than you might think. We spend our life with the wrong one trying to make the best of it. Thing is, now Dan's coming to see me. Now I can't help worrying."

"Why? I mean I wouldn't."

"You would in my shoes. For one thing, somebody already got dibs. Their wedding was some kind of a big country club whoop-de-do. And most likely all he wants is to check up on me, make sure I'm doing okay. You know, with Felix gone. He's like that. Dan's always been like that. He has the kindest heart. Day after tomorrow, and I still don't know what to do. I almost told him not to come. I feel like that same crazy kid again with the same crazy crush."

Friday morning, Elizabeth walked to work. She'd had other jobs. One in a psychiatrist's office transcribing terrible secrets off a dicta-belt, making her feel a little better about her own lot in life. Dr. Hudson had been disappointed when she gave her notice. After that the dreary job at the school board. They'd been about to terminate her when she quit, and all those temp placements in one-man offices with never enough work and too many lunches in with somebody's lonely husband. But this new job at the town library in Felix's aunt's old position had possibilities, not including the bronze plaque commemorating thirty years of devoted service. At thirty-three, she'd gladly taken over the smaller of the library's two offices behind the big circulation desk, Felix's aunt's office with the slip-covered easy chairs and the window with a view.

It was Dan's idea calling for her at the library. Dan, well-known in the community ever since his first book *Grady* became such a hit. What wasn't known was the well-disguised boy in the book was the assistant librarian's younger brother as well as the author's second cousin — that Elizabeth Donlon and Dan Crist shared a family history. In his second phone message, he said after drinks in town, why not drive out to a camp on a lake. Walking shoes would be in order, maybe a warm sweater for when it got chilly. After dark this time of year it got chilly. Juliet thought it sounded romantic. Elizabeth didn't know what to think.

Fortunately, Friday was the weekly staff meeting, though any meeting would help hasten her day along to its end. After staff meeting, the puppet theater troupe due in for more feedback got her all the way to three o'clock with still two hours left to go. By then she'd run a comb through her hair three or four times and checked her reflection twice in the bathroom mirror. She'd been replaying Dan taking her aside at Felix's funeral, his hands on her shoulders, nothing about it to suggest he meant other than to console. Still, how very close she'd come to telling him she'd only settled for Felix; she never loved Felix; that all she ever wanted from Felix was a home and a home life, Felix always about the boys.

The four other library staff had left by the time Dan arrived at a quarter past five. He seemed preoccupied, putting her even more on edge. He suggested crossing the street to have their drinks at the Old Orchard Inn. She'd have a frozen daiquiri, he a dry martini. He liked her hair style and thought a short hair style suited her. Had wearing her hair long been to please Felix? She didn't know what to say. She wasn't clear anymore what had pleased Felix, only that he liked her naked.

He pulled a picture from his wallet. "My girls," he said. His wife was a dark-haired beauty; his daughters Becky and Sarah seven-year-old fraternal twins. Both girls looked like him around the eyes, their hair darker than Dan's, more like their mom's. He looked sad looking at their picture. Over another round, he confided his family life was on the skids, his wife convinced he was having an affair. Lately, she'd been saying he had to make up his mind; he had to choose. He told her it's not that simple. Is there anything simple once you have kids?

"I probably shouldn't be telling you my troubles this way," he said. They were in his car going slowly south on the old highway. "It's just we've always been able to talk. Even when you were young, you were grown up. You lived in your own world. You wrote all those love poems. How old were you back then?"

"In 1963 I would have been thirteen."

He lifted his foot off the throttle. "You seemed older."

"Only because I wanted to be."

"You had a boyfriend though."

"No boyfriend. I didn't have a boyfriend."

"You had to be writing those love poems to someone."

"You don't need a boyfriend. All you need is imagination. And I was just writing them to be writing them. I thought I'd be a writer like you scribbling away in my notebooks."

"We're here. This is it. I have a cooler in the trunk. Don't forget your sweater. It gets cool once the sun goes down now that summer's over."

She had the feeling walking in she was some place she'd been before. But how someone of her background would get invited, she didn't know. Donlons just never were invited any place nice — not her mother Dixie, not her Uncles Colon and Kelly, nor her or her brother James. Only Dan's mother, Darlene Donlon, had escaped the Donlon curse. Cousin Darlene married one of the Crist Brothers, owners of Crist Marina. Darlene was the new proprietor of the old dance pavilion on the lake. The Crists weren't exactly money people, but nobody messed with them.

Had she come here with Cousin Darlene that time? And had her mother been invited too?

In all there were three buildings: a stable buried in brambles, a board and batten bunkhouse, and a massive three-story main structure with two tall chimneys in the end gables, casements in front opening on the lake, and in back on an apple orchard and hay meadow. She'd possibly been here to a party once, instinct shushing her, warning not to ask whose party and why would she have been invited. Just those few more steps and she could see water, watch the speedboats vanish in the distance, feel the tiny wings of tiny critters brush her cheek.

Once inside the house she knew, or thought she knew almost if not precisely when she had been there before. To a party, to an all-girl party, to some kind of swimming party after dark. Only a young girl at the time, but maybe a year or two older than what she'd always think of as her "camp summer", because weren't they living over Benz Men's Wear, her mother on the wagon then working part-time at Newberry's? Didn't someone come to town to pick her up?

"This place... this place is huge, like a mansion."

"That's how the old families built them then, for all the cousins and the maiden aunts. Now nobody comes, not like they used to, and only Badger and her brother Paul stay longer than a week. This summer Badger has Hugh to keep her company in the city. And Paul stays pretty busy too with his dance troupe. But Badger was here the month of June. Ever since June though, it's just me and my two girls, and only on weekends. Weekdays nobody's here at all."

"Did I know her? I feel like I've been here before, but a long time ago."

"If you knew her, it would have been when your mom rented the trailer over on the camp road. Badger taught arts and crafts at the old girl's camp, the same girl's camp I bought a year ago."

"Now I remember her. She wore her hair in a braid. She made pots on an old kick wheel. One time she made me cry. She told me I shouldn't ignore my brother. My brother was lonely. Couldn't I see how lonely my brother was? And I remember this room and us playing records on that old-fashioned record player over in the corner and all of us going skinny dipping together after dark. And I especially remember this one girl, this one really nice girl. She worked in the camp kitchen and lived upstairs in the staff house. I would write her verses and give her snail shells and pretty stones. She was my best friend then. I didn't have many friends then."

"What was her name? Do you remember?"

"I don't remember. All I remember is her telling me stories and making things out of wood. She knew how to make benches and she made me my own bench. She was the nicest person, and the party I came to here was for her birthday and that's why I was invited, because we'd been writing each other letters. I think it was her 20th. It was in June. That much I know. And her and her mom celebrated their birthday every year. I thought that was so cool. I remember her crying because it was her first birthday without her mom. I figured something must have happened. Her mom must have died or got sick. But the rest of the time Sophie kept us in stitches. I remember Sophie's name because Felix's aunt's name is Sophie."

"I knew. I always knew. I had a feeling all that summer. I paddled out from the marina once hoping to find her, but no one was around."

"You knew her?"

"I still know her, just not by the same name. Your friend's name was Jane. We fell in love when we were nineteen. Remember the girl I was so in love with the winter I lived on the camp road and I'd get lonesome for her and you'd come and keep me company? Well, that girl was Jane."

"But I didn't know you were in love. I just thought you were lonesome. You were living all alone, writing all those sad stories in your notebooks. And I know I never knew you knew my friend."

"To me she's *Sparrow*. That's the way she wanted it. She had her reasons and why I can never think of her by any other name. What my wife doesn't seem to understand is how I can still love her. But sometimes there's no putting love behind you. You're looking in the wrong end of the telescope if you think you can. Just this summer she was here. Here one day, gone the next. But that's her, that's Sparrow. With her you never know; all you know is to stick by her. That's all that counts really. Let's eat. Why don't we eat something? Like I said, I stopped at the deli."

Elizabeth's memories of her year lived on the camp road were different from Dan's. She remembered him writing and writing, always writing. She remembered how eager he'd be to read to her from his notebooks. There was a song he made up to some old tune playing on his car radio. She'd asked him if he would write the words down for her. Now she asked if he had ever written any other songs, and all he could remember was something Sparrow wrote. Not a poem exactly, but like a poem. If he could find it, he'd show it to her. It begins: *all I'm doing, my darling, is putting your words on and wearing them around, looking in the mirror seeing how they fit.*

Later over coffee Elizabeth told him she knew his song by heart. Then she told him she'd taken it to an engraver and had a plaque made for her brother's tombstone. She told him she couldn't sing it but she could recite it. She wanted him to appreciate it, appreciate it for how true it was.

You get about 80 trips around the sun
Then you're gone so you'd better have fun
And share the trip with someone you love.

And when it's done and the trip is over
You'll spend eternity in the clover
Hopefully, with someone you love.
The ride goes fast so you have to hold on
Before you know it the time is gone
You'll look back and smile with pride
If you didn't screw it up for the others on the ride
You can't get another ticket, you can't get another pass
Or ride again by going to mass.
So get on the ride and hold on tight
You'll have a great time if you do it right.
Don't be judgmental or pass out blame
Because when the ride is over we're all the same.
No one will know your past or fame
You'll be lucky if they even remember your name.
So it's about 80 trips for you and me.
I can't believe all there is to see.
If the trip is good it will end with a smile
Remember you only get to ride for a while.

She watched him smile at places, roll his eyes at others.
When she finished, he stood and stared out at the lake. He began
recalling her brother James trailing along behind his big sister
pulling his three-legged beagle in a little metal wagon, little James
carefully laying up kindling teepees in the big stone fireplace,
James standing on a chair reaching for a Milky Way on the
mantle, James being read to, James skipping down the camp road
doing his best to keep up with his sister.

A night he'd never forget was the night Elizabeth pounded
on his door, yelling, "My brother... is he in here with you?
Because he took his blanket and wrote his name in big letters on
the pad by the telephone. I keep calling him and he doesn't
answer. We have to hurry and find him before something
happens to him. It's cold out and I'm afraid he'll freeze."

They found him finally at Galvin's Amoco behind the retreads. That was the first time, but the last time he never made it back. That was when he died in a little town far from the little town he came from, and his big cousin Dan got the brilliant idea to write a book about him. That was it, wasn't it? His cousin James, still so young he couldn't raise a mustache, dying alone and far away because of something Dan could have done but didn't do to save him. Dan hadn't gone looking for him till he finally found him; Dan hadn't saved his cousin James from himself.

Elizabeth couldn't believe her ears. Dan really believed her brother's accident was his fault? What could he have done to save him? What could anyone have done when James was always very determined? If he wasn't to blame then, why wouldn't she talk to him or even look in his direction, all those years never meeting his eye? She didn't know what to tell him because she couldn't tell him. How could she tell him she couldn't meet his eye because she loved him, that it scared her to death she could love anyone that much?

"Someday there's something I'll tell you," she told Dan on the drive back to town. "But not today, I can't tell you yet. It's something I have to think about."

"Something you'd sooner die than tell? I know I shouldn't tease. I just hope I didn't ruin today for you. But I won't bug you. And any time, Elizabeth. You call me any time. I'm just glad we've patched things up between us. You said you didn't have any friends back then, but you had me. I was your friend then, and remember no matter what, we're Donlons and always will be. That's the important thing."

She'd turned on the news and then the phone rang. It was Badger calling from Brooklyn to say she'd just got off the phone with Dan. Dan had called her about his cousin Elizabeth, sure she remembered a birthday party she'd been to at Badger Point. Absolutely, summer of '63, the summer she had Sparrow here helping her to build the bunkhouse, the summer Sparrow turned twenty. And yes, she remembered the party and Elizabeth coming out from town and Sparrow's friend Sophie coming from somewhere far away. Oh, what a glorious day it had been, and the most wonderful party, nobody wanting to leave, a party to remember.

Almost too chilly for a dip, she put her swimsuit on anyway. Badger had gone in swimming before breakfast and urged her guest to swim before the breeze picked up. This late in September even the least breeze could make a difference. After her swim, they'd have lunch on the patio. If Elizabeth wanted more tales of Dan, she had some doozeys, beginning with the time her mother came up from the city and found a canoe pulled up on their landing, a young boy asleep inside on their couch. All he had with him was his bedroll, his canteen and compass, a flashlight, some matches, and his .22. For three days he'd been living off a sack of moldy bread left in her bread box, some apples found in the orchard and squirrel meat roasted on a refrigerator rack in her fireplace.

That was the first time, but her mother had found Dan to be endearing rubbing sleep from his eyes there on her couch, not giving anything away about who he might belong to and yet polite, surely the most well-mannered little housebreaker in the county. He was handy, and he excelled at plumbing, and he wasn't afraid of heights. Only two things he was afraid of, he confided; he was afraid of his mom at times and afraid of snakes. Only much later did he mention his mom going off the deep end after getting the regrets letter a year to the day after V-E Day. But he did really love his mom. He loved his mom a lot. He'd do anything for her. So far, living on his own was the only anything he knew how to do.

It was later over coffee, the sun starting down the west horizon, the supper dishes cleared away, and she and Badger in search of sweaters. "Dan says you write. He says even when you were a kid, you wrote poetry. My mother always wanted to write, but I think most people are afraid of it. Afraid someone will read things into what they write, things that aren't there. What do you think?"

"I don't think about it. And I don't write anything anymore anyway, not in a long time."

"My mother was a strange duck. She'd always worry what will people think. But maybe we all do. I have a boyfriend you know. Did Dan tell you about Hugh? This old moth-eaten sweater is his. We met two years ago. No, maybe it's three years ago now since we first met. Anyway he's older. At seventy, Hugh understands the important things, such as the pleasure of being naked together even when we're not young and silky. Am I embarrassing you? It's just I like talking about pleasure, now that I finally understand it. Before Hugh, I never really understood the simple thing it is. Now I say, why wait till you're old and gray? Still, maybe not for everyone.

"You warm enough? Let's go in. I have something up in my attic I want you to see. I don't know what happened, but something happened between Dan and Sparrow. Dan doesn't talk about it. I just know something's changed. Here we are. Take a look at this photograph of Sparrow and her husband Ruben. Isn't he handsome? He's as handsome as she is. I wouldn't call her pretty, but she never changes, does she? I guess we're all a little in love with her. There's just something about her."

Elizabeth sat at her desk mending book spines. She'd ask Dan along the next time she went to the cemetery. Felix's aunt had been in with her blue agapanthus in a pretty pot, explaining when Felix died she'd been at her sister's in Connecticut after that traveling to the Maritimes to visit more relatives. She traveled often now. In addition to the handful of Crumb kinfolk still living in the area, she had nieces in nine states, nephews in seven, two brothers in Canada, and two in Europe. Still she managed to keep up commitments, the historical society, church circle,

Scrabble club, services performed as a volunteer. Nearly eighty now, she hoped to live to ninety, the life expectancy of the Hale side. Felix's side had a tendency to die young of those awful coronaries.

Elizabeth would call Dan after supper. They'd go Saturday or Sunday. There were two graves — her mother Dixie's grave and brother James's grave, but no family plot. In death Donlons were as scattered as in life. Her two uncles were interred in neighboring states, one across the border in Vermont, the other in Western Massachusetts. Her mother's sea captain father buried in disgrace in New Jersey with only a footstone to mark eighty years on earth, far removed from his wife's marble sepulcher in New Brunswick, dead of childbed fever at age twenty-nine. Ever since her day with Dan, Elizabeth felt lighter, her burden lifted, her dear cousin back at last. Wasn't that what mattered? Someone she'd know all her life, trust with any secret.

In his voice message, he said he'd be honored. Either day was fine with him, but for a few more weekends he'd have to be at Badger Point. "Soon the last of the summer people will have gone for the season," he said. He went on to list tasks still to check off as if he were the last of the procrastinators putting off stowing porch rockers, draining pipes, getting a man out from the marina to haul out the boat. But before too long, he continued... well, he'd be the first to admit it. He loved every minute of it. Winter bringing tranquility, winter rarely disappointing. She played his message back. She tried to envision him as her 'sorry-to-miss–your-call' came on, a last wishful moment perhaps waiting for her to answer? No, of course not, the wishful moments all on her side, not to mention other more important and serious things he had to reckon with, all matters she could live with.

How long had it been since she'd ridden somewhere on a bike? She couldn't remember, but when Felix won his five-speed that year at the fair, he'd gone out and got her one. Three years later, two more for the boys for the family vacation. She couldn't remember the combination to the lock on their utility shed, but with any luck she'd still fit under the back wall where the hill fell away. Felix's brother Frank's garage door concern had been a big boon to the Crumb family. Felix and Frank built the bike shed using a dozen steel garage doors and then trading their extras to friends with something to offer in exchange. Three weekends at different camps and one day-long outing on a motor boat, now all of that history with Felix dead, Jason married, Michael far away.

After sponging off cobwebs, Elizabeth pushed her five-speed to Galvin's Amoco. Chuck Galvin inflated the tires for her and asked for news of Jason. He always asked about Jason but never about Michael, though he and Michael had gone all through school together. But most people forgot Michael, just like they forgot James. Later on, she'd drive out to the cemetery and try out her five-speed on the service road. Women her age can lose the knack for things and out-of-towners take the curves too fast. *Stick to the back roads; get there in one piece;* that was what her mom taught her, what she herself taught Jason and Michael. She'd have her chef's salad with Felix and Oralee, her slice of carrot cake with James, lie down in the grass by her mother's side, and get those forty winks in before heading home.

She'd seen the girl on the scooter here before. She lived with her uncle out on the dairy road. What was Elizabeth taking a picture of? Taking a picture of a song her cousin wrote. What's the song about? All about our trips around the sun, and then we're gone, so we better have fun. What else? About getting on the ride and holding on tight, and having a great time if we do it right. *Did he do it right?* Did who do it right? *The one you were talking to.* Oh, you mean my brother James. Yes, he did. Yes, James did, as right as he could get it, as right as anyone.

She was at her corner when she caught sight of the big station wagon in front, loaded down with boxes that laid the leaf springs flat, the boxes labeled *Grady,* the best-selling book about

James, the book that James's famous cousin Dan wrote about him. But what was Dan doing at her house on a Saturday when he was to be at Badger Point?

"Dan?" she called at her back door, "Dan?" again in the hall. Finally a sound, Dan asleep on her porch glider. Still, he didn't look great — a two-day stubble, circles under his eyes, his station wagon weighed down with boxes of books, seats draped with winter clothes, boots and shoes piled high in the foot wells. Where was he going? What was going on?

"Once I tell you the story," he warned, "I can't un-tell it. Just so you understand, you might not like me as much once you know. But let me just say it's not what I want. It's Cindy. She's sorry now she ever met me. She knows, she says, and she knows everything, so I can just quit playing Mr. Nice Guy. I was sure she meant Sparrow. But no, she was talking about these. Remember these?"

"Your old notebooks?" She hadn't known he had that many. Three bags of them? She waited for him to go on.

"Look," he said. "Look at the dates: November/December 1961/January 1962. This bag goes through July 1963. This one's August 1963 to January 1964."

"From when you lived on the camp road in the staff house."

"And you lived in the trailer. You and James coming to see me after school every day. Your mom was having her problems then. I remember it being quiet, not a whole lot going on. But I was writing. Remember, we talked about all this last time? Sometimes I'd read to you from my notebooks. You were my first fan."

She opened to the first page of the November/December 1962 notebook. "I remember," she said. "What's so terrible about you writing? I loved you reading me all those things you wrote about your friend. It made me feel grown up. I forget her name now. What was her name?"

"Her name was Carmen. Carmen and I grew up together. My dad was dead. Hers was always in the slammer for drunk-and-disorderly. My mom was depressive. Her mom left her with an aunt as an infant, a woman who disliked people in general, but her more than anyone."

"I remember you reading about when she worked washing dishes at the Leaning Tower."

"I read you that? About her boss putting the arm on her and her having his kid?"

"You told her you'd take care of her, that things would work out. You had your after-school job at Grogan's Grocery. You'd find her a decent place to live. She could give your name to her baby."

"I guess I did read you that part. But I know I never read you the ending, about us squatting at Badger Point those two winters? No, I didn't think so. I was a senior two months from graduation when Carmen went into business for herself turning tricks out at Badger Point. That's when I kicked her out. That's when I washed my hands of her. But that wasn't the end of the story. First the state came and took her baby. Little Freddie — Freddie the fearless we called him. Little Freddie was just two when she took Badger's mother's old Chrysler New Yorker and drove herself into the lake.

"Your mom told me. I will always thank her for understanding, but who else would understand better than her about Carmen, Carmen just another sad story for most folks. Cindy says there's something sick about my interest in troubled girls like Carmen and Sparrow. She says now it's affecting Sarah. Sarah being so sensitive is the first sign. Cindy wants happy lives for our girls. She wants them to want sports cars when they learn to drive and graduation trips to Paris. She says I don't want the same things for them when I do. She says it's unhealthy for them getting caught up in the things I write books about. It's just a trial separation, but I don't know. One minute she's sorry she ever met me, the next she can't go on without me.

"But the reason I'm here is this. Remember? I'd forgotten it all started with my so-called song. But I went to visit James Wednesday and there my song was engraved on his tombstone just like you said. Here, let me read this to you. When Sparrow wrote it, we were so very young.

> *All I'm doing, my darling, is putting your words on and wearing them around, looking in the mirror to see do they fit. Eighty trips around the sun, you tell me, each of us circling in our tiny gilded cab, our journey made sweeter by sharing even knowing our final destination is the end of all we've known and done. But shouldn't knowing our final destination is the end of all we've known and done make us sweeter, make that light you speak of come on sooner? Help us glide along more evenly, help us appreciate what we've come to know in our little time; share the beauty in everything around us, sing life is good knowing how good life truly is just waking to another day.*

Elizabeth was reminded of being up in Badger's attic room with all the beds in a row under the casement windows. And Badger saying that thing about being afraid they were all a little in love with Sparrow. Such an odd and unexpected thing for someone to say, even if it had the ring of truth to it. Sparrow — thoughtful, earnest, honest — and yet who loved getting the giggles more? who loved having the time of her life as much as she? And Sparrow so very similar to someone else she loved; Sparrow so like Dan. Was everyone a little in love with Dan as well? Was that it? Not really love at all, but making everyone feel a little in love with them, some kind of magical thing they did without even knowing, some kind of golden dream anyone would want to dream along with them to the end?

There was a story her mother often told, a story about Dan's granddad on his father's side. All she could remember now was him being an artist who lived on the lake near Badger Point. But there was more, a big secret that eventually got out and the reason her mother even told her about him. Did the secret have to do with Badger's mom? Was the secret somehow connected to Badger's mumbo-jumbo about her mom's dream about being a writer that time at the lake? Someday she'd ask Dan why he never said much about his granddad on the Crist side, never wrote a book about him.

Meanwhile he was hard at work on his fifth book. The book was about his great-grandfather Captain Horace P. Donlon, dead at eighty, dying all but alone in Highlands, New Jersey, with only his grand-daughters Dixie and Darlene and a very young Dan there for last rites. Very few remembered the story of the ship-wrecked *Estes Noonan*; in Dan's opinion, many of those who did remember remembering only second-hand. The story went the captain had been in his cabin drinking the night the *Estes Noonan* ran aground. Still, he'd managed to telegraph their location, help his crew ready the passengers for rescue, reassure them help was on its way. Too soon though, the ship was taking on water and help was taking too long to get to them. One by one they swam for it. In the end, only Captain Donlon hauled to safety by the brave men of the Spermacetti Cove Life-Saving Station. In the first light of morning, fifty-two bodies found in the pounding North Atlantic surf.

There was a line in Dan's song: *No one will know your past or fame.* Who was he thinking of? Was he thinking of their great-grandfather when he wrote those words? Was he thinking they'll forget your name unless your name happens to be Horace P. Donlon, captain of the *Estes Noonan*? All but the captain lost at sea one cold December night in 1909: 21 men, 19 women, 12 little children under the age of ten.

She asked him if she could assist him that same day he told her the story of the shipwrecked *Estes Noonan*. She would gladly give him a hand. As a library assistant, she could arrange interlibrary loans for him. She could help him sort through newspaper accounts on micro-fiche. Sometime maybe drive down to where it all happened. He was delighted. Did she really mean it? Writing a book can be very lonely at times. He assured her nothing could please him more.

Family Smile

ADIRONDACKS — JULY 1992

"I'M NOT CRITICIZING. I'M ONLY THINKING HOW SAD for you. Still, don't tell me anything you shouldn't. It's none of my affair one way or the other."

"More tea, Lindy?"

"Please."

Badger studied her girlhood chum across the table, at sixty-seven as cagey as at sixteen. Lindy must have heard the gossip concerning Badger Point from her cousin Harold who likely heard it from Badger's brother Paul, though Paul may have let something slip to a mutual acquaintance in Asheville — Asheville ever the busy trunk line for gossip with an upstate area code.

"Dan knew his bloodlines years ago," Badger assured her friend, "and long before we deeded Badger Point over to him."

"So he's known all along about your mother and the famous artist?"

"Mother decided the less Dan knew about his famous grandfather the better. The rest we could tell him after she was gone. Beyond that was up to him. All he has to do is ask."

"What I'll never understand is your mother taking so long to tell you. All the girls at school knew the story. Why not you when it was water under the bridge?"

"For the simple reason I was her daughter. For the reason some things you just know. But if you think it was water under the bridge, you're wrong. The man spent every summer here from 1921 when they met till 1940 when he left; 1940 being when Percy Point was sold out from under him."

"By *the man* I assume you mean your mother's paramour?"

"Call him what you will. By *the man* I mean my half-brother's father, the famous landscape artist, the man in my mother's life as essential as her husband, all one and the same!"

"You knew him?"

"Only Mother knew him."

"One can only imagine how awkward for your father when he had to deed Badger Point over to a Crist."

"Can one really? Well then, let me state there was nothing awkward about it. Father had no qualms. Not to mention we don't share your view of the Crists. When they see an opportunity, they go after it. Nothing wrong in that. And Father had three children — two sons and a daughter. He was as proud of Dan Crist as of us."

"If you say so, but turning you out of your own home and at your age!" Here she tuned Lindy out, the rest a recounting of the many summers shared at Badger Point up to the fateful summer when their long togetherness came to an end, the summer she took her first flying lessons, the summer she turned fifteen.

"Tell me, Lindy, anything else I can clear up for you before I get you back to George?" Damn if she'd give Lindy Babcock another minute, this woman with a sixth sense for the right moment to ruin an otherwise perfect afternoon. And just how would a catered-to, city-bred, only child like Lindy know anything about such matters of the heart, promised as she was to George from the time she was in water wings. Lindy's blueprint for life was a duplicate of Lindy's mother's: cast your eye no farther than your mate, no farther than your spacious home blocks away from where you grew up, from your summer home on the lake, your one child conceived there four years into married life.

Beyond all other considerations, Badger held Dan in the highest regard. He was her ally, her comrade in arms, the person she was closest to and not only here on the lake. Worry over someone else, Lindy Babcock! Not to mention she had Hugh who at almost eighty was as sharp as George in his prime. And Dan's twins who she'd taught to shoot a shotgun, reef a sail, all about the stars in the firmaments. By god, she didn't need Lindy Babcock or her pity. And likely someday, Lindy well might stand in need of hers.

But as fate would have it, her mother never told Dan he was her grandson. As far as he was aware, he was loyal friend of the family, in-charge person in the off season, reliable fellow marksman in duck hunting season. Never again would Badger prepare a wild duck dinner and not be reminded of that day in the duck blind, Dan downing a last cup of coffee, his shoulders hunched against the wind. Even now she could hear every syllable of her one impossibly long sentence telling him who he really was: the grandson of a famous artist, his father the adopted son of the Crist family and her half-brother, his grandmother and her mother the very same woman, Helen Badger Worley.

That last day of duck hunting less than a year ago, his brown eyes had pooled tears as he told her it was all too much to take in. Given his pick of kin, who would he pick besides Badger and Paul other than his mother and his cousin Elizabeth. He would never forsake them. Even harder for him to take in was that Badger Point would be his to pass down to his children. And if she really thought he gave a hang about a famous artist somewhere in his family tree, he didn't give one hang about him, whoever he was.

Now with Lindy gone, she had three days to sort the sacred tokens of a girl's enchantment stored in the attic room at the top of the stairs, casements opened to the sweet scent of raked meadow grass. This, her favorite room held much of summertime, of friends in books, of the chosen authors of her childhood, of all the lazy afternoons she and Paul watched summer storms cross the lake, their matching pairs of solemn eyes at the window.

She and Paul dreaming in the attic room, each tucked in their own narrow bed. To their way of thinking, the empty bed beyond each of theirs for the new brother or sister one day to join them, while in truth only for the absent boy whose gingham dog waited summer after summer. Still, neither one was made aware of this other child, the parents in their wisdom deciding such young children would never know what to make of it had they been told. They'd want to know how could there be an older brother when Badger was oldest? And how could he be their brother when he was never home? And what was this older brother called? And what school did this older brother go to? And on what day of what month was this older brother born? And if this older brother were truly *older*, older by how many years?

Badger was seven the day she had Sally over. She'd taken her chum up to the attic room to watch a summer storm cross the lake. At first she let poor Sally take the blame, explaining how frightened Sally was of thunder, the reason why she climbed in with the gingham dog and covered up her head. But that wasn't what happened. From the start Badger egged Sally on, urging who would care if they got in a bed no one had ever slept in. Her mother had been severe with her, giving her a whipping to remember. After that things never were the same again, always something not quite right between mother and daughter that couldn't be talked about and couldn't be fixed.

She sorted more books, skipping more sentimental birthday inscriptions from long-dead relatives. After the books, she sorted stacks of magazines, many from her mother's childhood that always felt terribly out-of-date for her and Paul. By mid-morning dozens of *St. Nicholas* magazines were hauled out to the burn barrel. By late afternoon piles of vintage *Life* and *Look* flipped through and discarded as well. She'd been about to call it a day when a 1940 edition of *Time* caught her attention with its promise of a Current Events Test.

In June 1940, Badger had just turned fifteen, as always passing for older. At barely four, people had taken her for school age; when only ten, quite often for thirteen. By July, she'd been flying for weeks with a bush pilot named Buzz, not many years older than he believed her to be, which by law was sixteen. Soon he had her convinced he could make her into a pretty fair pilot who one day might just rival another famous flying Amelia. As Amelia Badger Worley, she had the name for it after all.

The *Time* quiz covered every department: National Affairs, the Pictures, the World at War, the Arts. She checked the answers and could see how some review beforehand would have helped better her score. She could clearly recall civilians perturbed at the few seats available when all the new recruits filled the trains, but the politics of war had been lost on her once she left for boarding school. At her Virginia boarding school, there were more important things.

Unlike memories that even now remained crisp of her summers on the lake, few wartime memories remained about which she could say the same. The one memory she'd hoped for was the longed-for red-letter day, the day her mother would ask for her forgiveness and have the kind of affirmation-giving, soul-redeeming conversation only a daughter who feels terribly wronged will always dream of having before it is too late.

Dan's famous grandfather was the one who had blown her cover that near-perfect day. He'd been sketching, hardly aware of planes practicing take-offs and landings on a nearby airstrip. When he sat down to his lunch, they were still at it, then all serene as he stretched out for a nap. When it went down, he had no idea what woke him, but kept a long lens handy in his camera bag. He framed a shot of Helen's daughter waving in a spotter plane from atop the downed plane's wing. Her braid was his first clue, her long slender neck his second, the last straw her mother's smile — mother and daughter so very alike even if often so obviously at odds.

By God, she would never forget Lend Lease. At the Worley dinner table, always some back and forth on the subject, her mother leading the pro-side of the Lend Lease debates. No problem remembering mobilization. All the men rallied by the fireside talks, the roll call of fallen heroes, the war's long unbroken night. Yes, and always the fathers reading to their sons about war, reading from the June 24, 1940 issue of *Time*, the same lines she read again fifty-two years later in 1992:

> *For the French Army living in a shrieking, thundering, bloodshot nightmare, last week was a period of progressive disintegration. Swarm after swarm of planes strafed them. Herd after herd of tanks charged them. Columns of armored motorcycles machine-gunned them, storms of artillery shells and grenades burst among them. They retreated fighting, day and night, through a time-space that had no measure because it brought no rest and no features because the whole world was filled with smoke, noise and death.*

Every summer the entire Worley family — meaning all but the father — took the New York Central to Albany where they stayed overnight with maternal aunts. The routine never varied except for the year she came down with a serious case of impetigo, her father promising to fly her to the lake once her impetigo cleared up. Even now taking off in a Ford Tri-Motor from Floyd

Bennett Field was among the most vivid memories of her life, as was her memory of Lou, the feisty lady pilot in the cockpit.

Wednesday was Becky's day to help her out at Badger Point. Lately she could feel her niece closing in on certain chapters of past history, especially her questions concerning a local flying school started before the war. Had Auntie Badger known of it? Her mom had seen old photographs of pilots-in-training classes, and one class included a girl pilot-in-training, her dark hair in a single braid. In several photographs this same girl embraced a handsome pilot. The girl pilot wouldn't happen to have been Auntie Badger, would it? She'd dodged the questions that time but knew more were on their way.

Secrets were hard work. And poor Dan had lost patience once she refused him permission to write her story as it really happened. Her true story had adventure, a certain degree of danger, and better yet, turned on all-too-human frailties rather than on the old tried formulas. Not to mention that only her true story provided an opportunity to set the record straight. Still, 1985 had been such an unexpectedly satisfying year, not only the year she turned sixty, but the year she fell in love. The plain truth of the matter was that she hadn't been ready to tell her story to Dan and less ready yet to tell the world.

"This may take a while," she told her niece. "But you asked about the flying school, about the young woman in the photographs. I was the young woman in the photographs. I had to lie about my age to take flying lessons. The young instructor in the picture was Buzz Albright. He was twenty-one; I was fifteen. My first time flying solo I landed in the drink. Your great-grandfather took a picture of me and made the mistake of showing it to my mother. Not long afterwards, I had a new address at a Virginia boarding school, 750 miles between me and my flying instructor.

"But if they thought they could stop me, they were wrong. I continued my flying lessons at my room-mate's father's private airstrip. Still they did succeed in putting a stop to me flying at all when I was underage. Mother wasted no time. She got that part taken care of with one quick call to our congressman.

"Still, I'd logged more than enough flying hours. We were close to declaring war. Buzz helped me get papers under a false name, and I was getting ever closer to joining women pilots from around the world flocking to Britain to get in the fight. And by god, this woman was ready to get in the fight. But then what do I do? I get myself kicked out of school. Before I know it, I'm grounded in Brooklyn for the duration."

The next part of her story was the long middle part, the part that went on and on. Nothing going smoothly for her back in Brooklyn, her mother and her mother's friends always spying on her, watching from behind their movie magazines at the drugstore, listening in from the next telephone booth wherever she went to make a call. Like the Syndicate, every string she'd think to pull, somehow the Syndicate would get there first. Worse yet, while she'd been in Brooklyn, Buzz had become a flying legend overseas. He led the pack in missions, his legendary record taking her through the long middle part of her story to the beginning of the end. That was the part she dreaded telling and was just beginning when the phone rang. Becky was needed at the office urgently, giving her Auntie Badger a breather, a merciful hiatus in which to regroup.

Only after her niece left, did she get out the drawings. No one had seen them except for the French farmer who found them, and later Buzz's family and now her. There were maybe three hundred of them, all in pencil. More than a third of them were of Canadians: the teacher in Buzz's country school, the World War I ace who first took him up in a plane, his sisters, his parents, the family dogs. More than half were of her and of some good times together during flying school days clowning around at the lake, all done from memory. A dozen were of the bombed-out farmhouse in France where he'd survived for over a year. A single drawing of a French boy in a cap looking up at RAF planes flying east in formation, the only drawing with his serial number, his home address and her name and Badger Point address written in his hand on the back.

Several hours later Dan arrived. "Becky can't get away, so I told her I'd fill in for her," he said joining Badger at the table.

"Fill in for her doing what?"

"Wow, I guess we know who this guy is — Paul. It's got to be Paul. And this one. Is this my father beside the B-52? My father was a pilot?"

"I'm the pilot in the family. What's taking her so long?"

"It was me. I was the one on the phone. I called Becky to tell her I had to talk to you. There's something we need to talk about."

"Talk about? What's there to talk about? Yes, my half-brother — your father — was the navigator of the family. But none of us knew at the time who he was. I mean we knew Dan Crist. Everybody knew Dan Crist, knew him from the marina and knew he was the best damn slalom water skier anywhere around. We knew the whole family, the mother, the father, the three Crist girls and Dan. We just didn't know Dan was adopted. Your mother says your father himself never knew, and she only found out when he died in the war. And my mother got her first clue all those years later when you, my friend, showed up on our couch."

"He does look like you, you know."

"You think so? In the photograph your mother gave me he doesn't look much like me at all."

"He wasn't smiling in his photograph. Here he is. Look. The family smile."

"Mother always would say our smile was our downfall. I always say *what downfall?*"

"No mistaking it though. Becky has it, Sarah. I don't smile, so who would know? And your mother had it and so do you. What I came here to talk about was you living year round in the city. I mean I appreciate the sentiment behind deeding Badger Point over to me, but…"

"But? But what, Dan? For heaven's sakes!" She pulled the captain's chair out and squinted down the length of the table. She picked up the last envelope and dumped out the rest of the drawings. "And these! These are of yours truly. Look at how young I was. Not an ounce of flesh on me. Look at the hair!"

He leaned closer. "How pretty you are. Here you are dancing and there you are sailing, here playing un-horse on some handsome fellow's shoulders, in your big goggles here taxiing a plane. And here I am looking at a 4"x6" drawing of the father I never knew and only learn today that he was a B-52 navigator. Another missing piece of the puzzle. And here I am almost forgetting again," he said patting his shirt pocket.

"Forgetting what?"

"About these notes of your mothers. I was still a kid the day she gave them to me. All she'd say was someday they might mean something."

"My mother gave you some notes, did she?"

"I honestly forgot all about them. She kept asking wouldn't I rather be water skiing. You know how she could be."

"And just exactly what do these notes my mother wrote say?"

"Like I said, I forgot all about them. I only read them yesterday. One said deeding Badger Point to me was something they'd planned for a long time. And how sad for me I never knew my father, how he died too young, but how many did die too young, that sort of thing. If you like, you can read it. The other one is the one she wrote to you. I forgot about it because she told me it would be best to wait. She must have written it over and over."

"No need to hurry and read it right this minute then, is there. Is that what was so important?"

"I thought it was."

"A note from the grave?"

"One other thing too. I heard from Sparrow. Things aren't going well. Her mother had part of her stomach removed; I think she said ulcers."

"Her mother's in prison for life. I know that much. What about Ruben? Where's he?"

"She didn't mention him in her letter. She says she's going to write to you, but asked me to ask you if she could come for a week. She sounds pretty desperate. You know Sparrow, how she can get at times. But I'm worried about her. I really am worried about her."

"You have time tomorrow? I'll have some time tomorrow. We can talk about Sparrow then. Afterwards I'll give her a call. Now read me my note from Mother. One thing I don't need is more silence from her. Just go on and read it to me. What does she have to say to me after all this time?"

"Or... we could just leave well enough alone."

"Just read it to me. Read it and get it over with."

"If you say so, but why say she's sorry now. Love has such a bad reputation around here. What's wrong with it? She gladly went to her grave not saying a word about the man she loved all that time. In my house, if I even mention Sparrow, the world will come to an end. And you fell in love at fifteen with a man six years older. That's a crime? You're a criminal? You have to be sent away and for the rest of your life never speak the man's name? I just don't get it. Here she's saying she has much to answer for. I'll

say she does – as if we can spare anyone their pain. Just say stop
when you've heard enough.

> *My dearest daughter Amelia,*
>
> *I have much to answer for, but all you need to know is this. I
> wanted to spare you the pain of what I'd gone through, but
> then I didn't know what you would go through losing the
> man you love in the war. I've never been able to say this to
> you and so I'm taking the coward's way out to say it now in
> this letter. Of course, life is about losing, and we all lose in
> the end, but I lost you before the end and through no fault of
> your own. I beg that you forgive me and pray the good Lord
> forgive me too.*
>
> *With all my love, Mother*

"You crying, are you, Badger?"

"No, of course not, I'm laughing, not crying for Pete's sake.
That was the letter, the letter from Mother I've been waiting for.
We'll say no more of it after this. I wasn't in love with Buzz. I was
fifteen. At fifteen I was incapable of love. I didn't have a clue. All
I loved was flying. I was in love with the sky, in love with the
clouds. I was on my way to being a good pilot. Buzz always said I
could have been great. He did all he could for me. He believed in
me. He never gave up. Mother never believed in me even for a
minute.

"But we have each other, don't we? And we have Paul. You
have your girls. I still have Hugh. We have Sparrow and Elizabeth
and Sophie and fond memories of many others. And I have much
to be thankful for. You're the best thing to happen to me, and I
mean that with my whole heart. Enough said on the price of eggs
then, what do you say to that?"

"I say whatever you say. You're still the boss around here,
not me."

A Car without Gas

ADIRONDACKS & NEW MEXICO — JUNE 2002

SUMMER WAS HERE, OR SOON WOULD BE. Before summer's arrival their daughter Sarah was due in on the Lake Shore train. Since Dan seldom was the one to pick her up, Cindy's drive to the station became that rare duty mothers take on once her children leave home. As a rule, Sarah came with only her backpack, her trusty leather tote, laptop computer and camera bag. Each year she and her mother made quick work of their leisurely lunch together, with Sarah dispatching new glossies of her Maine coon cats, her mother ready with the old familiar stories from another life. Each nursed a frozen daiquiri; each took care not to invite long-buried differences of opinion to a place at the table.

This year Sarah's mother took possession of a New Brunswick rental house a week ahead of schedule. She invited old college chums to join her rather than have Dan there against his will. Dan seemed happy his wife had a new lease on life, bowing yet again to old college ties and good old days he had no part in. With Cindy occupied, he'd pursue Corvette #5 and finish the final chapter of his book, perhaps prepare another dad round on server-farm energy consumption — his daughter's brilliant idea for her master's thesis. With any luck maybe find some time for airing certain grievances he had with the state, among them

Albany's ideas about whom to tax and how to tax them, government largesse once again run amuck. He knew people in high places; he'd write another letter... these days any diversion improving his outlook on life.

Oh, but he hadn't been ready. It hit him like a cyclone. Like the girl in Wizard of Oz — not Judy Garland, the one in the book! The one named Dorothy, the one spun away in a funnel cloud, the same kind of preposterous un-survivable single event now spinning him away from everything dear, eerily similar to what came out of nowhere and caught Sparrow unaware. Sparrow had been living in such dread her mother would take her life rather than live out her life sentence, then her husband Ruben was taken in the prime of his life by that terrible disease. Meanwhile, his mother Darlene remained strong at 96, and Badger still not yet gray at the temples the day she fell out of her pear tree, four years shy of her eighty trips around the sun.

He'd leave early, drive the back roads and give himself some time to think. His thinking was done best with the volume turned up, some honest back and forth with the piece of work behind the wheel, the one who got things right most of the time, but oh brother, could he ever screw things up! What an asshole; and lately a worse one than ever. Or maybe just a candy-ass coward like at the post office earlier. But why did she have to go on about it? Okay, I nudged her. A little nudge, not a fatal collision, probably didn't feel a thing. I bumped her bumper, big fucking deal. But why not just admit it? That's all you had to do, asshole! Yeah, and did she have to say what she said when it had nothing at all to do with sex? Goddamn it, what's the matter with these crazy women these days anyway? Is that all they think about!

He'd gas up at Galvin's get a coffee at McDonald's. No, maybe he'd skip Galvin's. Chuck was such a know-it-all lately. He'd hit McDonald's for his coffee, gas up at the crossroads, and take the river road. He had hours yet till her train was due, maybe spin by the old pavilion. He'd heard Johnson Brothers had a man out looking at the bulkhead, heard a rumor roofers were checking out the roof, knew for a fact every last loser with a pulse was out spreading some damn rumor or other. He couldn't walk down the street without someone asking about the old pavilion or Badger Point. But that was Chuck Galvin for you. Some people never change, just get more like they always were.

Still, neither did he want to see his mother sell the old pavilion just to get out from under. Hang a For Sale sign on the old pavilion and it was open season. Anyone could buy it, and whoever bought it could as easily tear it down. Sell it to the wrong outfit and everything it stood for, it would stand for no more, as if all it had stood for never was. The age-old story: let a poacher from downstate in the door for half of what it's worth; prepare to see him flip it, by that time too late to see a better day. It wouldn't be the first time. Those types don't go away. Always seeking the next easy mark, always looking for the little brother of the big one they sold the bridge to.

He wouldn't put the top down, not today, not even close to warm enough, though maybe in a day or two. He'd hold off on the old pavilion, wait for Sarah. They could swing by on their way home or any other time they pleased. Four whole days to do things, this year without the usual interruptions. Cindy was too far away to dangle her girls-night-out treat or any other trick up her sleeve. Still, a change in the air this year and this twin more attuned; Becky easily embarrassed, thinking a father should know better, so like her mother, willing to toe the line, tread the well-trod trail. Sarah more like him, always a bit lost in time, always in search of something — something neither he nor she could name.

Her sleeping car was the second from last. He watched the attendant help an elderly gentleman off, assist a mother with two small children. It didn't surprise him; Sarah likely in a last-minute dash from the dining car to her sleeping car, after making an acquaintance met at breakfast into a lifelong friend. Some people just have a way with people. It was a gift like any other, like perfect pitch, like a green thumb or a sixth sense, or enough sense to stick with it and not ditch it, his own loosely cobbled together gift, for him filling the bill this far anyway. But here she was finally, his easy-going, dad-adoring daughter with the crazy smile. Not the Crists' smile or the Donlons' or even her mother's, but the Badger smile. She had yet to spot him, feet not yet on terra firma, miles and miles of rail from distant Corvallis, Oregon to Schenectady, New York.

"About time," he said taking her tote, playing the put-upon dad. "This old thing... is this all you got?"

"Mom says it's time I traveled properly, so she Fed-Exed me some proper luggage. Now we have to wait. Howsbyyou, Daddy-o? You're looking ready for prime time! Do I get my smooch this year or am I too old for that? Now turn around and wave to your fans. See them there in the dining car window? It's you they're waving at. I told them you're famous. I liberated eleven copies. Remember the time you never made it out to talk about your book?"

"What book was that?"

"Book number three, my favorite. Everyone's favorite."

"I've honestly never understood why that one was so popular."

"Why? Because it's a love story. At least Cousin Elizabeth knew a love story when she saw one. If left to you, who knows? Maybe the good ship Estes Noonan settles down with a mermaid at the bottom of the sea, your grandfather's love story one more casualty of his sinking ship."

"As bad as that, am I?"

"Don't look forlorn. Mom and I always eat some place fancy, but you know what I want?"

"Hot pastrami on rye, side of pot sal, side of slaw?"

"Nope, a blue plate special at some crummy old diner. Any ideas about where to go?"

Sarah's first full day *home* she was happy to hang out at the old house, the entire upstairs now her father's office. She approved of his skylights. She had two in her rental house in Oregon and an upstairs office as well, one upstairs room for writing her thesis in, the other one for other pursuits. And by the way, her new boyfriend's a South American, Dan not venturing questions as to this latest Lothario's status. All he knew was the last one lived in. Nathan, was it? Ethan? He could never remember who to say "hi there" to when someone with a deep voice answered her phone.

This daughter's high school boyfriends were all Toms. He'd been a classmate of the first Tom's dad; a team-mate of the second Tom's on the fastest relay team in the history of the high school. The last Tom's dad had been his best friend, that one's name incised in granite on the War Memorial in Washington. The first time they took the train down to see the War Memorial, they took young Tom along. Young Tom was a senior that year, Sarah a year behind. As far as anyone knew, one young couple guaranteed to stay together. He'd kept track of young Tom through Tom's mom Rose, soon to retire from Grogan's Grocery. Her boy moved west the year Sarah graduated and was making good money working for the railroad. His girl was stone broke working hard for her master's degree. They'd shake their heads. In high school no light came between them. After high school, neither one picked up a phone to call, even living in the same state!

On her second day home, Dan made his first mistake. "Your day to choose," he told her. "I was thinking we'd stop in on your old friend Mr. Thune sometime, but anything's fine. You choose what to do today."

Sarah wrinkled her nose. "I like Mr. Thune and he was my favorite teacher, but last time he got kind of personal. All the talk about Carmen. What was he, in love with her or something? No, don't tell me. Forget I said that. I know. Why don't we get a boat at the marina and buzz out to Badger Point?"

"A little cool still for that, isn't it?"

"My choice, remember."

"Maybe you and your friend Sue should go then. You'll have more fun. I'm not that much fun lately."

"You're fun. You're still fun, Daddy."

"Not really. Not lately."

"Auntie Badger?"

He looked away. Would the choked up feeling never stop? "I never thought I'd have to face life without her I guess. I must have thought she had enough gas in her to keep her going forever."

"Poor Daddy. I used to be afraid of her. She was so outspoken."

"Spoke her mind is all. She went to bat for you, you know. Your Auntie Badger went to bat for me as well. And for Sparrow and for your sister. Even for your mother one time, though she'd be the last to admit it."

"How is Sparrow?"

"I wish I knew. Did I tell you about Ruben? Well, now he's gone too. She loses Badger one month and the next Ruben. The big shocker though was Badger, for me and Sparrow both. I don't know who it hit hardest. But as long as we had Badger, we had each other, Badger keeping us in touch through all manner of trouble. Even the day she died, she was on our wave length. Now I don't know. Sparrow's gone silent on me lately. We'll be fine though — Sparrow and I."

"Will you?"

"She's a lot stronger than you think."

"I don't mean Sparrow. I mean you. Will you? Will you be okay?"

"Why? Don't you think I will?

"My honest opinion?"

"Sure. Tell me what you really think."

"All right. What I really think is you try really-really hard not to be, but down deep inside you're really-really sad. You are, Daddy. And I think you've been like this a long time. And it's not just me. Elizabeth says the same thing and she'd know better than anyone. Who knows you better than your cousin?"

"No more sad than anyone else. It's life, Sarah. I've outlived my dad by forty years, outlived my best friend by thirty, my friend Carmen by forty-three, my cousin James almost as long and now Badger's gone. Sure I'm sad, sad about losing my people, the ones I knew best, the ones who knew me. You'll be sad at sixty too. You haven't lost anybody important yet. But you will. We all do."

"You've still got us, you know. Maybe someday we'll all batch together at Badger Point. I dream about it. Becky says she dreams the same thing, but all Mom wants is for you to unload Badger Point so she and Grandma Crist can re-open the old pavilion. I think she's crazy. But we told her you'd never sell Badger Point, not for a million dollars, not in a million years."

"Of course not. But who knows how or where or who we end up with. You go on now and make your plans. I'll take you two girls out somewhere nice for dinner. I must have some email piling up I should get caught up on. I was about to do it last night, but then we got talking."

"Um, after you went to bed I needed to check the web for something. There was this email from Sparrow. Sorry. I didn't mean to read it."

"Email from Sparrow? Pretty safe reading our emails, toots. It's not like we're all that romantic anymore. Not for years. Go on now. Get going. Time's a wasting."

My darling,

I leave in the morning. I'll be gone two weeks this time, but you can email at the same address as last time. The new visitor support system is such a huge help. Some church ladies in town started it almost a year ago. Pat, the one I stay with, charges me only a very nominal amount for my room, but even better Pat's someone for me to talk to should things get heavy at the prison — which they do at times as you know.

But there's something else I want to say, something I never told you. All I can recall telling you about Ruben's mother Lil was that she was everything my mother wasn't and everything I ever wanted to be. "Free" I think is the word. And I wanted to touch the world with beauty like she did – lighten everyone's heart. She called me "her darling" and why I call you "my darling" now. Is there anything sweeter than being someone's darling? If there is I don't know what it is, and it could never be sweeter, only different. I just want you to know how Lil changed everything about me and my life with those two words, and how I hope saying them, or writing them — I do say them too —brightens your world for you. We've had some hard times, haven't we? First Sophie, then Badger and Ruben, and it won't be long before one or both of us lose a mother as well. And we're not getting any younger ourselves. I wrote this for us. I hope you like it.

Sparrow

Beneath This Our Lady Fern

Your arms around me I hear you say
Lie down with me beneath this lady fern
Here beneath her parted fronds
Her leaves as jewels upon our fingers
We're not as limber now as once we were
Our kisses more tender now than ever
Twined anew our afternoon together
You, my enduring ivy,
I, your abiding rose.

He read it through once, twice, read it again. He couldn't stop reading. First the letter, then the poem, then the poem out loud as if her words once sprung from the screen would grow roots, send up shoots, her verses flower not for a season like before, but forever. But then he tore himself away from her invitation to lie down with her and drove the two miles to Galvin's. Chuck wouldn't be a minute. They'd go to lunch. Why not? He'd wait in the office. But then the scanner picked up the collision on the highway and then the call came for a wrecker. It was a fatal, his friend Chuck saying maybe not such a good day after all. They'd do lunch some other time. Was it Chuck or was it him or was it the fatal accident on the highway? Whatever it was it took all the shine off.

Sarah's last day she asked her father why was he so secretive. Why couldn't he just come out and say what he was thinking, what he was feeling? Why put on such a big act? Sparrow's beautiful poem — what was the matter with him? If anybody wrote a poem for her like that, her feet wouldn't even be touching the ground. They were out in the garage inspecting the shiny new Corvette, his, on trial all week. Well? What did she think? She had to think a minute. The shiny new Corvette was unlikely to change much in his life, but if he let Sparrow back in his good graces, she just might change a lot. Trust her. Trust Sparrow. He had to trust somebody sometime, didn't he? Had he even answered her email yet? No, she thought as much, but knew he would in time.

Dear Sparrow,

What is a car without gas? It can be anything from a pile of rusted junk to a work of art. But when you add gas it grows a spirit, and it becomes a means of transportation. And through the life of that car it takes you places. It takes you with your friends and family. You see things you'll remember; you meet people you'll never forget. It adds experiences to your life. Not because it's rusted junk or a work of art, but because it has a spirit.

What is a piano without a pianist? It's a piece of furniture; maybe beautiful, maybe not. But when you add the pianist it too grows a spirit. It produces music that can change your mood, make you remember things from the past or dream of the future. Not because it's a beautiful piece of furniture, but because it has a spirit. It adds experiences to your life.

What is a television set without electricity? It's an interesting technical gizmo, but when you add electricity it instantly has a spirit. It can take you away from reality, show you exotic places, educate you. It has a spirit.

And when the useful life of these things is over, what you remember is not the rusted junk or the piece of furniture or the ugly gizmo, but the places the car took you, the music the piano produced, the favorite shows that came to the screen of that television. For when it's all said and done, that's all any of us has; the experiences of our lives.

Now what are we? We are a body that has one single purpose. That is to be a support mechanism for our mind, our spirit. Like the car that needs gas, the piano that needs a pianist and the television that needs electricity, we need a body to have a spirit. Our body takes our mind to places, puts us in situations, and dares us to be open to the unknown.

But Sparrow, I must admit to being at odds with what I'm about to write after you wrote your beautiful poem. Still, I have to be honest with you. I couldn't take it in. When I read your note and your poem, it felt almost like the day Badger told me she and I were kin. I thought how can that be when I'm a Crist and she's a Worley. When I read your note, all I could think was how can Sparrow be telling me this when she told me I had to stop thinking about her, I had to give her up, that she was no good. And I did that. I gave you up, but not because I wanted to. I gave you up because you gave up on me. You shut me out. You closed the door on us forever as far as I was concerned. I just wrote "Our body takes our mind to places, puts us in situations, and dares us to be open to the unknown." How I wish my mind could follow my body to your lady fern. There's nothing I wouldn't be willing to do if you could convince me I truly was your enduring ivy, you, my abiding rose. But you'll have to convince me. Twice wounded, twice shy, I'm afraid. How I wish it wasn't so.

Dan

Nothing could surprise her anymore, but Dan's reply to her email coming late and with little encouragement left her close to tears. She shut down her laptop and went down the hall to shower. Past nine when she went outdoors to finish air drying her hair, she debated if it was too late to bother Pat with this new trouble. Still, Pat being a Christian lady, might she not think ill of what she'd written Dan a little over a month after losing Ruben. How to explain Dan to Pat, explain Dan to anyone?

Maybe start by answering which side of herself she was showing him. Was it a different side now from when she got his call about Badger's deadly fall from her pear tree, their dear Badger's bones just too badly broken, no one in hearing distance to answer her cries for help including her nephew and best friend Dan? Then another call from him and then another, while at the same time Ruben was calling her from the patio. And now was she the only one breathing new life into better, happier times? Or was he doing it as well, his contributions less obvious but no mistaking them — that same summer, those same places, those same songs, those same longings...

Dear Dan,

You're right of course. I can't argue with what you say. I did do what you say I did. I gave up on you when you were willing to face terrible consequences just to be with me. I'm speaking of your children, sacrificing your beautiful children. Still, that was never my object, nor is it my object now all these years later. I won't pretend. What I want is for us to be as close as we once were. I want to find a way back into your good graces. To use your words, "I want to be open to the unknown again", hard as that is with so much water over the dam. Still, I understand your reluctance. I worry about all this at least as much as you.

Maybe for now we catch up on each other's lives. We don't talk on the phone. We don't visit. We email. I ask you what you're working on, about your girls. You ask me whatever it is you want to know. I promise to tell you everything.

I'll start now. Why not? When I turned twenty I spent the summer with Badger. That's when I got to know her and Badger to know me. That was the summer we built the bunkhouse together and Sophie came from Nebraska and everyone threw a twentieth birthday party for me and I never laughed that much or cried that much. It was beautiful, the most beautiful day in my life except for the day I met you.

Following that summer, Sophie and I moved to NYC and got our apartment together and found jobs. We stayed just short of six years. We lived at West 103rd by the post office just off Upper Broadway. Sophie played the field for six years. I had a lover. He was older, married, and off-limits for all practical purposes. I wouldn't say I loved him, more I needed a body next to mine, between me and too many lonely nights.

After NYC I followed Sophie to Colorado where she took up a career in aviation mechanics and where I took up nursing. We congratulated each other; we were amounting to something. Up to then we were playing with fire, not losers exactly but living dangerously. I was Champ, she was Ace. At best, we were two single girls bumbling along, not at all sure what life was all about. She worked in a man's world and had her own way of seeing things. I took care of sick people, but learned men are still men even in a hospital bed, and a woman's body is what they think about more than anything, even when the ones they try hardest to impress are still always men.

But I'm going to stop. As I re-read this, all I can think is, what am I doing? Setting you up to say all those things Skip swore any man in my life was always sure to say about me, that I was trash! But I have to come clean, no more pretending, no more fairy dust.

If I never hear from you again, I don't blame you. But dare I hope in telling all, the door I closed on you will open. I go back home day after tomorrow. I'm quite sure I'll never see my mother alive again. I think we celebrated our last birthday together. Remember me telling you about "our" birthday. You said, and I quote "no need to explain". That's how we started. You trusted me. I trusted you.

Sparrow

Dear Sparrow,

I remember your mother reading a romance novel, you sitting across the table from her nursing a beer. You looked so peaceful. I didn't want to disturb you as much as I wanted to dance with you. I liked your mother all right. I think she might have liked me too under different circumstances. I know how much you mean to each other. You showed me the thunder eggs she found in Oregon as a young girl. They were your earthly treasure you kept under your bed in a box. When your mother dies, I want you to call me. I don't want you taking her ashes back to Idaho all alone. I'm serious. That's one trip we're making together. Promise me, you'll call me. No excuses accepted.

I'll answer your email later after I give what you've said some thought. I can already appreciate how honest you are. In the meantime, take your time driving home. Find some good music on the radio. Think of us dancing together the last time we saw each other.

Dan

Pat was up at first light to fix breakfast, pack a lunch and find Glen Campbell's "20 Greatest Hits" CD for her friend to sing along to on her drive home. "Call me. Your mama will want to know you got home safe. The fried pie is on top, a ham sandwich and some Cokes underneath. Should hold you till you're home again. But aren't you a pretty picture all in blue today! We pray for you and your mama. And we pray for Ruben too, God rest him. He was a good man, but then that's something I don't have to tell you about now, do I."

No one had to tell her Ruben was a good man. It wasn't possible to love somebody as long as she'd loved Ruben, go through all they'd gone through, and not know what a good man he was. Still, long before she realized something was haywire with him memory-wise, she knew there was something the matter with him otherwise. When he'd look at her, it was like he didn't see her, like she wasn't there — not a woman to undress and take to bed, more like a voice on the other end of a telephone call.

As a young boy, he begged her to stand up to her stepfather. Had he felt later he hadn't done enough? In those letters he left unanswered, had she told him what she was up against and where to find her — in New Mexico in the mountains and not in California? How she wished she could remember. Then Sophie meeting him saying she couldn't help but like him, anybody would, but it was almost as if part of him were unconscious or dreaming, and hard to tell which. Even so, Sophie saying her friend had all the luck, first Dan, then the married one, last Ruben, all handsome, all clever, all devoted in their way.

Sophie was first to register the change in him. The three of them were on vacation hanging around the house Ruben built in Deming when he said he had in mind a car trip. He wanted to romp with Jane in the Texas bluebonnets before it was too late. He wanted to race through the wild blue-eyed grass with her, lie with her on the Indian blanket in the Texas hill country. He was in love with love; he was in love with life, in love with his beautiful wife. Sophie was sure he meant something terrible loomed just over the horizon, Jane sure he meant before spring was over, before the wildflowers wilted and died in the heat.

Whether he'd been speaking of spring flowers wilting in the hill country heat, he maybe didn't know himself or know exactly what he meant by "too late". But the first sudden change in him was the difference between day and night, when the day dawned and he saw his wife with a man's eyes. It was like a switch thrown and all his sleeping senses streaming out at full bore, as if the words "too late" were all the reminder he needed that there was one day less today to get enough of her than the day before. Even her mother noticed. "Before he was always reserved with you, Janie, not like your other one." Her own mother who had never spoken of these things to her ever!

With tears streaming down her face, she hunted a place to pull over. She couldn't have said who she missed most. She missed so many people. She missed Ruben. She missed Badger. She missed her friend Sophie. And she missed Dan; she wanted Dan. But at this moment the person she missed most was her mother. And now she knew why she missed her. She missed her because only one person knew the only two men in her life she'd ever loved. Only her mother had known Ruben as the young boy she spent all her time with; only her mother had known Dan as the young man who was so in love with her daughter.

She didn't have much of an appetite. She took one look at Pat's fried pie and wrapped it up again, then a few bites of her sandwich. She drank one Coke and then another. She was thirsty, and very lonely. They were cruel, these last months, as she and Ruben grew closer than they had ever been, he raging at his fate, submitting only at the very end to slip away finally, his hands in her hands, hands rarely idle from the time they were children. And now she didn't know who she was or what she wanted other than her mother. She wanted to talk to her mother, hear her mother say "It's all right, Janie. Go ahead then if you're sure", knowing no matter what her mother said to her, she wasn't sure about anything, not anymore.

It was still light when she unlocked the door and went straight to bed in the shorts and top she drove home in. She didn't want to dream. She wanted to sleep without dreaming. When the phone rang at eight the next morning she was sound asleep, thinking she was still at Pat's visiting with her mother at the prison. It was a relief being at home; a relief hearing Sophie's daughter's voice on the telephone. "How'd it go, Auntie Sparrow? Did I wake you? I bet I woke you."

"No-no, Lara, I'm glad you called. I'd have slept till tomorrow. It went well. We had our birthday as usual. They keep her on tranquilizers now, she doesn't say much to me anymore. She did ask about you though. I told her you're thinking about college a year from now. She remembers your mother. She always admired your mother's spirit."

"But what can I do? There must be something. School's out and I have a week till I start my job at the bottling plant. I really want to come see you, but only if you want me there. We thought you might be lonely."

"I am. Very lonely. I have a lonely heart. I think I always will have. Your mother understood that. So did Ruben. And Badger. And Dan. Now I'm down to Dan. You were just a little girl when we all drove east together. Do you remember the big house on the lake?"

"I remember a lake and riding in a motorboat. I remember you water-skiing."

"That was your mother. Anything involving speed she was good at. When though, when can you come? I have to look for work soon, but I have this week."

"I can be there by dark tomorrow. I have Mom's picture albums. Do you remember the summer you worked in Kentucky? There was this terrible flood, and you and Mom just hopped in a car and went down and worked there for free. There's another album from when she was in high school, the summer you came through High Road. I'll bring that one too. And some other things of Mom's I want you to have. One is a photograph of her in an old World War II Spitfire she'd been saving for Auntie Badger. Another is something she wrote the week she and her new boyfriend left on the canoe trip. Every time I read it I think maybe she knew she wasn't coming back. It's sorta spooky, Auntie Sparrow. She called it 'When Love's in Charge'."

"She did? Did she really? That's perfect. That was your mom all over, Lara. She was always saying that. She said those exact same words to me the first summer I met her. That was how she saw life: once you fall in love, love's in charge, and there's nothing you can do about it. I'll look for you tomorrow night then. I'll fix chicken and dumplings and hold supper. Sound good? Oh, and bring your guitar. We'll sing to the coyotes. I love you, and you calling me like this made my day. Now I can get up with a smile on my puss. Gotta go now. Dan just dinged me. Drive the limit, no faster than the limit."

> *Dear Sparrow,*
>
> *According to my calculations you got in late last night. I've had you on my mind since getting your email. I think I'd forgotten all the blank years between visits. Mostly I had no idea where you were. I'd imagine you all kinds of places, and I'm sure New York City crossed my mind. You didn't mention Badger during those years in your last email, but I'm sure you must have seen her from time to time. Badger was good that way. She never tattled on us to each other. She probably felt unless asked to do otherwise, she should keep any confidences shared with her to herself. But I'll have to admit the part about your married lover did set me back a bit. Not that I sit in judgment; I don't judge you. In fact, I think I might understand why you would choose such a person, especially following so closely on the heels of us. The one I really envy though is Ruben. After all, you went back to him.*
>
> *Now I'll follow suit and tell you about myself. Two years of working in old man Geary's blueberries was enough for me. For six years after that, I divided my time between working at the marina for my aunts and uncles*

and at the pavilion working for my mom. I forget just how many, but probably for four or five years, Chuck and I worked as booking agents for my mom, bringing in some pretty big names and drawing good crowds to the pavilion. We thought the sky was the limit, but then we had some new regulations like when the drinking age went from 18 to 21. What it all boiled down to was the big names stopped signing and the crowds stopped coming. One year we went dark half the summer and the next summer the lights went out for good. And then my best friend Tom died in Nam. Tom was a writer even in high school. After he died, I made up my mind to pick up where he left off. He'd go around reciting "Ozymandias" and could write poetry as good as Shelley's. If only you could have known him, Sparrow. Tom and I were in synch. We thought alike. He was just much smarter.

You may as well know about Thora. She lived on the lake and I'd see her at the marina when she'd bring her old Chris in for repairs. She had ten years on me. She leased one of Mueller's lakefront camps on the north side. We met her second year teaching flute at Strahan's Music Camp. I never actually lived with her, but I might as well have those three summers. She never told me this, but I was her cure for somebody important she was getting over. She was very nice and discreet about when she was having company. She was from Boston, but not all that proper, if you know what I mean. But before and after Thora, there wasn't anyone in particular till Cindy. Just some old friends from high school making the usual mistakes kids make growing up.

But I promised Sarah I'd ask you a question. Sarah says I try my best to hide it, but in her opinion I'm sad, and I've been sad for a very long time. I've already asked Becky, and she says she wouldn't call me sad as much as contemplative. I prefer being contemplative to being sad somehow, but then I think I have reasons in my life to feel sad, so why not admit it. Just please tell me what you think. Was I sad when we were together? I honestly can't remember. All I remember was I was in love.

Dan

Dear Dan,

You are sad at the moment. But you're sad now because of losing Badger. It was a terrible shock. But even before losing Badger, look at your life. It's like a road map to tragic dates and places. Here Dan lost his father, here his cousin James, there his friend Carmen, there his best friend Tom, over here his sweetheart disappointed him and disappeared, and then reappeared and disappeared again. Meanwhile he married under not the best of circumstances, had twin daughters and did his best being a good dad and husband. I agree with Sarah, not that you're not contemplative. You're a writer so, of course, you have much to contemplate.

I've known from day one how alike we are. I don't know even now whether that's a good thing. It could be we're too alike for some things but just the right amount of alike for others. I don't see being sad as a major stumbling block at our age. We've both been through the mill enough to know those times run in cycles and that the best way to feel better is to feel close to someone, even if you never get to hear his voice or look in his eyes or see him smile.

By the way, Sophie's daughter arrives tonight. She lives with her Aunt Goldie in Nebraska, not far from where I met her mother the same summer I saw you for the first time having a beer with your friend and playing Ray Charles on the jukebox. This is the last "Dear Dan" letter I write. I'm taking you at your word, and I'll call you as you made me promise when my mother dies. From now on my emails to you begin "My darling". If that's too much to bear, think again about us going to Idaho together. I'm quite serious. It's not too late to change your mind.

Sparrow

The house-cleaning went fast, faster than she'd have thought. She found one last whole chicken in the deep freeze, and then went after the mess in the guest room. The last person to use their guest room was the night nurse they hired to help Ruben toward the end. But every spring before this spring, Elizabeth had been the regular guest in their guest room coming for a week from rainy upstate New York. How Elizabeth loved her spring visits, loved everything about them.

But the best part about her last visit was what she was able to inspire in Ruben, patiently sitting down with him each day to describe in some detail a scene from one of *their* walks. Before long Ruben was busily sketching, turning his tablet her way, asking is this like the trail we took, are these like the ferns we saw, are these cedars like the giant ones rising straight and tall along our trail? Is this like the rocky cliff face high above the valley below? Is this our rustic lodge and these our porch rockers? Are these all our foot-sore and weary hikers with their boots off drinking wine?

Ruben's last good days of his too-short life were when Elizabeth stayed over for a second week, a not-quite-finished Ruben Baker mural in their guest room, the rising sun writing anew his final signature each morning on their east-facing wall.

Then just this morning Elizabeth's email coming. Not such a big surprise that Dan would leave Badger Point to Elizabeth in his will, saying he owed her for helping with his book about the Estes Noonan and telling their grandfather's love story, a story he would have missed if not for her. But also a thank-you for being there to remind him who he is — a man who seeks understanding of what drives a cousin like James and a friend like Carmen and even someone like her so that he can put a little of each one in a story, pass on some small amount of understanding to others. She tucked in her nurse's corners and plumped her pillows. Her first tears fell as she measured flour for her mother's dumplings. Dan's email arrived just in time:

Dearest Sparrow,

I think I understand now what you mean when you call me your "darling". It's when you "talk" to me, isn't it, when you see an eagle soar or hear a certain song and you want me to be a part of it? That's when I'm your darling, and what's wrong with that when our circumstances limit our options for being closer than we are. You are correct. Why would anyone object to being someone's darling. And no, I'm not about to change my mind. Just call me. I know it can't be long now for your mom. I just hope her ulcers aren't giving her more pain than she can bear. I'm glad you asked her to draw you a map. I can just see us trying to locate such a remote place without one. It's going to be very special – standing on the ground where you were born.

Felix's son Michael will be with us for a few days. Elizabeth is away on one of her trips, so Cindy and I will be first to meet the prospective bride. At forty, he's finally settling down. Is that what you did at forty, Sparrow? Somehow I don't think it was like that for you and Ruben. I think you did exactly what you were meant to do.

Now I'll be the one shaking things up by agreeing with you that this current running between us is real. You didn't make it up, and it won't go away just because it's not convenient. We both know better. And this time, we can't go to Badger for her blessing. I went ahead and made some edits in your poem. I'm fairly sure I don't have to ask if you approve.

Dan

Finally we meet
Beneath your lady fern
Her leaves jewels on our fingers
We're not as limber now as once we were
Still our kisses sweeter now than ever
Twined our few hours together
You my darling forever
I your darling too.

Other Stories of Altered Lives

This Hard Land of Dreams

THAT A TIME WOULD COME when she would forsake the Wild Rose Ranch had never crossed Ivy's mind. Not on the day when old age forced her aunt and uncle off the land, not some years later when the main quarter section was sold to Portland people likely to vacation there no more than a week or two once or twice a year.

But that time did come. At the end of a long tramp up the cliff road switchbacks beginning at her Uncle Fritz's doorstep just the far side of Wild Rose canyon.

Afterwards, she'd recall seeing a dozen mares and some knobby yearling colts move off as she rounded the Jump-Off and hit the straightaway. Then surprising more mares cropping their way down slope and seeing that none of these were trailed by their spring foals. She'd remember buzzards tipping overhead, the feel of her legs churning under her, her dread growing by the minute that she'd find any spring foals picked clean. But the trail of desolation she found strewn in the cheat grass was so much worse than anything she could have pictured. She vowed she would never go back, knowing in her heart that day would come.

By then seven more winters had melted away, the waxwings returned in as many seasons only to vanish after a single false spring afternoon, and after her Uncle Fritz had been laid to rest beside his kinsmen in Peck Valley's tiny settler cemetery. For Ivy, the days and months and seasons of life seemed to follow one upon the other till news came of her husband's death on a distant Virginia highway while she was away mourning her uncle. Even through this sudden stinging loss, she managed to shore up and keep going. All that summer the old tried reserves of grit and determination were there for her to fall back on, as dependable at sixty as in youth.

But then came September with its lonesome hunter's moon and early morning fogs. One such gray morning she took in a hungry dog for company, though soon the hungry dog moved on. Next she took in Billy, the big bay quarter-horse to board. Then late in October she awoke, knowing that the day she knew would come was upon her. She threw a saddle over the big bay's back and took her time on the all-but-vanished wagon road. At the water tank, she led the horse to where the main barn squared up across from the remaining granary, where a pick-up knelt on flat front tires.

"Go," she whispered, nudging Billy past the pick-up into the barn's main bay. When she dismounted to lift the latch on the big stall once shared by her Uncle Arthur's Belgians, she had to dive out of Billy's way. On her feet again, she looked around to see what could have spooked him.

"I scared you, huh?" said a small girl in pigtails, dusting herself off and stepping out of the shadows.

"More likely you scared him," Ivy answered, reaching for Billy's reins as he backed farther away. At the same time, she watched another small girl in over-sized boots and baggy coveralls edge a step at a time through the side door. To Ivy both the girls and the wild-haired woman framed in the opening seemed more uncertain than unfriendly, but once again she was surprised.

"I had no idea anyone lived here," she said, trying to gauge the person facing her in the big barn's afternoon haze. Feet spread, the woman had a swagger to her even without saying anything. "But not so long ago," she went on gamely, "my aunt and uncle had their cattle ranch here."

The woman took a long sober drag on her cigarette. "Where they at now?"

"They died. After that somebody came and torched the place."

"What kind of people would do that to a cool place like this?" the woman said, her voice rough, though somehow sympathetic too.

Ivy tried a shrug, as if none of what she'd just been saying mattered anymore. "That we'll never know," she said, not mentioning that whoever did the deed didn't stop with setting the house and granary alight.

"Quit messing with her horse! Both of you! Quit!"

"Now I live across the canyon," Ivy said, pointing with her chin toward Uncle Fritz's house and barn. "But when I was your age I lived here," she went on turning to the two little girls, their feet firmly planted still no more than an arm's length from Billy. "These big stalls were for our Belgians. See there, that's where we carved their names."

When she got home she had just enough in reserve to put Billy up for the night. But the pall had lifted. The Wild Rose of her youth hadn't vanished after all. And even sore from diving out of Billy's way, she felt herself almost float up the porch steps. Still, she would have postponed calling her cousin, were it not for the worried sound of Gracie's voice on her answering machine. "I thought you weren't ever going back."

"I did go back though. What's up with you?"

"A change in plans. It'll be Thanksgiving before I can get out there to see you. But tell me, was there anything left of our poor old Wild Rose?"

"Actually some people are staying in the bunkhouse. They fed me supper."

"Staying? Staying for how long?"

"They didn't say. But Kathleen did a couple of stints in the army. Now she has a job operating heavy equipment down in the valley. She has some really smart little kids, Audrey and Evie."

"Just her and the kids then? You sure this Kathleen is on the up and up?"

"Why wouldn't she be?"

"Because why would anyone live there who didn't have to? It's so remote. A mom with two little kids? For me that would be a red flag."

"All I can tell you is they do live there. And you may not think so, but as far as I'm concerned, people are the best protection. Trouble-makers make their mischief after people clear out. Anyway, Jack's coming with the splitter early in the morning, and I'm dead on my feet. Don't worry about it. Thanksgiving will be fine. By then I hope to have Uncle Fritz's in some kind of shape."

The next morning Jack drove up just as Ivy stirred the last ingredients into her soup. Jack and her husband Corby had been best friends since childhood. Then, as newly minted high school grads soon to leave for boot camp, they had stood up for the other in big country weddings. Now she watched as Jack cut the wheel to round her uncle's barn. For as long as she could remember Corby had been the one to get in her uncle's firewood. And for all those years, only when her husband was away filing stories from a war zone or when her uncle was down with an illness, did time feel measured in life spans and not in too-long waits between letters.

As recently as May when Uncle Fritz called to ask could she spare him some time, she'd had no inkling how *a lifetime ago* and *only yesterday* could mean the same. That she could leave Corby in the east busily pursuing a new project and their friends Jack and Brenda could be so carefree picking her up at the airport; like so many other times, their talk mostly idle. And then, with unimaginable swiftness, not only her dear uncle gone, but her husband gone too. Corby's run ended abruptly on a foggy Virginia highway. Now, suddenly, winter looming once again, the steady cadence of loved voices lost to her forever.

Still, what she'd always known remained as true — there was balm in work, even when the work involved a whining splitter making talk impossible. Shifting the lever as Jack wrestled the heavy log rounds into position, the two of them taking turns, working in tandem. The next weeks were followed by more hard work and just as good medicine, whether stacking stove wood under the eaves in shoulder-high double rows, putting up storm windows, wrapping pipes, or caulking cracks.

Even as she wrestled storm windows in place she knew other jobs awaited her attention, one of them being Uncle Fritz's studio hidden from view by a screen of broad-trunk cottonwoods. She'd come close to going in only once. She'd been wool-gathering in a porch chair, a rustic one Corby had fashioned from slab wood the time they stayed all summer, the summer he sat for Uncle Fritz with crippled old Jeff beside him asleep on the floor. Each evening they'd go out before supper. She'd snap beans as the sun slipped down the sky, alongside her husband so fit then from all the ranch work, his freckled hand on Jeff's head the same shades of tan as the old freckled dog.

Even harder to face was the matter of Corby's trunks. She'd had no ready answer for Jack, Jr. the day he backed the U-Haul up to the porch. Two seasons on though, she knew the small company of army foot-lockers still waited in the room at the top of the stairs, one filled with mementoes and manuscripts, another with trousers and shirts, a third with the sweaters she'd knit over the years of his long career reporting for small dailies and wire services and too many cold damp news bureaus overseas.

Soon enough though, Gracie would come. She'd be less daunted by Corby's trunks and by their uncle's nostalgic family portraiture. In the meantime, she sought out old school friends and volunteered at the library. Over supper she paged through books, and a few times looked up to see Kathleen's pick-up make its way up the last grades to the Wild Rose, spilling pools of light before disappearing from view. With the days growing ever shorter, she envied her neighbor the job she had to go to each day, and chose to forget the Waterloo she faced, that fraught time between clearing away her supper dishes and first light.

The day her neighbors finally came for the old mattresses she'd promised them, she was slow to get going. She had rolled out of bed early enough, but then stood in front of the mirror debating what to do with her hair. No mistaking what had once been a nut brown had since faded to dull beige, and was quickly turning the color of soap flakes. And worse, it hung down to her shoulders. She snipped off a few quick inches and then a few more, and might have gone further yet had she not glanced out and seen Kathleen's oldest girl Audrey cradling a marmalade kitten on her porch step.

"What in the world?"

"He's for you!"

"But how ever did you get here? Did Kathleen bring you?"

"She said tell you we came for your old mattresses and she's gone to turn the truck around. Who's that with you in the picture? Is that your little girl?"

Ivy didn't have to look around. Inside the door was her uncle's painting of her sad-eyed mother, little daughter Ivy asleep in her lap. "Oh, but that's not me! My husband and I never did settle in anywhere long enough for children."

Audrey stepped past her, still cradling the kitten. She gave the painting a long thoughtful inspection. "But the lady is you! I can tell, because she looks like you."

"It's not though," she said, evading again. It was one of those times; she never knew when to expect them. Only the day before she had blinked her morning cobwebs away, certain the sad-eyed woman in her uncle's painting downstairs was about to appear. Other mornings she would wake before daylight made a bureau and a wardrobe out of the dark forms across the room, certain she had become the unwitting vehicle for her uncle's lifetime of wishful thinking, that one day soon his beloved sister would finally come home.

"Here, would you take him now? Cause I have to go help."

"But I don't know that I want a kitty."

"So why don't you like him?"

"It's not that. He's very nice."

"Evie calls him Freddie, but I call him Mickey after your old horse."

"Well, take him with you now, and tell your mother I'll be right out."

"Okay, only she's not our mother. Kathleen's only our aunt."

Ivy lifted her heavy barn coat off the hook, feeling in the pockets for her gloves. Of course, the phone would ring. It surprised her though, Kathleen and the girls just taking off and not testing her further about the kitty. Not that she'd take him; the dog hadn't lasted a month. But then she had to shake her head. After all, what harm could there be in telling little Audrey that she was the sleeping child in the painting and the young woman in the picture, with the long hair turning a premature gray, her mother; her whereabouts unknown for going on fifty years.

For the first time since the holidays, Ivy had no visitors at all. Winter had begun in earnest with heavy snow coming the week after Christmas, followed by a thaw, more snowfall, and plunging night-time temperatures. Only when the storm clouds lifted and daytime temperatures hovered at zero, the horse water refreezing in minutes, did time seem to stop. Days went by; then a week. She put on more and more clothing and kept round-the-clock fires burning in both kitchen and front room stoves. She read; she started knitting a sweater; she baked bread. She tried not to think about a narrow stretch of Wild Rose road with barely room for one vehicle and none for error, where new snow often hid ice from the unsuspecting driver.

Then one early morning she opened the back door to find Kathleen and two chilled-to-the bone little girls standing there. No one spoke a word, not rambunctious Audrey, or easy-going Evie, or even Kathleen. They just stood mute till prodded through the doorway to her warm front room. She heated cocoa in the kitchen and hurried back to where the woolly steam off their sweaters filled the air and Evie's heavy brown braid dripped a steady stream of water on the carpet. She had the girls strip down and wrapped them in blankets. At last Kathleen's speech returned. "I kept making them get up," she began.

Later, out of earshot of the girls, Kathleen gamely stumbled through the details. It all started when she told them to get their things together, that she'd found a better job closer to their mother. But then they'd had the ruckus and she'd given in to one more day, though in one more day the weather turned and that one day more nearly got them killed.

"Kathleen," Ivy said, by this time thoroughly alarmed, "what happened?"

"You don't want to know."

"But I think I do know."

Kathleen hung her head. "We were almost down."

Ivy set her mug aside, the cocoa suddenly too sweet on her tongue. She made herself not blink when she asked, "How far?"

"Maybe thirty-some feet. Then we just stopped. I thought we'd bought it."

"I kept having this feeling. I didn't know why, but I'll call Jack. He'll get your pick-up out. Then you can call about your job while I see about the girls."

After the shipyard agreed to hold the job for one more day, Kathleen told the rest of the story. After their quick trip down, it was all slow going getting back up again. They'd make it up a few yards and slide back down. She'd have to carry Evie on her shoulders because of the footing. Audrey was down more than she was on her feet and both girls worried the cats couldn't keep up. Back at the cabin finally, there was hardly any fire wood and all their bedding was still in the pick-up. Their total food — two candy bars.

"But you made it," Ivy reminded her. "And the Wild Rose never was a good place in winter." She didn't say what else she'd been thinking lately. That just maybe the Wild Rose wasn't a good place most times of the year. Especially not in winter, being so far from anyone. Not in spring, with melt water and rainwater spilling down the steep hillsides, churning all the way to Peck Creek and the river, but settling for whatever was cupped enough to hold it. Not in summer, lest the most a person had to do was tend a small garden before or after the heat of the day and didn't have to go out on custom work to make ends meet or build a fence, cut poles, work on the road or patch one or more of a dozen roofs. Certainly, it was as good as it was going to get in autumn, but only if the surrounding woods didn't dry to kindling over a summer's drought and neither man nor nature set it alight come September.

She pulled the last of Uncle Fritz's wool blankets from the shelf in the upstairs closet and the feather bed out of the cold cubby. "Get some sleep," she told Kathleen. "We'll talk again in the morning. I'm happy to keep the girls here while you get things squared away. You can take all the time you need. They'll be fine."

Once Jack winched the pick-up from where it had come to rest on the ledge and Kathleen left for her new job, the scary slide down the side of the mountain faded from the girls' minds. Audrey brought it up only a few times and Evie only when probing the bump on her forehead. Ivy alone remained mired in the experience, repeatedly searching her conscience for answers. Why hadn't she strapped on her snowshoes and gone over to check on them? Why had she let Kathleen talk herself into staying the winter when she, of all people, knew what winter on the Wild Rose could bring?

Still, in her day the root cellar was well stocked. There were Jerseys for milk and butter, hams hanging in the smokehouse, and wild game when they wanted it. They'd been so self-sufficient they never had to leave. And in her day the cramped former bunkhouse Kathleen and the two girls called home had always been a playhouse. The refuges of her memory were from before she came to live on the Wild Rose, too many of them in damp rented rooms with never enough heat.

As Arctic winds tossed the cottonwood tops outside her window, ruminations like these made Ivy's nights restless ones. She was first to catch cold, then Evie, though it wasn't till Audrey came down with it a few days later that the trouble began. Still, she distracted them, keeping Audrey busy with her drawing, finding yarn hair for Evie to paste on paper-bag dolls, coloring in red lips and green eyes and purple forehead bruises to match her own. Even then they seemed much too quiet. And one morning Audrey turned especially gloomy as they stood washing breakfast dishes at the sink.

"She's not ever coming to get us, is she, Ivy?"

She dipped a cup in the rinse water, rattled by an unwelcome concern of her own that was being voiced so soon. "What would make you say that?"

"Because she's not. I know she's not. She'd be here by now."

"What I think, it takes time finding a place to live."

"But I mean what if she doesn't ever come back?"

"I think we shouldn't worry. I think we should be patient." After all, why wouldn't Kathleen come for them? She'd left little more than a week ago. And she did call and leave a message that time they hadn't made it to the phone. And, hopefully soon, Kathleen would be getting a phone of her own and they could call her.

"That a girl, Evie," Ivy said as she watched Evie dry the last cup, realizing what they needed was a place away from the telephone. Each time it rang, both girls froze in mid-sentence, as if playing a worried game of Statues.

Why not go to Uncle Fritz's studio and say hi to all the friendly ghosts waiting so long inside? In the fall she'd started there twice. And then there'd been that strange day in November when she, Gracie, and Jack's wife Brenda walked up the road and turned to face the studio. They'd been chattering away, catching up on each other's news, when she saw how the setting sun pooled a fiery-red glow in the crow's nest windows — this for only the tiniest fraction of a minute. In another minute the studio was shaded and dim, the chill air setting cottonwood limbs to chafing in the woods behind. That was the third time she'd turned around and not gone in. It was the kind of thing that got worse the longer a person let it go on.

"Okay, ready? Hup, two, three, four. Hup, two, three..." Her plan was simple. Together the three of them would visit the place she'd been unable to visit alone. They would build a fire in the big stone fireplace and sit down beside it to eat lunch. After that they'd set up an easel and paint. She could almost look forward to it, like a treat she'd been saving up for just the right time. But then poor Audrey's tears flowed from the minute they sat down by the fire. For the longest time, all she could do was cry, unable to get anything out, though with Evie's urging got the worst of her worries out in the end.

That night after tucking in the girls, she called her cousin. "Now I understand why Audrey's so worried."

"Why is that?"

"Because for one thing she dumped Kathleen's stash down the outhouse. For another their mother's in prison serving time for dealing drugs."

"Oh, my goodness."

"I knew they'd had a ruckus because Kathleen told me that much. And I know how difficult Audrey can be. She knows just which buttons to push, believe me, and not just Kathleen's."

"So what about now? You still think Kathleen is coming back for them?"

"She said she would."

"I know what she said. But what if she's changed her mind? What if she thinks they'd all be better off in the long run if they stayed with you? With her they live like little refugees, no real home. And where will she park them while she's at work?"

"She won't park them, Gracie. She'll leave them with a licensed service like she did here. She's very responsible. She loves those kids. That I don't question."

"For their sake, I hope you're right. Still, you should talk to somebody official. This could get messy. There could be more to this. There could be worse still to come."

That night Ivy stretched out in the room across from where she'd tucked the girls into her own bed. She switched off the light and turned on her side, expecting another restless night. As when

Corby died, Gracie was adamant. She was so sure. Then her advice was to return to the east and let the high-country homesteads return to nature. Let them be scenery for the artists among them, not a bitter pill for extravagant country girls in such a hard land of dreams. *Like your own mother, Ivy.* That was the real message, her own mother who at sixteen was so desperate she ran off with the rural electrification man and spent her whole life on the run.

Still, she'd never once thought of letting Uncle Fritz's return to nature. Her uncle's ranch was second only to the Wild Rose in her heart. And now the question at hand was even more serious. Now the question was the well-being of two frightened little girls. What, if anything, was she to make of a delay of a few weeks, of even a month, if in the end Kathleen came for the girls as promised? And if Gracie's doubts proved out and Kathleen never came for them at all, would it be clearer then, or as foggy as now?

The next morning she awoke to the pelt of raindrops on a house strangely cozy and warm. By her third mug of coffee, the rain began changing to snow and then thickened to a wooly and impenetrable blanket of gray, straining a person's hearing as well as her sight. It was weather neither girl cared to venture out in. Still, they had their routines, regular chores being good for everyone in her book, especially for Audrey whose ears stayed tuned for the sound of Kathleen's return.

It was late when a truck ground into compound low down on the valley road and split an otherwise ordinary afternoon in two. The girls had been quietly grooming Billy while she shifted hay in the loft and did her best to ignore a steady static of more heavy rain on the roof. Audrey and Evie were first out the door. She hurried down the ladder after them, followed by the cats. Huddled at the foot of the driveway, they leaned in the direction of the straining crash-box transmission lugging slowly through the switchbacks and from there up the three grades. How long had they stood there waiting in the pouring rain? Was it as long as it seemed before the phantom truck fish-tailed out of a river of slush, before the pinto blotches on the driver's door slithered past and the single tail-light blinked out and disappeared again in fog?

That night Ivy helped Audrey settle on a book before she sat Evie down to trim her waist-length hair. Later she told Evie not to worry so much about leaving Mama Kitty just yet. "Remember what I told your aunt? I told her you girls are welcome to stay here with me till she has everything over there squared away."

"I know, but she says we can't take Mama Kitty, not where we're going. She says where we're going we can't take a cat."

Ivy patted the stool. "Hop up here and let's get that hair of yours braided. And then you can take Mama Kitty upstairs and we'll start a new story."

"I like the one when you come live with Gracie. I dreamed about it last night. I like the stories that come out right."

Ivy pulled the last few inches of Evie's pigtail through the rubber band, feeling tired, as though she could fall asleep on her feet. The nightly routine got harder with the steady drip of ever-more worrying concerns — that bit at the supper table about Kathleen's threats to re-enlist in the army. Was it true? Had she really been threatening to re-up? Was it some army post where they couldn't take their cat?

She squeezed the sweaters drying on the banister and called Audrey to come back down. Audrey had taken to tending Uncle Fritz's wall clock that hung on the landing. One night she'd tell the story of its long journey to America, first by sailing ship and then by rail. "Everything in this house has its own story," she mused aloud as Audrey nudged the big brass pendulum to start the old clock again.

"We like the story about when your uncle was little and he went on the cattle drive and got lost in the snow storm. And everybody went looking for him and kept on looking till they finally found him."

"I'm glad you like it. I like it too."

"And we think you're the little girl asleep in the lady's lap in Uncle Fritz's picture down in the kitchen."

"I *am* the little girl in the painting and the lady is my mother. My uncle painted us the year we came home for her birthday."

"Was your mother really famous then?"

"Do you think she looks really famous?"

"I think she looks really sad."

"I try not to think of her as sad. But I don't think of her that often, to tell you the truth. She was sad though. Beautiful, but sad."

"I only get sad when people get mad at me. And I get even sadder when they don't want me around."

"It's getting late, my friend, ten minutes past ten. Time for us to go up and get ready for bed. Tell your sister I'll be along in a jiffy."

"But once me and Evie understand some things, then we'll be okay. We just have to understand we're not the only ones. And it's not like Kathleen planned on raising us two kids up 'cause the army's the only life for her. If you want, I can show you a picture of her making sergeant. We got to see her make sergeant. I was five and Evie was four and our mom was there too. We got to eat a steak and have strawberry cake and see them all march in the parade."

"So she's a sergeant."

"Just don't *ever* call her Sarge. She hates it when people call her Sarge. But if she comes back, we're gonna obey from now on and do every single thing she says. And we're not gonna criticize her 'cause she hates it when we criticize her, and she hates it more if I hide her weed. But what I don't get is how come hiding her weed makes it okay for her to go off and just leave us. I don't think that's right. Do you think that's right for her to go off and just leave us, Ivy?"

"No, I don't think it is. I don't think it's right at all. Up you go now. And brush those teeth." Were it not so late would she have said more? Would she have gone on to say that nothing they had ever done or could ever do gave Kathleen the right to leave them? But it was late and she was tired. And like her friend Audrey, she'd had to apply her wits as a child to the difficult business of trying for a better deal, doing whatever she had to do to forestall the worst while hoping against hope what had come to pass already was just a bad dream.

Even all these years later, still fixed in mind were the broken rhythms of Tacoma's night shift. Still in her head were the sound of the big clock tower clock tolling twelve, the grain cars shunting in the yard, the great racketing outbound trains tunneling into night, the imagined cries of mariners doomed and drowned. Forever rooted in memory were all those long hours waiting for the welcome relief of a morning's commotion, for the cheery chuff of a city bus, for the newsboy at his corner, the day shift workers jostling past to the shop floor and slaughterhouse and loading dock, for the children her age at the cross walk crossing to school.

Only toward the end had she begun to see patterns in her own life too. One being how she said things all but guaranteed to drive her mother away. Always accusing her, even knowing how her poor sad beautiful mother kept an eye out for a more wholesome line of work while others taking money for it just never did bother. And in her line of work, looks were everything. She got all that. She understood everything about it. She knew if they ever were to get ahead, she would have to put her own petty desires aside and be more patient, be more willing to wait a little longer for the baubles so coveted at the Five and Dime.

Still, these things were very private, so private she might never have told Mrs. Figge, had Mrs. Figge not knocked on their door. Who would she have told that her mother abandoned her and it was all her own fault? Who would she have told of her long wait up on the third floor of the old apartment house as dusk faded to night again, night lifted to dawn? And what if Mrs. Figge hadn't noticed the unaccountable quiet in the next apartment and hadn't known Miss Eunice at the community house? What if there had been no Mrs. Figge and no Miss Eunice? Just how would she have got to her better life at the Wild Rose? But for those two women, her life would have gone otherwise and almost certainly less well.

Thinking Audrey still in the bathroom, she went to see if Evie was even awake. She found the two of them curled up together on top of the covers, fully dressed, and sound asleep. She pulled Uncle Fritz's goose-down comforter up over them. Little Evie liked sleeping under goose-down because it was like sleeping in a cloud, and sleeping in a cloud gave her only good dreams. Sometime in the night, one of them would wake enough to wake the other. Come morning quite often, Ivy found both girls under the covers still in their clothes, the surest way to be ready when the big worry in life was being left behind.

But this business with Kathleen had gone on long enough. In the morning, she'd have to get the whole situation straightened out for the simple reason some situations never will come to a proper end unless someone steps in. For the girls' sakes, she'd call the shipyard and give Kathleen the benefit of the doubt. Then, if no one named Kathleen Yates was on their payroll, she wouldn't hesitate another minute before calling Jack. As an army reservist, Jack would have contacts. He'd be able to find someone who would know just how to track down Kathleen.

In her room, she sat down in front of the vanity. Her crow's feet met her laugh lines in the middle now. Not even Corby would be likely to say she looked younger than her years. At sixty though, she had more left to do in her life, and much more left to give than she thought.

Higher Math

TOO OFTEN SUMMER LASTS ONLY EIGHT OR NINE WEEKS in our town. Sometimes summer never comes at all. But who worries about weather once school's out with all those lazy days of summer vacation waiting? All the time in the world to do as we please. Anything, that is, but racket around inside while hardworking breadwinners catch up on sleep. Somehow though, those days of shift-workers and day-sleepers and kids taught to keep the noise level down seem so long ago. But were we so different? Have times really changed all that much?

In wet weather, we did have to hunt a dry place to go. Sometimes we'd hoof it downtown to Woolworth's, four skin-and-bone belles in short shorts, swinging to Aretha singing R.E.S.P.E.C.T. as if we already knew all there was to know. Other times we'd huddle under the overhang of the little plank church where nobody went anymore and tell stories about who we'd be in ten years' time. Besides me and Merrilee, it was mostly just Melanie and Pauline Montgomery. We all four lived on the same block in nice painted bungalow homes with climbing roses and pink camellia bushes in front, green garden rows of pole beans and collard greens in back, porches swept so clean you could lay a table on them — me in 1430, the corner house, Merrilee in 1432, the Montgomery twins in 1434.

Mostly on those rainy summer days under the church eaves, we'd stick to the usual tall tales about fame and fortune and falling in love with different neighbor boys. But sometimes mine would go all the way back to when Daddy was just a little shirt-tail child in East Tennessee and all his aunts and uncles and cousins so close by that conversations were carried along as on a telephone wire from one porch to the next. Other times I'd go to telling some crazy thing that just sprang out of my head, and then have to admit I made it all up.

Most of those Tennessee tales I told were to paper over a time I wanted not to think about. I was eleven and Daddy wasn't going to his job anymore. The sad fact was there was something bad wrong with his heart, and warehouse work was just too great a strain. But he'd keep busy out in his workshop making bird houses and keep-sake boxes and corner whatnots to sell. Evenings Momma would have me go out and call him in to supper and he would holler, "Comin' Carrie, on my way," in that cheerful way he had. To my ears, he'd always sound the same, and I will never know just what went with me the day he didn't answer, how I could just stand there dumb as a crutch and Momma calling Mil-ray! Mil-ray! over and over till she completely gave out.

But more good times were in store after the summer Daddy passed. Like when Momma's sister's youngest girl Chessie came to live with us. Momma said the day Chessie came to live with us felt like the end of a long wait for reinforcements. At the time, I didn't take her meaning, but now I do. When we're young we don't see life as columns in a ledger. We simply make room when someone new comes along, close ranks when someone's old place sits empty. We learn adding a person is better than subtracting. What we had yet to learn was what Momma called higher math. Not till we waged and lost a battle of our own did we graduate to higher math.

Over time Daddy's lonely grave opened my eyes to what Momma meant by a long wait for reinforcements. Each time we'd go, she'd fret he has no kin to keep him company, no familiar names to remind him who he is, no creeper, no whippoorwill's call, no cool branch to dip our feet in of a summer's day. In this country, we Buttermilk Road Carneys from East Tennessee were all on our own till Chessie came, just when we needed her. And her being a Little Horse Creek Lytle from East Tennessee meant our Lytle kin would lie down beside us Carneys for all eternity, our dearly departed balm for the living in life's long journey.

And there were those losses too that feel like a death in the family. Our Woolworths closing down felt that way. Weeks and weeks of close-outs and final clearances, of last lunches at our old lunch counter with old friends, always with the feeling this may be the last time, not so different from any other visit with any other loved one in failing health. As with much in life, there was no way to be ready for our last Woolworth's lunch.

Still, it would take more than Woolworth's closing down to move me closer to higher math. The summer I turned sixteen started out gloomy. with nobody on the street, nobody calling me on the phone, only little Chessie to run around with, once the twins left on a family trip to visit Texas cousins. My friend Merrilee was kept busy by new boyfriends. Sometimes just the one boy coming over, other times two. All she would ever say about it was they were some boys from her Sunday school class; just don't say anything to her momma.

When you're older, you look back you see yourself in a different light. But when you're young and a girl and all the boys call you "Stilts", you think there's nothing left to live for. You think your life is pretty much over. I know my life was, but then Coach Comer got me to running the hundred. I will never forget him telling all the boys what they were looking at was the next Wilma Rudolph. I was that fast. And I remember believing if I trained hard like Wilma Rudolph did, I could be the next great Olympian. All that summer I believed. It became my summer of firsts and of fame and of my picture in the papers, the same summer Merrilee's momma got engaged and got married and changed all our lives overnight.

But once again I didn't see the changes coming. Only later would I link Merrilee's momma's big church wedding to life shading into something different from what it had always been, even more so than when Daddy died. I'd link her momma's wedding and their move down to sunny California to our block breaking up, one home at a time, followed by a long parade of fancy new people marching in behind. I'd link it to my best friend getting knocked up and dropping out of school, to two kids to raise on her own before she was twenty, to her free fall from a brilliant future in engineering to no future at all. I'd link it to my own hard times, not that I was worried then. As long as we were in our bungalow home, and as long as the next school year was a whole long summer away, and as long as my times satisfied Coach Comer, then everything was fine.

Only now, as a woman of thirty with a young son of my own, does something run the clock back to the summer I turned sixteen. Very likely it's Chessie at my elbow, by this time nearly grown. But whatever takes my thoughts back, I'm a younger Carrie with yet another plan to get down to California to see Merrilee, fair summer breezes blowing as I scheme on our porch. In a very different memory of that time those same summer breezes turn suddenly foul as the first claps of thunder announce a long bad patch of stormy weather.

October was all but history the day the real estate sign came down at 1432. By then Merrilee's house had stood empty since June. Momma was ready for new neighbors, but not me. I didn't want anyone over there — not on their porch, not in their kitchen, not in my friend's attic bedroom. I didn't want to see lamps burning or have anyone under that roof waving to me like we're friends. But I would bide my time and wait for Halloween to throw a rock through their window. And I would wait for

Thanksgiving to be over with to be done with everything else, and that included getting up mornings and going to school.

The one morning I did get out of bed was when Momma made me go with her to an appointment at the big public building downtown. I must have pitied her knowing how her sugar weighed on her and never more so than after the hospital cut back her hours. But still I needed her to understand some things too. I needed her to understand I would never be her, good at the things she was good at, such as playing the piano and getting up in front of people. And neither was I going to make an engineer like my friend Merrilee. And it wasn't because I lacked ambition as she seemed to think. It was because my two biggest fans had been moved from the plus to the minus column — Daddy from our midst to his grave, Merrilee from next door to faraway California.

Still, I went with Momma and sat down beside her in the reception area. I listened while she explained to the man caseworker that her daughter wasn't on drugs, didn't hang with a gang, was never disrespectful in the home, always had been a good student and out of the blue decided she'd had enough school. When she finished talking, the man turned to me and asked why I wasn't going to school anymore. I told him it was because Merrilee moved away and I just couldn't go. I told him the truth.

"Very well," the man said. "Now if it's all the same to you, why not tell us the real reason you quit school."

So I told him again what I told him before, and he just sat there looking at me. It's that look they give when they're playing with you and trying to get into your head, only you're not playing their game. When the man caseworker left and this lady caseworker came in, both Momma and I picked up on that pretty quick. To us it was plain which way their wheels were turning. They had it in their head some boy had got me in trouble.

But I knew something they didn't know. I knew Momma's look — the look that says *here come another lesson in higher math*. By then I got that *higher math* wasn't math at all. Higher math was about seeing what makes us do the way we do. Still, it didn't start out like a lesson in higher math. It started out with her asking did they want me to tell them why, or were they going to tell *me* why I quit school? The reason being I might just know more about it. Still, all I knew about it was that school and me were finished. I wasn't going without Merrilee. Then Momma put in her two cents about how a best friend moving away can set back a smart girl like me. It took a minute, but then I got how this wasn't higher math. This was about me needing reinforcements. Aha, Momma did have a clue after all.

Now I've forgotten how we got through my home school years. But I had regular lessons to prepare each day, plus I had elocution lessons. I had elocution lessons because Momma had them under Miss Alta and, under Miss Alta, had gone on to win a major elocution prize in the state of Tennessee. And Momma's goal was for me to speak with the conviction of Barbara Jordan, the African-American senator from Texas. Now, finding her State of Tennessee certificate as I get ready to leave our beautiful bungalow home for the last time, I hear the ring of hard shell certainty. I hear Momma's bred-in-the-bone belief. "Now it's all up to you, Carrie Louise, just when you harness that mind of yours, but you will do it!" I have to hold back the tears.

Later it was the whiff of old suitcase smell that turned the spigots on. We were on a bus trip back home. I was eight years old. Momma and Daddy were sharing a seat while I watched the scenery go by from across the aisle. In my memory, it was all dry mountains and empty deserts, but then we crossed the mighty Mississippi and after that got to the long leafy state of Tennessee to where we climbed down from the Greyhound bus one more time. There we were met by a sweet-smelling fruited land and waded in a warm brown river of kin and were washed in a soft rain of remembering, Momma and Daddy so unlike themselves, cutting up and flirting and carrying on.

Was it the two of them as they had been on that trip that I expected to find inside their traveling bag? Or was it a new improved version of myself I hoped to shake out as I undid the snaps and took out Momma's wedding clothes? Some days I can feel so weighed down carrying all this trouble with Chessie, thinking how I spread the door open to trouble, how I say, "Trouble we're here; trouble come in when she comes home with new make-up and jewelry, when she'll be high or be gone," and once in the door, more troubles come crowding through. Some days I don't want to look in the mirror and I don't want to answer the door, because I'll be thinking of Momma. I'll be thinking how she wouldn't stand for it.

I remind myself when our mommas were raising us that the unwritten law was to keep your children to the straight and narrow, and that was from coming up with Jim Crow and learning at an early age not to stir the pot. It was from wanting your children to live to see another day, from getting a nice Christmas basket one day and a crack on the head the next, from knowing you can't sit here and you can't swim there, and nothing was ever going to change for you, so abandon all hope.

Then I'll remember Daddy saying, "Even if it's not as bad here as back there, that doesn't mean it's not here." Prejudice may have had to cross a continent to get here, but when it got here, it found opportunity the same way he found a job. It just kept looking. And even if we'd like to think we can stamp out prejudice once and for all, we can't. It just lies dormant for years and decades and even generations and then springs back to life. It goes underground and waits us out, and while we're thinking the worst is over, prejudice is in the next room changing clothes.

Daddy said even someone like my momma who left the known world to blaze a trail of advancement couldn't stamp it all out. Even after all her years of trying, she couldn't win more than one battle at a time. And soon it would be down to me and Merrilee and what we'd teach our children. That's what he'd tell us. I'm just glad he never lived to see *three strikes and you're out* transformed from a day at the ball park to life in prison for the children of folks he knew.

Now I can hear my taxicab down on the street. Here on this same porch is where Daddy told the story about the first Carrie Louise Carney and her flock of laying hens, about her going to the henhouse and thanking each one of them by name. Thank you, Ada. Thank you, Bessie. Thank you, Charlane, Daphne, Effie, Felicia, Georgia, and Hattie and on and on till she'd thanked every one of her laying hens, A through Z. And this same porch is where I snuggle down with my little son in the same glider and tell him the same exact story Daddy told me.

The first Carrie Louise Carney would surely hate leaving this porch of ours behind, although nine steep steps would be a chore for her to climb now at past a hundred. Still, in my mind she pins those same plaits up in those two big buns every morning just like in the photograph on my bureau top. And when she goes to town on market day she sits up high on the wagon seat to drive that mule. They never grow any older, these Carney kinfolk of mine, or the Lytle side either.

Yesterday though was for saying our good-byes, not that we're moving all that far away. Only five blocks to a larger rental home my godfather found for us. First Pauline came over with her son to give my son the Big Wheel he'd outgrown. Then later Mrs. Montgomery and I went out to dig up Momma's Prince of Persias and box up Daddy's hand-made bird houses. I gave her the one called Old Tennessee Smoke House and kept Granny's House by the Buttermilk Road for myself. I'm saving Whippoorwill Hotel for Merrilee. It's always been her favorite.

Merrilee and I quit writing back some time ago, but when Momma died it was Merrilee I had to talk to. She got me caught up on her twelve-year-old Robert being so good at math and her ten-year-old Avery being musical like my momma. When I told her I had a son now too, Kenneth Milray, age four, she remembered not only Daddy's Christian name *Milray*, but my godfather Kenneth Coffey. She asked was Mr. Coffey still known as the Archon of M Street. I told her only a very few would know that about him, because most of those activist folks had already passed on.

"But here lately," I told her, "new blood's coming from all around the country about every day of the week." I had Jim Best in mind, come all the way from New York City to start a movie theater. "Remember that old church we'd go to and get out of the rain? That old church is a cinema now! And you remember Coach Comer's daughter Althea, don't you? Well, pretty soon our Chessie will have her job at Althea's Hilltop Café. Me? I've been working at Best Cinema full-time for a while now, the best job I've ever had."

Such a long wait Daddy had for Momma to come keep him company. But I'm sure he'd wait even longer, long enough for Momma to see Merrilee again and get to know Merrilee's kids. Both my folks always said how Merrilee was like a daughter to them, always as proud of her as they were of me. Nothing would please them more than her coming back home to the Hilltop to be where she belongs.

Come morning we go meet them at the airport. My son's so excited he'll have a big brother and sister living in our same house. Chessie's just happy she'll have someone on her side. There's no use repeating it's not about sides, but about putting forth the effort. In our house that's the way it's always been and always will be too. But now I sound just like Momma. I know. I know. Everybody says.

Between Corn Rows

JIM HELPED HIS ELDERLY VISITOR BACK TO HER CAR in wet snow. During the last war, she'd been one of three young army wives sharing the bungalow that is now occupied by Althea's Hilltop Café. She was apologetic digging in her purse for the pictures, the first of three little white boys in striped jerseys, their fathers in uniform behind them looking proud and in charge. Not one of the men made it through. By war's end, all three wives were widows, left to bring up their sons alone.

His friend Kenneth came in as he slid the pictures meant for Althea back into the envelope. He kept out 'three lady pea-pickers in dungarees' for a second look later on. The one with the bamboo rake could pass for his own mother, a teller of tales known to shower cheer down on every dull chore. But his mother would die young, too young to look back on a full life in old age. Not that many pictures of her, and none of his father. He'd never known much about his father. She didn't talk about him, and he didn't ask. He just knew his father was a black man; that much was obvious.

"Go on in and have at it if you're hungry," he told Kenneth. "We're closing early on account of the snow."

Kenneth pulled out a stool, unfolding stiff old man's legs one joint at a time. "I'm not the man I think I am. Any part I still can move hurts like the devil when I do."

"What brings you out then? You get a call?"

"They call me; I go. That's how it is in the burying business. I carry my man to the mortuary and that's about the time I see a light burning at your old movie theater. And I think, why not drop in for some friendly conversation."

"You talk to him? He say when he plans to open up for business again?"

"Just soon, and you and him need to talk."

After Kenneth left, he switched off the OPEN sign and absently slid the packet of pictures onto the shelf under the cash register. He took his time walking the six snowy blocks to his apartment house, as perplexed as ever at how rarely the new owner of his old cinema sought him out. He'd been expecting him to drop by after school to talk shop — a memorable directing effort, a slick jump-cut, anything at all. But the new man just rolled up his sleeves and went back to work even after a hard day of teaching, still strong, still silent, still singing *ki-yi-yippy-yippy-yay*. Or at least that's the way it seemed.

Christ, how he missed it, and not just his creation, but his flock who spread the word from the time that he'd begun salvaging the derelict church, with him through the thin years and a desperate 'Save Our Cinema' campaign. His true believers who hung with him after the show and helped carry out the trash! What was up now? If there was a snag somewhere, what did it have to do with him when he was no longer in the picture?

Another week went by before their meeting at the cinema. By then he was prepared for the tug in his gut when the new proprietor reached in his pocket for the ring of cinema keys. The tug was what Althea had warned him of before he ever put Best Cinema up for sale. "Just an itch," she told him, "like everyone in business gets sooner or later. We think we'd rather have the money, but what makes us happy is the business, because the business is what we make happen every day."

The burglar alarm disabled, the two men stood in the before-noon quiet of the cinema lobby. Jim was a brindle-eyed, call-the-clock Cincinnati Kid, playing opposite a stony-faced, chisel-cheeked juror #8. At the far end of the lobby a not-quite-life-sized Claudette Colbert and Clark Gable swung on a sliver of moon. The movie was Frank Capra's 1934 comedy "It Happened One Night". With his nose inches from the photo, Jim launched into a description of Gable giving Colbert lessons in how certain things were done — how a man undresses, how he dips his donut — an actor so popular with the public that when he claimed he wore no undershirt, the undershirt business nearly went bust.

But the business uppermost in Cap Ussery's mind that day was getting his opinion on switching from second run to an art-house platform. "Carrie and I like the idea. But we'd like to know what you think?"

Jim shrugged. By then they were down in the office, little changed with the exceptions of a new chair and the four framed glossies of a bony young rodeo rider squinting across at them, this time from lower down on the wall. To Jim's eye the young rider had a familiar look. The chair, unlike his coffee-stained swivel one, was a brand new straight-backed teacher's chair.

"When I first came out to Tacoma," he began, "the first person I met was Kenneth. We met at work. The second was Althea. I met her at the café. Then I met Carrie at Althea's, and it turned out she was Kenneth's godchild. All three were from the 'hood and knew everyone. I looked like I belonged, but I didn't know anyone. When it came time to open my cinema, they got everybody around to beat feet to my door."

"So what are you saying?"

"I'm saying first, give people what they want to see. Next I'm saying give thanks first-run theaters pay the advertising. Last I'm saying always keep in mind the mass market movie is a good fit for a neighborhood cinema like this one."

Cap put his fingers together in a steeple. "I enjoy the projection end of the business. And now that Carrie's getting the knack for the booking end of it, and neighborhood folks are coming out for Movie Night, thanks to you, it feels like the right time to try something different. Still, what you say makes sense too. We always need a decent house to break even. Any changes we'll be taken a step at a time, believe me."

Later that day he began feeling out of sorts and lost his temper with one of Althea's regulars during a busier than usual late lunch trade. He accused the woman of not understanding plain English. Still, what should it matter if the old battle-axe ignored the *Staff Only* sign when Althea's sister and Kenneth sailed past the same sign through the same swinging door into the same restricted kitchen area every day. At least this time Althea sided with him, if not saying which one was lacking in plain English. Sad to say, ever-practical Althea still hadn't made up her mind to keep him on as assistant manager, even after four months on the job.

But just what manner of foul fog had descended on him, made him feel free to blast away at anyone crossing his bow? First the cheap shot at Cap's conceit that art house fare is superior. Then the primer on how to survive in the 'hood. And last the down-and-dirty plug at a poor unsuspecting café customer while he shrugged off both his seller's remorse and his nostalgia — a nostalgia only heightened by film cans in the lobby, one-sheet tubes tossed on the counter, the chatty soft-drink delivery man double-parked outside. Then, that hardest-to-shake of all his old head-tapes — of house lights coming up in a Bronx movie theater and standing beside his mother in broad daylight on a cold December Saturday savoring some silly bit in the last movie she'd ever see, waiting all these years for a different ending each time the house lights dim.

At midnight, the streets of Tacoma were dry, a breeze out of the southwest just starting to kick up. He paused on the corner of Pacific and 9th to pull up his collar. He knew it would rain, as he knew old habit was what took him down the steep flights of worn wooden stairs to under the 11th Street Bridge and the broken-backed wheat warehouses of another age. He'd photographed many like behemoths back on the east coast, but none in the west. Here he had no partner in crime, no sharp-eyed little daughter reporting her high-fidelity child's view of the world. Here he'd just walked when the itch came in the night, clicked off forty some thirty-six-exposure rolls bleakly documenting the birth of his cinema.

Were his daughter's anxious letters turning his thoughts back to a time when the living was never easy for long, or did it come down to the rest of his life slipping randomly away at a twenty-four-frames-per-second clip and nothing to show for it? Back in his apartment, he got out a sleeve of saltines and drank down a glass of milk. The clock said five minutes till two. It was later than he thought.

"Just my usual," Jim told the server. For the third time that morning he turned his attention to Claire's senior portfolio. Her pastel "Front Window" evoked the view from their apartment on the Lower East Side, a time when too briefly they'd been a family of three fighting for independence from Nina's mother and the entrenched expectations of her elite black sisterhood. But yes, the flowering tree Nina had coaxed back to health, their bright-eyed little scamp Claire and her best pal in corn rows and matching muumuus, the street busker from down the hall cradling their cat in their bean bag chair. Same cat and chair, same muumuus still luminous after a decade of washings? His sly daughter invoking collapsed time and the message it's all still here when, of course, it wasn't. Nothing was.

He stirred sugar in his tea, reminded too, of Nina's first Official Class all those years ago. Her front row students — Tonya, Tyrone, Taz and whiz kids Thurm and Von — all armed with attitude if still naked to what rained down on them, doing what they had to do to survive the scrums on the narrow side streets off once Mount Morris now Marcus Garvey Park. How old were these most senior of Nina's students? Still bright-eyed and mischievous, still curious, fiercely loyal, parents themselves with kids in school? Did they remember the friend they'd had in their teacher after so long a time? Remember Mr. Jim and his cameras, the movies they made, the wall of fame behind Miss Best's desk, their too-fleeting junior high dreams?

After lunch, he walked the block and a half to finish prepping Kenneth's new white elephant. House-painting never could be a good career for him either. Too often he'd misjudge where to reset the ladder, among those tricks of the trade that pros have which aren't shared as part of a repertoire. The pain working up from the soles of his feet was the worst part of it, not that skittering around on the roof like a crab was exactly a favorite pastime either. Nothing he did these days was. And Kenneth checking up on him like he did each afternoon? He could honestly do without it. Especially the whistling, world-on-a-string Kenneth like the one coming his way now. Not anyone he wanted to see, not in the mood he was in.

"Aw, come on, man. You got to at least look. Come on through and hold it there just another minute. It's hard seeing till your eyes adjust."

They stood in the back hall, Jim peering dubiously through an elaborate gingerbread divider separating two parlors, feeling he'd already seen enough. "I sure hope you're not crazy enough to rent out a place like this."

"Now go on further and try the staircase. And check out the stained glass on the landing. I heard you, I heard you. And no, I'm not crazy enough to rent this out to just any old anybody, no.

But five-hundred a month will get you twenty-one hundred square foot of living space for you and that little genius daughter of yours, plus you get more wall space for your pictures. You could even set up a nice little dark room in here somewhere."

"Why so cheap?"

Kenneth pulled on his chin. "Why does a man not get all he can get? A man is greedy and nobody asks why, but just let him share the wealth... well, come on. We're not anywhere near done yet."

"Thanks, but I've seen all I need to."

"Not till you see the big bedroom with the tiled hearth and the period mantelpiece and nice floral wallpaper."

"I honestly don't like moving."

"This from the brother that moved clear across the country to a place he'd never been to before!"

"That time was different."

"Different? How about curious? You ride the dog thousands of miles and get off not knowing anybody and all that gets off with you are two boxes of pictures and one change of clothes."

"Those pictures were ones we took of New York's working waterfront."

"I could see that."

"We'd go down Saturdays. Just Percy and me mostly, but sometimes Doc would tag along too."

"Friends of yours?"

Jim shook his head. "Not really. Percy rented darkrooms out by the hour and ran the projection equipment repair business I worked for before coming out here. Doc? He was just a guy who liked inventing things."

"And I'm just a guy with a thing about finding a decent place for you to set up housekeeping. Still, if apartment living suits you, fine. You ever think back on those sessions of ours at Browne's? Our come-to-Jesus sessions. Hell, when's the last time we had one of those?"

"Not since they shut the place down."

"But you know what I'm talking about? Digging down to the nub of what matters in life. Two brothers putting their house in order. Remember?"

"Not really, no."

"Sitting in the dark with the fishes and our pitchers of beer? You remember the fishes there at Browne's?"

"I remember our pitchers and spreading our glitter around and drowning our sorrows."

"It wasn't like that."

"Whatever. Whatever you say it was."

"You really don't remember? What it was about was declaring independence from the man and getting some skin in the game. Any of this coming back?"

"Some, only what's coming back is me going in the hole."

"The problem with you is all you see is the hole."

"And the problem with you, Kenneth, is seeing my profits as seed money for more of your schemes."

"The difference between what's done and what still can be done better? It's called opportunity. That's just the truth."

"For you maybe. The truth for me is Claire about to graduate high school and I'm still out here futzing around on your roof."

"The way I see it, we're both of us in a funk. And rather than go on like this, why not come over to the house and leave me do the cooking for a change. Let's make it for breakfast and make it soon, soon as in tomorrow morning at ten. And don't go being late on me this time!"

As far as he knew, the only house Kenneth had ever lived in was the house on M Street. Before M Street, Kenneth's address was more than likely his troop ship bound for the invasion of Japan when he was still so young he had to fudge on his age to enlist. In Kenneth's war, recruiters ignored a problem if a recruit proved able-bodied enough to make it through a day's march. Later in civilian life, interpretation trumped regulation every time. A man either took charge of his destiny or paid the price — the kind of thinking that was giving Jim second thoughts about Kenneth's command breakfast.

Still, forgetting to set his alarm wasn't planned. He'd overslept after a late run to the mall for a new sports jacket for his daughter's graduation and a later trip up the freeway for a plane ticket to New York. Besides, Kenneth was the one with the plan. And Kenneth's plan would almost surely include a come-to-Jesus moment on the old life he'd bailed on back east, a life he didn't care to talk about. He took the six steps up to Kenneth's porch, pausing to gather himself at the top. He could hear Kenneth's TV, then a husky voice hollering, "Who's there?" when he knocked, a voice too sweet to be Kenneth's.

"It's me. It's Jim."

"Jim? Jim who?" the voice came back, closer, and clearly a woman's voice.

"That's fine. Just tell him his friend Jim came by and I'll catch him later."

Behind him he could hear the lock tumble. "Come on in if you want," the woman said, her tired young face disembodied from the rest, still mostly hidden behind Kenneth's front door.

"That's fine I can just give him a call."

"I only just got in myself, but feel free to wait back in the kitchen."

"I uh… don't have anything that pressing."

"He fixed some coffee and stepped out to get some food in the house. That's where he's at."

"So he *is* expecting me?"

She took a half-step from behind the door. "Let's just say it isn't you he was expecting."

He spotted the note under the sugar bowl and waited for her to go back upstairs. The note was for him. *I honestly didn't expect company. Meet me under the big cedar in the garden on Oakes. Just give me time to get our breakfast.*

Kenneth's kitchen at times had an autumn smell, even a bitter smell. To him it had that smell now. And even if his friend believed he personified modern man, the mere fact he boiled his chicory in a saucepan and drowned the grounds with egg shells told a different story. Still, the taste and smell of Kenneth's chicory was all of a piece with everything else. His friend Kenneth speaking in tongues would be little different from the language Kenneth always spoke. Even this late in the game, the young woman with the tired eyes wearing Kenneth's blue flannel bathrobe would be one of Kenneth's grand-babies come home for a visit, and yes, Kenneth's friend Jim would have to fall off the turnip truck one more time.

Rare though it was, the garden on Oakes brimmed over that morning. From time to time he'd catch a glimpse of cheery pre-schoolers roped one to the other for crossing busy downtown streets. These though were free-ranging, slightly older children feeling each bud and flower with even more zeal yet after a boisterous group reading of a hand-lettered sign requesting "Please, oh please, leave us flowers in peace!" At half-past ten, the garden's one other adult visitor sat down to read in her Bible and make underlines in her *Awake*. At ten past eleven the children dispersed. Only then did it register that the young Jehovah Witness at the other end of the park bench was the same white woman from whom he'd purchased the sport coat only the night before to wear to graduation.

Later he'd try deconstructing the observation he made about the children in the park, saying how a little adult supervision never hurts, how it comes down to parenting in the end. He'd analyze saying that he wasn't a believer and never would be one, then deciding the time had come — the time to begin his story. Begin by saying what happened, happened a long time ago. How he'd been ten years old and they'd just come out of the movies and it was cold out and they stopped to button their coats. How this mugger took his mother's purse and then he stabbed her to death.

He watched her out of the corner of his eye, not to see would she register the dark-skinned Size 42 shopper she sold the sports coat to, but what if anything she would show him now. These moments were why he nixed telling his story, nixed explaining the closed off way he lived, because people have a way of hearing what they want to hear, hearing what happened to him as if it wasn't too late when it was. All shrinks in their own minds, sure they can fix him, even Kenneth. But at least this lady had helped. She'd helped him find the right coat.

"What happened then?" she said finally.

"They had to put me in a home. What else could they do?"

"But they caught him, didn't they? He didn't get away Scot-free."

"As far as I know they never did catch him."

"That's a shame," she said, ending the conversation, she going back to her Bible study, he to waiting for Kenneth to come with something to eat. It was a story never quite told through to the end, a story that arced from bad to very good to very complicated. The next part he'd told only one living person. But it was the one part he told his mom in her nice posh hotel in eternity:

> *This woman came to get me. The same woman you kept house for with the big library and the two big pianos. But you never did tell me much about her. All you said was "Betty was nice and she had five boys and a girl named Nina." And this nice woman who came for me never said her name was Betty or anything about her five boys or her daughter named Nina, and since you never said she was black like me, not white like all the other people you worked for, I didn't have a clue who she might be. All I knew was I wanted this beautiful woman to adopt me. I wanted to go home with her. I didn't know why, I just did. I hope that's okay.*

The one living person he told this to was his seat companion on the through bus from New York to Seattle. Feeling on the verge of new beginnings, he'd got out the photograph. She'd picked him out among the six Best brothers right away, the shorty in the middle she took to be twelve when he'd been fourteen, and she took her time with the picture too, counting heads, counting six boys and no Nina. How come the girl's not in the family picture with the rest of you? What happened to Nina?

That back and forth had ended when he moved to another seat. Not that he minded talking about the family, just that he'd feel so drained having to think about poor Betty digging in with her "a change is a-coming for the better" routine, code for a return to old ways long overdue. And feel even worse reflecting on how Betty's character was forged on an anvil of southern tradition while Nina's flowed upwards from a well-spring of the soul, how they'd been bound for a fight to the finish from the beginning, a fight fought over him, mother versus daughter, winner take all.

Still so fresh in his mind were all the times Nina crept around the stairwell and climbed in with him. How she cradled the half of a whole boy he'd been after his mother was killed, bucked him up with his poor dead mother's tales, picked up the thread of her own vainglorious "Bela Brindesi" venturing forth into misty realms where damsels of her sort never dare go. Bela Brindesi — the girl he was fated to fall in love with. He'd been a boy then, a mere child, nowhere near childhood's end and blissfully unprepared for contretemps soon to come over long idle school vacations, the maternal aunts nodding off in wilting heat on their wide side porch in sleepy little Bright Forge tucked in Virginia hills.

But that was then. Those times were gone; what was there left to say about them? He nodded at the saleslady from The Bon Marche pressing creases out of her *Awake*, leaving Jehovah's certainty down at her end of the bench. In the old days, he and Nina had made light of such hand-outs, calling them "The Believers Guide to the End of the World", but that was before — before Nina quit her dream job teaching eighth grade English at her beloved junior high school, before she left their seven-year-old daughter for him to manage on his own, before... so much.

Past hunger when he got home, he was as tired as he'd ever been. He'd fallen asleep in his chair still trying to decide whether to call Kenneth or wait for Kenneth to call him. He must have been dreaming it, though it had seemed real enough, Kenneth saying, "You going to come down and let me in or do I eat this by myself?" But Carrie's tone said it all when she called to tell him. Not that Kenneth showing up at his door about to have the big one hadn't happened before; it *had* happened and more than once.

That night he went to all the places he and Kenneth had gone — first to the house on M Street with a funeral wreath already hung on the porch rail, over the 11th Street Bridge to the mothballed St. Regis plant where they first met, along the industrial waterway where he learned history not yet in history books from a man who took up life's every bitter challenge. A good man, perhaps a man whose friendship he could never truly deserve being as concerned with his own troubles as he was.

At Kenneth's funeral, Carrie spoke of his long close friendship with her parents back when Kenneth was The Archon of M Street. Then Brother Glover from the mortuary recited those famous lines from Sophocles, lines Jim had studied in school: *The long unmeasured pulse of time moves everything. There is nothing hidden that it cannot bring to light, nothing once known that cannot become unknown. Nothing is impossible.*

Next Althea said a few words in praise of Kenneth for his leg-up when starting her café. Following Althea, the new mayor spoke and the former mayor and the mayor before that. At the end, Cap's surprising announcement: soon the Kenneth S. Coffey Gallery would be dedicated in the big downstairs room of Best Cinema. That was when he learned the young stunt rider in the glossies was Cap's father, a man who lost his sight before he was twenty-five.

Were Kenneth alive, would Kenneth be first to hear his story through to the end? Was change in the air? Was it late, but not too late? Would the long unmeasured pulse of time pulse on with Claire's graduation just days away? Other than Betty and Doc, eldest brother Edmund Jr.'s family was expected for Claire's big night. And Afton was due in from Zimbabwe. Nina was flying in from Mexico with her usual reports of hectic third world Kingdom Halls. Davis was coming down from Troy with wife and kids on the train. Of the boys, only Arthur sent regrets with an advisory to expect a package. Claire saved a place for Jackson; no word yet from Jackson. Jackson's life had become a mystery not even Betty could solve.

Of course, Betty's sisters were coming — the Smith sisters of Bright Forge whose company Betty dreaded and Doc claimed came in the door nostrils a-flare and smelling of foxhound, company they were obliged to welcome once a year at holiday time. And welcomed they were, even if they all showed the strain of certain awkward chapters in family history, one when Betty, from a long proud line of landed black Virginians, accepted a dubious dealer in marine fasteners from a rough band out of parvenu New York. As an adult, Jim could accept this shifting along of a hot pot, but as a boy, he'd struggled with certain Smith family expectations — the ones where the children are to be born accomplished adults, are to be grateful for all that's given, as parents in their own right, are to imbue the same hard shell expectations all over again.

"Hello there, Betty. It's me."

"You arrived early enough."

"I'm not actually there yet."

"I asked Thelma to get your room ready. But you should know Nina's on her way here too."

"Don't even bother about me. I'm not who's important."

"I would never say that. Only you would say such a thing."

"It's to be Claire's day in the sun. Did she fill you in?"

"If you think she tells us anything, you'd be mistaken. All she tells us is she has no intention of ending up like her grandmother, and you sold your movie theater at a profit."

"I did sell at a profit. Not a huge one, but a nice one. Are you ending up soon then, Betty?"

"Not ending up soon as far as I know."

"I'm glad to hear that at least."

"It takes its toll. Nina. Then Claire. So often I've asked myself how someone of my background can turn out two such headstrong girls."

"But not now?"

"My battles were over hemlines and bare shoulders, over my first name. How I despised the name Cabel! But I could never invent a Bela Brindesi or dream up half the things Nina dreamed up. Like her white girl sleeping out in the corn crib. Where would she even get such an idea? My poor sisters were beside themselves till she confessed she made the whole thing up. And to join up with the Jehovahs when that's not who we are. Then to infect poor Afton with it when he's the one with his father's gift. And to leave you and leave her own daughter."

In his bottom desk drawer was a letter – a letter Nina wrote the day she was awarded her high school diploma in Bright Forge, Virginia:

> *The sad part is we want only what everyone else does and stand to lose it all in the end. Three years now down in Bright Forge, three years with my mother giving not even the least thought to me at all. But you must see you were her big project, Jimmy. You were the one she could do over and show off, her adopted little mixed-race street-urchin son brought home from the slums, her bronzed and beautiful trophy boy she could stamp 'for display only' and keep for herself. So now is the time to run for the hills while we still can. She's got them convinced I'm not just a girl with an imagination, but a girl who will bring shame on them all in the end. I've been so afraid of what she'd do when she found out about us. And now that she knows the truth we don't have a prayer. If you want to tell them I was made class valedictorian, be my guest. I give my valedictory later tonight. I love you forever and ever.*
>
> *Your Bela*

All there on one side of a page in black ink, this letter so long preserved along with the tell-tale ringlet lying inert in his palm; a letter read simply as a love letter by a young man blinded by love still in his teens. And Nina correct about his being Betty's project, a boy plucked from a life in the slums, given a family to love, be loved by, and still miss more than he wanted to admit. So many good times in those airy upstairs rooms with the four older boys and little Davis; Davis alone standing with him, the others yielding to pressures as word got around about his infatuation with their sister — an infatuation lasting eleven years plus one sad year more spent in a doomed effort to restore what had begun so well.

As for the white girl, there was never a white girl! The corn crib was their place, his and Nina's place, up six rungs of a rough ladder to a low-roofed and secret place with moldy straw and a view out of the hills.

He slid Nina's letter into a book about film he'd been reading the day he was to meet Kenneth. As a youth, he'd turned to Hollywood movies for escape, later to art film for insight into the human condition. As a young father, he'd take his little Claire along on photo shoots and down to Percy's repair shop and out on jobs to install new lamp houses and fix problem projectors and out-of-date sound systems. Back then anywhere he'd gone, she'd gone too.

And then one day he'd made up his mind to leave her with Betty because she'd need someone like Betty more than she'd need someone like him. Because Betty could teach her to play piano and to sing harmony and to dance the waltz. Because Betty could teach her what she should wear and where she should wear it. Because she could teach her all the things she could never teach Nina. Because it would be good for Betty and good for Claire and good for him. He still had the letter beginning, *I still love you, Daddy. When are you coming for me? Mama says I can expect you very soon.*

From time to time he'd take out the snapshot of the young army wives left for Althea the day of the snow. An idle sort of thing perhaps, these strangers kept in his wallet opposite the picture of Claire with Nina's brooding nature showing through in equal measure with Betty's love of good breeding in his same sad eyes cast at some vanishing point now long gone. Only the sassy stranger with the bamboo rake returning what he recalled of his mother's durable Ulster spirit, something he hoped yet to find in Claire — Claire pinning so much on his coming home and being in her corner, going with her to the Smith sisters down in Bright Forge, spending a last summer before college with her.

Off Cape
Disappointment

LEXIE'S NIGHT OF RESTLESS REST WAS OVER even before the phone rang. This time she let the caller have it, both barrels, "You have any idea what time it is? Because if you don't, it's four in the morning!"

She lifted the stove eye and dropped a match in the firebox. Outside a drenching rain made tender maple leaves turn on new stems and the sword ferns high in the branches over her roof flatten under more weight. In another hour, Rodger-Dodger would open the retail house. At six o'clock her workday would begin, her friend Bea's day a half hour later, seasonal help all in place by seven. Poor Bea, just fifty and the planets lining up against her, not that Bea's wasn't the better job. In the greenhouse biz, the retail end was busy at times and other times not, while bedding plant season in the transplant house stayed hectic. Overall though, it was the usual worries — quirky wet-side weather, trace element problems, finding and keeping good steady help.

At five Lexie put eggs on to boil. She brought the hard-cooked eggs and dessert to work, Bea the sandwiches. They each brought a thermos of hot tea to warm them as they huddled in chill spring air to take up each confounding new wrinkle in Bea's situation one more time. Bea's mom Iva had become such a handful Bea never had any peace once she got home. Practically none since her husband turned toes up and Iva parked herself in the porch swing for the duration.

At exactly six, Lexie slid her car even with Rodger-Dodger's delivery van in the greenhouse driveway. "Where you off to?"

"Indian country," he said, meaning the U.S. 101 loop: down to Shelton, up to Hoodsport, Lilliwaup and Quilcene and back. She'd made deliveries herself a few times. She liked driving. She especially liked driving along the canal. Still, Rodger-Dodger hired her to be the whip hand on the transplant bench. Time was everything on the transplant bench. Deliveries he could sub out to his wife. "Get your crew on the six-packs. Lobelia first, then alyssum. Impatiens, when you get time. Bea will get the phone. See you when I see you."

So far it was a typical Puget Sound kind of spring. In the low fifties till mid-March, then some warm sunny days hitting sixty-five after that, urging every damn fool gardener on the peninsula to set out tomato plants in cold wet ground. But as her friend Bea said, you can only get a person to hear what he's willing to hear. *Don't argue with them* was her advice. When customers slap cash on the barrelhead for their flats of tender tomato starts, they envision rows of rosy ripe fruit. They're in the grip of a fever no ounce of prevention can cure.

Over lunch Lexie told Bea about all the phone calls. "Whoever it is never says a word. Not hello or who they want to talk to. Once I answer they hang up."

"How Gordy and I hated the sound of a telephone ringing. He always said, all they're here for is more bad news." Bea nibbled the cream cheese frosting from a piece of cake, her dark eyes blinking back tears. Lately, nobody in Lexie's life warranted that kind of missing, at least not since her ma passed away. And while she did still miss her last boyfriend at times, she'd had heartbreak to spare from that messed up stoner. Who but a lost cause like him would keep fishing in shipping lanes after two close calls? Nobody she knew with any sense.

After she got home, Lexie climbed up on the roof to check the new leak by the chimney. Her phone rang two rings, stopped, and rang two more. She didn't think about going down. With her left hand flattened against the chimney, she eased into a crouch. She could feel more moss than shake in places, one of those thin spots being over her kindling box in the original end of the old Badger cabin. She'd have to patch that one over too. Till this year, her fifth year in these parts, the nearly century-old cedar shakes had soaked up enough moisture to seal off any gaps.

The next time the phone rang, Lexie was up to her elbows in the dough bowl, making the palm-size rolls that Bea was always after her to bake. Just rye flour, some corn meal, a little salt, yeast, and molasses with a splash of buttermilk. She'd doubled the dough to keep Bea and Iva in rolls through the coming week, well past their regular Saturday supper. And now that she understood standard fare at Bea's was soup, she was ready for whatever ended up in Bea's pot, ready for any root, fruit, or shoot, any fish, flower, fungus or bivalve.

"Anybody going to talk to me this time?"

"It's me. It's Bea. I've been calling you and calling you. I finished it. You know how it is when you almost have one in the boat? You're close, but you keep finding better ways to bring it in. You're afraid. Landing a poem is slippery business."

"Like I said, I only do lists. But I could get your poem about the life cycle of a moon snail. That one I got."

"This one's more paradoxical. This one's about my Croatian grandparents answering the call of the west. The wheat ships seemed like the big break they'd been waiting for. They'd been down in the mines too long, probably thinking, oh, to labor out in the light of day. But I can't quite make up my mind about the title. Let me know what you think."

Past nine when her rolls were cool enough to put away, Lexie carried one out to the table-size cedar stump in the woodshed where a black and white dog lay sleeping. "So what's your game?" she said, absently sharing a piece of roll with him. Later though, it annoyed her he was still hanging around, sprawled by the stump like they'd come to some kind of arrangement. "Shoo you! Get on!" she told him, letting him know she for one wasn't buying any poor lonely dog stories.

When she got to Bea's the next day, she found a note. "Taking Mom in. Soups still warm. Sorry, B." To Lexie, Bea's handwriting had a pinched look. Once when Bea's mom took a spill, Bea had to put her in the hospital for tests. That time poor Iva couldn't breathe, and they made her breathe into a machine to measure if she was getting enough oxygen. And that time she was. But what was going on with her this time? It seemed like it wasn't so long ago Iva climbed into one of Gordy's double-enders and went on that voyage halfway to Joe's Bay before a south wind turned her back.

Bea's soup of the day was wild asparagus cut over a year ago and kept in the deep freeze. Bea had talked of making her famous Low Tide soup. But with Iva ever more on her hands, when was there time for fishing and foraging? One more reason to keep the Queen moored down at the marina and let her friend Lexie have the use of her. That's all she'd say about it over lunch the day she reached in her pocket for the distributor rotor and handed it over to her friend. "Just drop it in the distributor," she told Lexie. Now Lexie kept the rotor in her pocket like a lucky charm. She could feel it there as she blew across a spoonful of dusky wild asparagus soup now barely warm.

Later she set Bea's new poem aside a second time. A strange car had crept down the drive and pulled in to the upper turn-around. She stood watching, aware telltale tatters of wood smoke haze lay low over her friend's hand-carved Cedar People camped for the ages behind a bright scallop of water's edge. What was she doing waiting so long for Bea and Iva when she could have gone home? If she were honest she'd admit mostly waiting for another tale of young Iva Lusich braving the wild amidst the heathen years ago. She loved Iva's tales of olden times, loved Iva and worried bad things would come to her. She watched the strange car creep back up the hill again. When Bea tracked in at past midnight, Lexie had the fire banked for the night and the kettle on.

"Jesus, Bea!"

Bea tucked her chin and stared down the front of her sweatshirt, as if noticing the dried blood there for the first time. "Sorry," she said.

"You in a wreck or something?"

"I wish," Bea said, her fingers only partially covering the wound on her neck, a raw weeping one, a wound only a strap can make, a strap or a pair of weapons even more unthinkable than a strap such as someone's bare hands. "Mom had the nerve to tell them I started it. I told them no daughter wrestles her mother lest she's seriously provoked. But at least they're keeping her there for now."

"Keeping her where?"

"St. Joe's. I'd gone out to the shop. I had it in mind I'd trim more off my cedar lady's hat and I'd need the adze. But then I hear this sound. At first I thought it was another escapee. You know, from the prison."

"Only it's not?"

"No, it's her. It's her lying in wait."

"And that's when she gets in her licks?"

"She thinks I'm my father. I tell her I'm not Anton, I'm Beatrice. 'You think I don't know you?' she says. But now, my friend, one thing I know is I can't think another thought. Not tonight. Not till Monday."

For Lexie, Sundays could feel like waiting out a long cold April east of the mountains. Maybe she had sensed Bea should never have been left on her own, not with her colors muddied, not with her breastworks breached — images from an earlier poem stored in memory. Yet leave her she did when Bea stood so composed in the doorway, insisting she'd be fine, really she would, don't worry.

Later, as the last embers dropped through the fire grate, as hour and minute-hand loomed toward twelve on the nightstand, lines from Bea's new poem "Drowned Ship" drew her back from the verge of sleep: *Is this sweet tide come to take back the water's edge?* asked one line; another, *Is this where the drowned ship sleeps?*

On Sunday Lexie went about her usual chores. She finished her laundry. She made her run to the store. She combed the beach, hauling in a size-eight boot, half a life preserver, and a nice moon snail for chowder. All day Sunday she kept busy. On Monday, half-expecting Bea would call in sick, she found Bea's Ford Falcon tucked in behind Rodger-Dodger's step van at five before six in the morning. Bea, whose greatest challenge was getting to work on time! What Lexie had given the slip all day Sunday, come Monday lay waiting at the greenhouse step. She could hear the two of them going at it just inside the panel door, Rodger-Dodger sounding nowhere near as reasonable as Bea.

She counted to ten, searching her mind for a joke before she went in. Amazingly, her friend Bea, dressed in a summer shift with a loop of floral scarf around her poor wrung neck, looked much improved since two nights before, even if her outfit didn't add up. "You sure are looking dressed up," she told her, when what she wanted to say was, "Here you are all rigged out when I can't sleep a wink."

"I've just been telling Rodger he deserves better than me in the office. Now he says he should be the judge of that, and that's all well and good. But my bones say go someplace warm. I don't know where — south though, down the coast somewhere. I guess

I'll just have to know it when I get there. But don't worry, I'll be in touch."

And that was that. Out Bea went with her geranium in one hand, her road map in the other, as if they'd never worked side by side and weren't the kind of friends who talked things over. Just zipped out the door, slipped behind the wheel and shot down the driveway to the highway. The last anyone saw was her turn signal blinking.

Rodger-Dodger was just as bad. "Good thing we're nearly done," he said, and picked up the phone. And she'd thought Sunday was the longest day.

By now she guessed she was used to it. At thirty she knew how the game of life was played. You're born. With any luck, you get a decent ma in the deal. Then one day your ma signs for the quarter section of prime Ponderosa, knowing her timber rights had already been auctioned off in the Great Depression resource grab. Still, you tell yourself you're lucky. You tell yourself you live in a forest and you do live in a forest till they come log it off. Later, you make a best friend in town. You dream away long high-desert summers and rise like slender shining trout over the cool clean Similkimeen, till all your really good times are used up.

That night it rained a river down the windowpanes, splashed over the top of the one big kettle she'd set behind the cook stove. She forgot to be hungry, but then fried up the last of the apples. It was those apples that got her remembering better times, like when she and her sisters did their triplet routine and won the trick-riding prize at the Lost Lake Stampede. The same summer she fell for K. T. Florian's line and to this day can sniff out a load of bull better than anyone. She guessed it was the fried apples that made her fall asleep so soundly.

Three long days went by before word came from Bea. When she did call, she called the office, so naturally Rodger picked up. She needed to ask him a favor she said, and that was to go to her house and change all the locks. Just subtract what it costs out of her paycheck. He never thought to ask why change the locks or ask where she was calling from. His excuse was she called from a pay phone, as if a minute more would matter. By this time, Lexie could barely keep from spilling her guts about Iva and Bea's bloody and terrible fight.

That evening Lexie decided one remedy was to go out cruising on the Queen. Early May and finally even the late trees leafed out, the sun warm as she tipped the cover back off the inboard and dropped the rotor in the distributor. She waved at Mont, rigging hand gurdies on the Katie C, as she shoved her stray mutt into the stern. The bay was flat. She let Bea's 16-footer drift into the cut where she could hear a train move along the stretch of track hugging the far shore before turning inland. She called it the *mainland* because she was from east of the mountains. Everyone else called it town. To her ears though, something about how Bea would say *town* seemed to say all that need be said about it.

She sat in the stern and pulled on the fish stick. Her friend Bea would certainly approve; she knew Bea was known for ending hauled up on some lonely beach, not in summer — too many summer people — but in October, or like now with each evening longer than the one before. Sometimes with a tarp and quilt stowed below deck, but mostly on the watch for what the tide would carry in, like when she towed in the name board from the scrapped tug "Nell Finegan". Still, it was always the old homesteads her friend seemed to gravitate toward: *his hewed cabin collapsed under hop vine, her tidy kitchen yet a cold keep*. Bea could make even the plainest of plain everyday things into a poem. Where did it all come from?

By this time, Lexie was inside the pass separating the peninsula from McNeil Island and the prison, the tide nearly slack when she noticed the big rowboat riding low in the water with a much smaller double-ender in tow. She could make out five people in the lead boat and no one in the double-ender. The shipped oars in the second boat, more than anything, were what set off the alarm ringing in her brain. She angled toward them and killed the motor, letting the Queen drift closer. They were kids, two girls and three boys, probably no more than junior high age.

"What's going on? You need any help?"

The girl in the ball cap did the talking, her voice sounding out of breath as if she'd been running. "We were on the beach," she said. "We see the boat out in the bay. There's somebody in it and when we look again nobody's there. We don't hear anything. Whoever's there just goes overboard."

"When's all this? Just now?"

The girl shook her head. "We had to go find a boat first."

"But you called it in, didn't you?"

"Every place we went to was locked up."

"Hop in. When anything like this happens, we have to call in."

It was already dark when she got home, her nerves much too frayed to do anything more than go over it again in her mind. The hospital seeing that Iva was gone, alerting the sheriff, the deputies searching for Iva at Bea's house, Rodger there changing the locks by then, Bea's husband Gordy's double-enders still in their boat house cradles where they belong. They looked in the all the sheds and anywhere else they could think of to look, including the graying board and batten cabins perched on the bank. Only after all the looking, did they put out the All-Points-Bulletin to get hold of Bea.

For the time being, all there was for Lexie to do was worry and wait. Lately, nothing was predictable anymore, not when poor old Iva could wake up on any given day, take one look at her daughter and see only Bea's father Anton staring back. Not when Iva was surely drowned and Bea down the coast, no one knew where.

The next morning Rodger was waiting for her, looking like he hadn't slept either. For once he didn't have the radio on. "You'd better come in," he said.

"They find something?"

"They found her body not far from where they said she went overboard. But it wasn't who we thought it was."

"Who was it then?"

"It was Bea."

"But it couldn't have been."

"She'd had to have been somewhere nearby when she called yesterday is all I can figure out."

"Bea wouldn't fall overboard. She would never fall overboard."

"What if I told you this was no accident."

"How do you mean?"

"What I mean, is it an accident when you weigh yourself down with sacks of concrete blocks?"

"But Bea's in California. They sure it's not Iva?"

"They picked Iva up in town on the corner of K and 15th."

"I don't get this. I really don't get it."

"The way I see it, she was watching the whole time! There in the woods while I was changing her damn locks! Can you even believe she'd do this, as far back as her and I go?"

From her pie-baking year at Dottie's Dinette, Lexie got to know many of the crossroads crowd — the smelt dippers, the barber, the hardware boys, the feed store philosophers — who on this day seemed to include Rodger-Dodger, since no mistaking his step van parked out in front. Thus, she pressed on, all her wits engaged in quartering wakes of missed intuitions brought on by a single poem of drowned ships at the water's edge and by too many mysterious phone calls in the night. Finally, she fell in behind a tangerine-colored minibus with a load of carefree, straw-brimmed Kansans. A slow day at the Vashon/West Seattle ferry landing, to her it felt like more late winter with no sign of spring.

Of course, it wasn't the sort of thing someone would make up, so it had to be true. And even if he was a little different, Rodger was no liar. And besides, just how would she feel were she the one on the receiving end, the one linked by the favor to the deed and by association to the plan? Wouldn't she be more than a little pissed too, because Rodger obviously was very pissed?

But still, why didn't he ask Bea, with Iva in the hospital, who would we be locking out? Or ask, why so urgent? Or consider the phone call was never about locks in the first place, but one more call of desperation from Bea's private wilderness? Or so she could say sorry to let the side down, but how would I ever convince you I'd had it! Bea calling the three of them *the side* – Bea, Lexie, Rodger — sounding another lost note now that there was no *side*, not without her. So much going to the bottom that Bea never would have meant to take with her.

Usually comfortable with solitude, Lexie dreaded the house Bea had taken her to see only four short years ago, telling her its history. First the Badgers lived here, then it's our family's humble little home. After that, just sitting so forlorn and empty. They'd gone from work, from the Tropics to the Yukon, one of them had joked. Nearly dark at four and so frosty inside that they'd gladly have fled the minute the flashlight gave out. It would have been point season, or the beginning of bedding plants and far too cold to snow. Even now, the sound of their boots on frozen ground came back, as did the hollow ring of Bea's regrets. Was that the one and only time Bea ever mentioned Anton by name to her?

The father who never did pass the mother's muster, because why? Because he couldn't abide living in town?

Lexie was outside when Rodger drove up. Her plan, such as it was, had been to skip supper and take her refuge in sleep. Still, it surprised her he even knew where she lived. She watched as he backed his van in beside her pickup. "I had to wing it," he said, waving a fifth of bourbon at her.

"Sorry. I never could drink the hard stuff. You coming in?"

"My wife's real upset about all this happening with Bea, so I told her I wouldn't be long. What parts of this do you already know? Bea ever tell you how far back her and I and her husband Gordy go?"

"Back to when you were kids. I know that much."

"She ever tell you she lived right here? We were six, maybe seven, so '33 or thereabouts. My old man had a shack just down your bank, and when I'd see their light I'd come up to hear Iva's stories about the wheat ships and the lumber carriers and the little white-painted house she hoped to build in town."

"Most of what Bea told me was about you and her and Gordy going on the road together with some kind of gig just out of high school."

He shook his head. "She tell you whose idea that was? Because I just wanted to go to trade school, and all Gordy ever wanted was to build boats. Still, she could have talked us into anything, I guess. We both were that crazy in love with her."

"But how was that going to work?"

"It wasn't. We got as far as Eureka, and after three or four months Gordy and I couldn't get out of there fast enough."

"What about Bea?"

"Bea? We hardly ever saw Bea. She'd got something going. In fact, she'd moved out and stuck us with her share of the rent."

"You just leave her?"

"The truth is she'd pissed us off enough that neither of us cared anymore. We were her ticket out. She only needed us till she found something better. But before I forget, the deputies gave me this to give you. They found her Falcon down the next fork in the brambles. They found this lying on the dash."

She lifted the envelope flap. A tiny black and white snapshot fell out, a young Bea Lusich looking oddly glamorous in a halter-top dress with her dark hair piled up. She leaned toward whoever snapped the shutter in a pose of "I just dare you to try!" one hand clasped around a porch post by the steps of the house in town where she and Iva lived. Lexie knew from stories that next door was the attic room where Gordy and Rodger boarded during four years of high school, a house entered from an outside staircase, their way out and Bea's way in. Other than the picture dated May 1945 were the few lines penned in perfect cursive on Bea's standard powder-blue writing paper:

> *I must have been quite young. I know it was summer and there were many canoes fanning out from all the different tribes. Even today I can hear Gordy's aunties saying look up, Beatrice, look up in the treetops... so many eagles, such a blue sky... and I can see my father's big shoulders... me wearing my little cedar hat. And at the end the welcome sight of the bonfires strung along the headlands, and then the bonfires growing dim till finally we can't see them at all and we're home...*

At twilight, Lexie took her rolling papers and can of tobacco out to the woodshed. It was dark by the time she came back in and curled up in her chair. By then each reading of Bea's lines was reminding her anew of the beauty she'd gazed out on herself as a young child, a natural world still so little altered she rarely had to look out on a spoiled mountain or swim in a spoiled stream, never had to cringe at the sight of yet another forest laid down by an even better-equipped bull-of-the-woods. *And I can see my father's big shoulders,* Bea wrote. *And me wearing my little cedar hat.* So much made sense now that never made sense before, not that it mattered. Her friend Bea had cut her losses, made her last soup.

The next day the crew kept mum about Bea, which Lexie took to mean they knew the whole story. Besides, when she gave them extra work, they jumped right on it, though Gail, the only new seasonal worker Bea had asked Rodger not to hire, hung back as if she had something important to say, as if choosing her moment. She had run the tape twice when Gail rapped on the door. "If you'll give me a minute," she said, not stopping to look up, waving Gail in to wait at Bea's desk in Bea's chair.

Gail was one of their better workers, careful, efficient, always looking for more work once a job was done. Another plus was she didn't jabber like the others. The one conversation she could recall ever having with her was when they stood in line at the hardware store, Gail telling her how they were short some rebar for starting the foundation for their dream home in the woods. Now Gail looked nervous, or maybe not nervous so much as upset.

"I'll never be as quick as Bea," Lexie told her.

"Bea was so smart."

"You knew her really well then?"

"Just my whole life. From the time our moms worked together at the Sash and Door. And maybe I shouldn't be saying this, but we could see this coming. Iva always did like her beer. She worked hard and drank harder, but she had big plans for Bea. She wanted her to be somebody. Mom will always say Iva drove Bea too hard."

"But she didn't mean to. Her mind was going."

"I don't mean now. I'm talking about then. But the worst one was Anton. Anton, The Indian, Bea's dad."

"Bea never would say much about him."

"Because Anton was her downfall. Because Anton made them live in those terrible shacks and hop from island to island and break bread with that lazy bunch of Indians. Anton was as white as the rest of us with a perfectly good job on the wheat docks in town! Is it any wonder Iva never had a good word to say?"

Lexie wasn't sure whose idea it was to bring a picnic to the cemetery, but suspected Rodger's wife. She was the kind, though it may have been Gail. But ever since their talk, Gail was someone Lexie avoided. At the same time, she avoided saying what she actually thought — that worse than the lazy man is the man who over-values what his paycheck can buy. Still, she signed up for a salad, writing in 'Lexie's Similkimeen Salad' on the sign-up sheet, not knowing yet what would go in it, but liking the sound, knowing Bea would approve. Bea who said Similkimeen sounded more like a whisper than a river, the same time she said if there still was a town named Nighthawk, it was where she'd like to live.

The late spring sun streaming in woke Lexie the day of the memorial. She could hear men's voices down on the water, followed by the sound of their outboard kicking over, after that their unison cheer. Their cheer lifted her spirits somehow, as if their cheer were a cheer for her, as if they knew like a good dog knows just when to give comfort.

Later she was debating what would go in her salad when she heard a door slam outside. She knew it could be only Rodger, even though he'd had fair warning not to expect a speech out of her. Today though, he looked as weary as she'd ever seen him. He looked ready to break down.

"I thought I could do it one more time," he told her, "but each one takes more out of me. And today's makes three."

"Gordy. Now Bea. Who else?"

"Anton. But you never knew Anton."

"And I didn't know he was dead either. I thought he was still out there doing his best to annoy poor Iva."

"Not for a very long time."

"What happened? Did he go and drown himself too?"

"No, but he did go down making a last go at pleasing Iva. Iva wanted him with her and Bea. She wanted a better life for them all. What happened to Anton was he got crushed to death on a loading dock in town. He'd always been so clear about how *town* would be the one thing that would do him in."

"Bea never told me."

"Because she never could face it. Those two were so close you couldn't tell where one started and the other left off. And that move to town didn't just kill Anton. It nearly killed Bea. It took Gordy and his family years to bring Bea back from the brink. Anyhow, come out to the van and I'll show you the bowls Bea and Anton learned to carve from their Indian friends. Bea was sure something would happen to their bowls once Iva moved in."

After the memorial, people said how well it went, probably because no one wanted it to be over and have to go home. There were fifty-some people present, which included the entire crew who showed up combed if not tamed. Besides the crew, some church folks came with their broods, and there was Bea's neighbor Finley Swope, Jr. with his. Dottie came from the dinette and Ken from the hardware. The night before, four Nisqually elders who looked to be eighty or more came with their boughs of cedar and coolers of salmon. Anton's Squaxin friends from down Devil's Head never showed this time, though Rodger recalled them coming in force to Anton's paddling two big journey canoes. Gordy's Ollala cousins all came, as did his only living relative on the Belfast-shipbuilding-Nicholson side. Gail showed up last with her mother on her arm.

No one exactly decided to keep religion out of Bea's memorial, but keep it out they did. No priest, no scripture, no prayer, and no hymns unless as many verses of "Acres of Clams" as they could sing counted. After Rodger said what he had to say, Lexie stood up and recited Bea's poem "Off Cape Disappointment" which, since her death, seemed less about a coast-wise lumber carrier that foundered on the Columbia Bar than about a family swept terribly off course. Next she read her own poem "No Place in Nighthawk" after which they spread camp blankets and quilts and sat down on them to eat, going back for second helpings till the food was all gone.

Back home Lexie took her friend's bowl out to the stump in the woodshed. She traced the trail of the crooked knife along the rim and down the sides, recalling the motion Rodger described, the patient persistent curling motion that takes away only a thumb nail's worth of alder wood at a time, the motion Bea's and Anton's Indian friends taught them long ago. But as fine as Bea's bowl was, Lexie could feel the broken promise in it, feel the straight tight grain become the vessel into which Bea would weep her own tears. She could feel this, because where she came from was also a trail of tears and broken promises, where whether she'd ever been willing to admit it before, it was plain that all but the mightiest lived on a reservation of bad faith, which seemed to happen when earth itself became private property to be bought and sold and divided into the rights to its minerals, its timber, its salmon, and water.

It was late in the season for starting a garden, but she spaded up a piece of ground just the same. She planted parsnips and turnips, golden beets and carrots. In the evenings she and the dog still went out on the Queen sometimes. Come autumn they'd go on a journey of their own, north to Lesqueti, the pristine island where her sister Lucy went to homestead with her Canadian boyfriend. It was now ten years since their famous ride in the Lost Lake Stampede, five since their last visit.

No one had lived in the family house for a long time, not since their mother died and older sister Moira left to live free in Alaska. *And even were they to return,* she wrote Lucy, filling both sides of two ruled sheets, *nothing would be as they remembered it.* She added a postscript: *what has gone before only poets can preserve.*

After addressing the envelope, she took a few quick Polaroids of the dog. On the back of one, she inscribed "Smokey 1977" and slipped it in with the letter. It was time she named her dog.

In Lieu of Flowers

ROY WAS ABOUT TO HAVE VISITORS AGAIN. If he wasn't mistaken, it was the same Dodge Coronet muscle car as before lunging up into the last tight turn. He watched a great long mare's-tail of road dust drift out over the valley, a sight that often was his only warning in this high dry country. He lived on his own now that Sam Skelly was dead. Sam Skelly dead and gone, going on a month since a chilly morning in a cold May of a late spring when he didn't get up at first light, his usual time for beginning a busy day.

"Come on and let's get a move on then," he told the dog. Lucky was Sam's dog, a cattle breed, and as lonesome as Roy was for Sam's call. But this time Lucky stood in place rather than follow Roy up the draw to wait out their visitors. He tipped his ears toward the plume of dust, whipped his brushy tail in short hopeful swipes, his way of saying he wasn't giving up.

Roy's wait up in the aspens lasted a good long while that day. When the slicker finally left, Roy didn't like the look of cordwood stacked for a look inside. This time he'd left a note; Roy found it folded in the door jamb. *I can see now what they mean! Van Dale.* What they mean? What who means? And who was Van Dale? Some war buddy of the boss's just getting the news, or maybe somebody out cruising old wagon roads to nowhere anybody didn't need to be going in their Dodge Coronet muscle car anyway.

Of the two men, Sam Skelly had been the sociable one. He would never run to the draw or hide in the barn to wait out a visitor. Up to the end, he was often a visitor himself. Even when his eyesight gave out, he'd saddle up Sonny or Sadie for a ride across the canyon to Big Henck Vogelsang's place just east of his own set-up. At Christmas, he'd trade twenty pounds of cut-and-wrapped deer meat straight across for a steaming platter of Mrs. V's pork roast. Mrs. V's pork roasts had been their regular Christmas fare since 1970 when Big Henck moved his family down from Cache Creek, B. C.

For a dozen years, Sam schussed over to boss the crew at Big Henck's steam-powered sawmill. Come January, he'd take out his grandfather's vintage skis and his leather aviator's helmet that strapped under the chin. He'd roll up work shirts, some trousers, and two pairs of warm coveralls and lay them in a heavy woven-wood backpack, leaving just room enough for camp blankets on top. One year, the coldest in memory, he took along his father's vintage ice skates as well. That year, each night Roy stepped out the door for more stove wood, he'd hear the hoots going up over across the canyon. In his mind's eye, he pictured a great strapping bear of a Dutchman and a fleet-footed, rusty-haired Scot circling the mill pond in the moonlight on long sharp spiral-toed blades, forged in another century a continent away.

During those months, Roy's main work was minding the livestock with an eye to overloads of wet snow on Sam's roofs. He'd be lonesome for a day or two, but not for long, not with his radio pulling in signals from all around the world. The way he saw it, a fellow didn't have to worry over a radio like he did a dog dragging itself indoors with a snout full of quills. Those months were the only time of year he could smoke and dream by his own fire. The rest of the time he'd work into the night — if mending broken book spines was work — while the boss read aloud or told "war stories" as he liked to call what weren't war stories at all. His war stories were about fighting a losing battle against lung disease in a crowded eastern city.

Exactly a week passed before this Van Dale fellow showed up for the second time. Only this time Roy caught a glimpse of a young woman tippy-toeing from the granary to the tool shed to the bunkhouse in high heel shoes. He never would understand women going around in the country in city shoes. Or understand whoever brought her driving a low-slung foreign job up a bad road like Sam Skelly's was. But he wouldn't see the note they left till the next day. *I don't give up easy!* Not even a name this time, but the same scrawl as before.

And the next time after that, Van Dale sneaked in on foot. Of the two roads in, local folks knew to take the lower one. It was common knowledge that the upper road meant a do-si-do with Sam's big bull. Sam's bull was known for keeping *office hours* there at the cross fence on the power line road. Worse yet, old Lem Tipton often was out to scare the underpants off anybody fool enough to set feet on Tipton land. The only good thing was that old Lem couldn't shoot straight, and Sam's bull never did do better than a fair job. Still, even Roy knew he owed something to both the bull and old Lem, or maybe he didn't owe them since here came mischief on the dead run.

"Lay," Roy told the dog, as a bright blur of white trouser pants pulled up a half-length from the fence.

"Phew. Does he shoot at just anybody? Sorry. I'm Van Dale, the Van Dale that leaves notes," she said, as she ducked through the fence corner, taking half steps toward Roy's cloudy sizing-up. "I thought sure I was a goner. Whoever was doing the shooting was out to get me, and so was his big old bull. I hope you don't mind me coming. My Grampa Dale sold this place to a man name of Skelly from somewhere back east a long time ago."

"In nineteen hundred and thirty-eight. Sold it to Sam Skelly and his brother Martin."

"To two brothers? And here I was thinking just the one man ran the whole show. But what do I know?" she said, reaching her hand out for Lucky to sniff.

"You here on business? 'Cause I got some critters croaked down the well."

"Just time on my hands. I work at the drive-in theater in town. It's nice meeting you though. You must be Mr. Skelly's right-hand man?"

"I do the work here. That's about it."

"My gramma knew Mr. Skelly. She's still living. But my Grampa Dale — he's dead. Gramma says Grampa just plain got tired of living. That's how come he went and drove his truck in the lake. But I'm going. Anyway, nice meeting you."

"Best not go that way."

"Got to go out how I come in."

He fanned himself with his hat, watching Van Dale's trouser pants make the turn where the road switched back in the pines. He waited to hear if old Lem would fire off more shots.

After that he climbed down the well lining and fished out two dead marmots. Then he killed ten or twenty minutes more before coming back up. Conversations made him go weak in the legs, a curse handed down from the old man's side. His mother's side didn't have it. His mother's side could yak the livelong day and do it in two languages, or so everyone said. That was the side he wished he took after, before he learned how they died young.

The next time Van Dale came by, he was up on the hay barn roof nailing down shakes. He had to lie low, at least as low as a short blocky man in orange coveralls could lie, or else face more conversation. Her idea that the boss had worked the place all on his own was nothing new, not to him. In this country, only the truth died young. In this country, lies and greed could live to a hundred. But hold on, wasn't somebody besides her sitting there in the front seat?

"I brought you some company!" Van Dale shouted up at him, as he made his way down and around to where she stood patting Sam's dog's willing head. "Gramma's been telling me about all the poles in your out-buildings coming across from over there," she said, pointing to Big Henck's side of the canyon. "She says her and her three sisters skinned the bark off every last one."

Van Dale's granny didn't mince words. "I'd heard there was a hired man here."

"Yes ma'am."

"A place like this takes more than one man to work it."

"Takes two for sure."

"It's not easy, this country. I couldn't say what is, but once you get used to it, you get so you don't want to ever leave it. You reckon it's just we don't know why we're here? Because we don't know, do we? We only like to think we do."

Leading them over to the house, Roy was surprised at how comfortable he could be in Van Dale's granny's company. He had thought her granny would be satisfied to stay put in the car and look out at the big barn she helped skin poles for as a girl. And he liked her not talking a lot or being curious about who he might be. He could get along with someone like her, feel comfortable saying, "It's not my house, but come on in and mind the step and mind the power cord down at your feet."

It was a month since the man came and pronounced Russell (Sam) Skelly dead, a month since the hearse backed up to where the purple lilacs bloomed by the porch steps, a month of the usual stone clearing and burning off of close-in fields, of watching the sky for the long V-formation of homebound Canada geese, for keeping his eye out for the check in the mail from Sam's nephew and his wife who had agreed to cover the cost of the plain dark jacket, dark blue necktie, and plain white shirt. They even wrote the note saying how they planned a contribution to the local chapter of the VFW, in lieu of flowers.

But for Roy, hardest of all was when Ellis, the UPS route man, came for the last time with the last two books that Sam would ever order. And the day the Jehovah's Witness couple came on the third Saturday of the month at the usual time with their Bibles and more solid evidence of mankind's age-old failure to create world government. And the day Chuck from the VFW came to pay his respects, a man who'd been held prisoner in the same POW camp as the boss. Always his job to break the news, his job to tell them, "Sam is gone; Sam's dead."

All those folks turning out for the funeral too, the Jehovah Witnesses and Chuck and his VFW friends, Ellis and those two UPS route men before him, Mrs. Vogelsang from over across the canyon — Big Henck Vogelsang being down with a toothache the day of the funeral — all those families down on the valley road also coming to the chapel with their memories and kind words to make the day the tribute Sam Skelly deserved.

"Gramma?" called a voice from upstairs.

"Yessum."

"Up here is just like in the picture books. There's a carpet on the floor and a card catalogue like in the school library and a big roll-top desk, even bigger than yours and Grampa's old desk was. You've got to come up. Maps that pull down! And books! You have never saw such books before ever in your life."

"I believe I've maybe seen a book or two."

"Not like these you haven't. These aren't Louis L'Amour westerns, Gramma. This is so cool. What does i-n-d-e-n-t-u-r-e mean? Because here on the wall is the most beautiful hand-writing that starts out *This i-n-d-e-n-t-u-r-e...* And it's real old and written on some thick waxy-feeling kind of paper."

That was the day Roy felt his tongue work loose, enough at least to tell Gramma what he knew of the man named in the labor bond. First that he was Sam Skelly's forbear, and the indenture paper had originated in London, England, and was held by a man in Ulster County, New York, for a period of seven years ending in 1787, and was written on paper made of rags. After that he just kept on going, though he couldn't have said later why he'd think they'd be interested in Sam Skelly's father skating on the frozen Hudson River from New York City to West Point and on to Newburgh, or that he had to maneuver tides making the whole adventure even more dangerous. That whole current of words rushed over his lips as unstoppable as Niagara Falls! In all his life, if he had ever got so many words out in a row, it was only to the great hunter moving down the night sky all those many light years away.

For the rest of the month — it was still June — no more visitors came to Sam Skelly's place up those four miles of lonesome track, though for weeks Roy half expected to look up and there they'd be. Ever since their last visit, he took more notice of the meadowlarks perched atop mullein weed or on fence posts. *Look at me I'm such a pretty bird.* Wasn't that what Van Dale's granny told him a meadowlark said? And wasn't it what she claimed she'd sing herself when she was young and handsome, her feathers still bright?

Roy missed the boss more with the passage of time. He couldn't go anywhere on the place it seemed without listening for the sure sound of his hammer ringing from the log house, the ringing of steel on steel in the woods. For thirty years, he had noted the older man's progress as he moved from chore to chore under high hot sun or blanket of winter snow. Even now, he'd stop midway to the woodshed, mid-stride to the bunkhouse, waiting for a sign to get his shotgun off the wall, look up at the billion stars of the Milky Way, or all around at the rime shining in winter.

In late June, his visitors returned in an older model station wagon, the model with side-by-side delivery doors in back. He'd been keeping an eye out, had seen them hit the bend in the road a good mile from where he stood with his axe and stone. He'd been sharpening first the boss's sickles and scythes, next his draw knives, splitting mauls, adzes and axes and hatchets. Once the boss finally got the come-along and straightened up the tool shed, it seemed the next order of business would naturally be sharpened tools in all their right places. Even after a busy morning, he'd had every intention of getting down under the flatbed to pull the oil pan and drain out the oil. But this time he was glad to be in plain sight as they drove up.

"Want one?" Van Dale asked, pushing her straw brim further back on her head as she pulled out a pack of gum.

"I might," he said.

"Gramma says to ask if it's all right us coming like this. She says she's not getting out till you say we can."

"Tell her it's no bother."

"She says it's got so hot at the rest home, they can't rest. And this time we brought Gramma's sister Ada along."

"Bring who you want to bring along. Once I worked in one of them drive-in theater deals. I worked on the grill most of the time, but I did all kinds of other work there too."

"Down at the one I work at?"

"No ma'am. This was clear down in Arizona in the desert where I come up. My old man's army buddy give me the job. But I only did work there to keep the old man from laying into me."

"Why? What did you do?"

"Likely I didn't do nothing at all. Likely he just hated the sight of me. I got so I'd just keep out of his sight the best way I could. When I got old enough to leave, I hopped the bus and come here. That worked out pretty good for me. If you like, I can carry those chairs."

He got out three folding chairs while she helped her granny get her sister out of the back seat. All three had brought their knitting; her granny was knitting up heavy winter socks; her aunt a pair of bright blue mittens. Van Dale herself was working on a black and orange scarf that curled at her feet like a sleeping tiger kitten. For some reason, the sight of the three women counting stitches there in the aspen shade in front of the boss's big log house settled him. He couldn't have said just why, but he took satisfaction in them and told them that if they wanted to look inside Sam's house, it would be fine with him.

The next day they were back. The temperature at the high school had hit a hundred and five. Was it all right them coming again so soon? This time there were four of them, and this time they piled out of a nine-passenger station wagon the same faded shade of mahogany as Sam Skelly's big bull, a wagon with hydraulic lifters that banged away in the distance long before Roy ever caught sight of it. And this time they'd fixed a picnic and brought along an accordion.

"We all of us play some, but Blossom plays best," said Ada. "I hope you don't mind hearing some accordion music."

He nodded his head. "I like accordion," he said, though he surely hadn't heard one in his years at Sam Skelly's. He hadn't heard an accordion since quitting tenth grade and leaving his girlfriend's grandparent's unit there at the tourist court where Chula's round little granny serenaded into the night. But now, would accordion music bring regret for his hasty adios all those long years ago? Or comfort like the boss's tractor brought chugging along home, hauling a hay wagon loaded down with fresh-sawn spruce wood for making more book shelves for more old books.

A little later, he was on his knees thinning the beet rows when they came to invite him to their picnic. And some time much later that same afternoon their plump red grapes put him fast asleep in the crotch of Sam Skelly's cottonwood trunks.

The next day a cold wave came in, dropping rain so hard and heavy Sam's pond filled up. He'd been out with a scythe clearing around the well, thinking the cold wave would surely mean the end of the knitting club. Still, in September, he'd have the usual seasonal work down in the valley, though even before that here came another visitor, this one poking along in a dented-in flatbed with a cattle dog riding the straw bales in back. He'd never met the neighbor to the east, but knew it had to be Big Henck Vogelsang. It had to be him and his she-dog Fritzie, because he'd heard his truck whining over east of him before shifting into low gear.

"Gettin' cool enough for you?" the man said, dropping down from the truck cab. With his hat off, the man stood nearly a full head shorter than Roy, who could only nod while trying to get straight in his mind who this fellow could be. The same as the big-shouldered, barrel-chested bull of the woods the boss talked of so much? And if this wasn't Big Henck Vogelsang, then who in creation was this sawed-off, apple-cheeked fellow standing next to him?

"If it suits you," the man said, reaching past the steering wheel to cut off his engine, "you can throw that old dog of Sam's in the back of the truck with mine and we can all go to town."

Roy squinted up at the morning sun and down at his boots. He looked around for Lucky, but didn't have to look long. Lucky never was the kind of critter to turn down a trip to town. "Well, okey-dokey we'll go if it's all the same to you," thinking a trip to town is a trip to town, even if a fellow don't lack for much and is not all that sure who he'll be going to town with.

Still, all the other times he had done the driving. The boss never drove. Said his eyesight was going, long before it got so he needed all those spendy new kinds of magnifiers for reading so much fine print. On the last trip they'd ever make, they'd hung a left on the river road and drove through forest land that went on and on for miles, some of it muddy ruts even late in May. For lunch, they'd ordered the shrimp baskets and the two slices each of home-made apple pie and sat drinking up a whole pot of coffee as they recalled different roads traveled down through the years.

This fellow, whoever he was, was a real talker, and not one to hurry along either. First they stopped at the south face with the view of the south mountains. After that they stopped for a smoke and the view down the valley. When they finally were making time on the county road, he slowed down to thirty or less miles per hour, this time to say, "What good country this is. Too bad that women don't like it for it being so lonesome. I mean look at Sam. He builds himself a nice big log house. Nice as it is, no woman ever cares to come live there."

Roy had nothing to say on the subject. All Sam's house was ever for was for more of those old books. How many trips had they made over the years to used-book shops up in Canada? Two a year, and some years three. Then add all the ones to second-hand stores and yard sales and to library sales in Wenatchee, in Walla Walla, in Boise, Bend, and Spokane, and some years as far away from home as Whitefish, Montana. While all the other cattlemen put their minds to building up herds, Sam put his to sniffing out more old books, so much so that his second story was floor-to-ceiling books, soon to flow down the stairs to the landing and from there down to the front room. Most of them with some pretty good age on them too.

"What I think is Sam was just different," said the short stocky dumpling-cheeked man, goosing the throttle pedal with his boot toe and lifting it off again so often it had Roy feeling sick to his stomach. "And don't you think after that long being penned up as a POW, his freedom would be what would have to count most?"

They'd come to the end of the valley road. In the canyon just ahead was where the big fire blew up that bad dry year for dry lightning strikes. The forest service had put local crews on the fire and made retardant drops, but finally called in the elite crews when it really took off. "Back in there is where a woods fire burnt half the summer one year," Roy said, hiking his chin to point just where.

"That so? And when was that?"

"Couldn't say when."

"Before you and Sam's nephew met up?"

"Him and I met up on the bus. He got on at the next stop and sat in the next seat. I'll just say all I wanted was to get the hell out of Kingman and maybe come up with some kind of paying job. But this nephew fellow wanted to tell me how hard he was going to work for Uncle Sam. Only Uncle Sam, it turns out, was Sam Skelly, not the U.S. service Uncle Sam, and his nephew wasn't coming to work all that hard."

"I'll bet that didn't go over."

Roy nodded, holding back on just how badly it didn't. The nephew couldn't stretch wire and couldn't split wood. Get him up on anything higher than the third step of a ladder and he'd turn green. He'd let the tractor run away with him and got the stove burning so high it set the chimney alight. And all day long was never long enough to get the least job done. But no, he wasn't going to talk out of school about the boss's nephew. All he did say was, "He didn't last more than that month or maybe two months at the outside. And much as I hate to admit it, I owe him. Without him I never woulda got here in the first place."

"Which nephew? Not the one Sam put through college? Not the one speaks five languages?"

Roy rolled the window down. In his view, it didn't much matter how many languages Sam's nephew spoke, not when he couldn't bother to say a few words in English over his own uncle's grave. He watched Sam's dog's shadow ride the cut bank, the wind in his ruff, a dog that mourned Sam more than Sam's own flesh and blood did, a dog that still went over each morning at first light and pawed at Sam's door. They had pulled over in the cottonwood shade at the city park where a crew of women worked sprucing it up for the annual Fourth of July pancake breakfast.

"Now you and me we should probably talk some things over."

Roy lit the last smoke he had rolled and ready, thinking this wasn't just a trip to town. This trip was about something, maybe something he'd done or not done. He concentrated on the split knuckles on the knob of the floor shift, knuckles he could now be assured belonged to Big Henck Vogelsang, as one of the boss's stories was about how Big Henck lost most of the middle finger on his right hand.

"So yesterday this nephew of his calls me. He says he wrote you out a check to cover his uncle's funeral expenses. He tells me you cashed it. And you are the man in question, right? Am I right about that? Only now you're calling him asking for more money? I can see you do know something about this business."

"Fact is he owes me."

"For?"

"All the boss had was just old work clothes. Not anything you can bury a man like him in."

Big Henck took his hand off the shift and turned off the ignition. "The wife told me there would likely be more to this story. And even considering how close Sam was with a dollar, I happen to know for a fact he was broke."

Roy shrugged and said nothing. He didn't want to comment about hard-working, hard-saving Sam Skelly having only his books, his bull, and a couple dozen head left at the end, and no way to turn things around.

"Believe me, Roy, your loyalty is commendable. And the fact of the matter is our friend Sam Skelly once told me he made all he needed to make at the cattle sales, just what he'd need to pay his taxes and pay you. And he'd have me pay him in kind every time. The reason for that was this nephew, this fellow with his hand always out for a contribution. Sam didn't ever say anything about this to you?"

Roy turned to face out the front window. This was one tricky business now with the boss gone. There were blank spaces where before any question asked of him he'd already know the answer. Besides, it wasn't that the boss didn't say anything. It was the boss said too much. How was he to pride himself on showing up the lazy good-for-nothing nephew in the boss's eyes with the boss cold in the ground? Besides, all that pride had a bad smell to it lately. "Only thing he'd ever say about it was rich men — trust not in wealth; gold cannot buy you health."

"How's that? Rich men, trust not in...?"

"...wealth. Gold cannot buy you health. Only somebody already said it before. Somebody back in the Middle Ages by the name of Nashe. But other than that, the boss only ever talked to me about books and about getting his brother and him out here for a fresh start. He wanted to get them settled in some place healthy like here with fresh clean mountain air."

"His brother Robert?"

"His brother Martin. But before he could get them out here, Martin died. And the other brother Robert, he died in the war. There was only the boss left. And this nephew."

"What did he die of?"

"Martin? His lungs gave out."

"*Trust not in wealth; gold won't buy you health.* Sounds like Sam. Something he would latch onto."

"The boss had a lot going on up here. You know, like upstairs," he said pointing to his forehead.

"He never would say much, not to me. He'd go out after supper and look at the stars, smoke a pipe or two, and come back in. By eight, it was lights out for him. My wife, she got better acquainted. She'd make it her business getting acquainted with the fellows, but I can tell you Sam Skelly was her favorite. Him and this one other fellow we had working for us, the one who took over for Sam. You ever know him? He was like Sam. Smart. Always had his head in a book. And what a skater, him and Sam both. Those two out skating on the mill pond that winter it stayed frozen... what a sight. My wife still talks about them out there skating on the millpond in the moonlight."

"The next time you and him talk, tell him forget it. Tell him we'll call it even. I won't be bothering him."

"Just close the book on it then? Fine with me. I need to pick up a fan belt. And I have this notice to post."

"Something I don't get though is how come he'd always call you Big Henck. Why'd he want to make out you stood seven foot tall?"

"I guess I didn't know he did. To my face he called me Henck, just plain old Henck. But like I said, Sam was different. Sam just was. And not in a bad way. I don't mean that in a bad way. I hope you don't think I do."

"I don't ever think much about how anybody thinks. But me and the dog we'll just get out here. Wait for you here in the shade."

"Look. What I wanted to ask about was would you have any interest in working at my saw mill? Sam always said if Roy Brown can't fix it, by golly, no one can. He said you have a knack."

"I'd have to think about it."

"I pay decent wages and Mrs. V, she puts on a good spread."

"I'd have to think about it, like I said. I won't say I won't, and I won't say I will. I have to think about it."

"Good enough. Be a half hour, no more."

"And the boss he always liked to joke around and call me LeRoy Brown. You know that tune about "Bad, Bad LeRoy Brown"? I forget who it was sang it, but LeRoy Brown was awful mean! And I never did know just how to take it. I just didn't know what he had in mind."

"Like as not he didn't have anything in mind. Like you said our friend just liked to joke."

"You reckon that's all the more there was to it? Used to worry me how come he'd think that way. I'll be over helping get them flags hung. I know some of those folks. They've been to see me a time or two. The girl she works at the drive-in theater. The woman there hosing off the picnic tables, she plays the accordion. That's her calling Sam's dog. See, he knows her. Boy, would you look at that dog go! Good old Lucky!"

It was early afternoon when he got down from Henck's truck at the route box. He had some work to do around the place, some things to work out. Like what next, once all the estate business was finally settled. For a month or maybe two months more, he could spend his days keeping everything in good working order, his evenings up in the boss's study reading aloud from the boss's books.

Something about it was a comfort to him. He would miss the big book-lined room ringing with all the words and phrases strung together by poets, dead and buried a long time ago. Not that he thought reading their words aloud made an educated man of him in the way Sam and his brother were educated with their Will Shakespeare and G. B. Shaw, their Blake, their Browning, and their Robbie Burns always there somewhere, handy to dip into should Lady Luck take a bad turn. He wasn't an educated man and never would be. But thanks to good fortune all those many years ago, he'd always have his own private shelf of good books, so wherever he'd go he'd never be lonesome. Each one of his books was inscribed:

With gratitude for your good company through the years, from your very good friend, R. S. Skelly.

The Decline of Duckpin Bowling

THE TROUBLE STARTED THE DAY we saw my sister off for Europe. If I know Sondra, she had excuses made for Pop already. In my opinion though, it was time for Rip Van Winkle to wake up. At fifty going on fifty-one, you'd think he would get what a big day this was for his daughter, be proud of how hard she'd had to plan and save. Besides, what could he be thinking? Sondra wasn't boarding a bus for a shopping spree in the city. Were we really going to just drop her at the pier and take off?

But I guess this was always his plan, because we sure didn't hang around. To say that it was a letdown to see her green fedora bob briefly there on the human stream, would be the understatement of the year. I'd pictured us staying at least long enough for the big tugs to muscle in, for me to blow brotherly kisses from the wharf as her ship was slowly nudged into the Hudson and turned toward the sea. What I never could have foreseen was us double parking and me unloading my good-hearted, hardworking sister like so much baggage.

Her letters home, nonetheless, did not once mention her unsung departure, not that Pop would know what was said in her letters dropped through the mail slot every other day. After a while, it got so I'd just skip parts because he'd never seem interested when I'd read them aloud. Still it was hard. Here my sister was having her one big adventure. It was going to kill him to hear about Mme. Latour's French class or about the Canadian girl across the hall at the Hotel Francois Premier?

Too soon her two months in Europe were over, and it was time to meet her plane. For me the Sondra swinging across the tarmac, collar turned up against the wind, was a changed Sondra. She brought a kind of sparkle to our crowded table-for-two at our dowdy little Schrafft's. Still, I was at a loss to put my finger on the change in her till we stood bunched at the curb waiting for the light, a moment she chose to casually say, "And then along came my Frenchman just in the nick of time."

Some will say I was too young to remember, but I remember when our mother died and Pop moved down to the basement. I remember tiptoeing out of the gable room to get under the covers with my sis in the big bed facing the windows that looked out at the woods. Now when I close my eyes and picture those terrible first months without our mother, what I see is Sondra tying her apron on over her school clothes and getting supper on the table each night. And I remember how early she'd have to wake up.

She didn't get up so early the next morning though, and I didn't go down before I had to. When I did, our old cracked Philco radio was tuned to Pop's usual morning programs. His back turned, he was busily packing his usual lunch of salami on rye, half sours, and a pear.

"Just so you know, I'm walking with Haskell," I told his back.

"Fine, just so you're there by the bell."

I watched him pull his collar up and button the three remaining buttons on his camel hair coat. To me he seemed no more or less distracted than when he couldn't remember something important from a long time ago. When he was out of sight, I went back upstairs, waiting while Sondra finished up in the bathroom, trying to invoke our old life, the perfectly good one we had before she left for Europe. Her job taking classified ads at the newspaper, Pop's teaching high school civics, and mine doing my usual snow job on them all at South Street JHS.

"Ray sweetie? Would you be a peach and bring me my robe? You were on the quiet side last night."

"I was wondering about the Canadian girl you wrote about across the hall at your hotel."

"You mean Ruth? She's still in Holland. But I invited her for Thanksgiving, if it's okay with Auntie Esther."

"And what about your Frenchman? Is he still in Holland too?"

The bathroom door swung open. Her snort could mean either I'd just said something too ridiculous or something she didn't want to talk about. "Hardly," she said.

"Why 'hardly'?"

"Because he gets on Ruth's nerves."

"But not on yours?"

"Raymond," she said, sending me a look. "I hope it's okay with you that I have an admirer or two. Come here and sit next to me. I missed you. Did you miss me too? You only wrote me the one letter."

"I wrote you two letters. I sent one with my poem in it to the American Express in Paris because that's where you said to send it. Is it my fault you weren't where you said you'd be? And for your information, Pop never did read your letters."

How could I say such a thing? I'd throw myself in front of a bus to save my sister, and here I just said her own father didn't think enough of her to read her letters. And not even to her face. I lobbed my little grenade and ran for the hills. In the process, I forgot to warn her about calling her friend Natalie at Natalie's parents' house. And now she would call and get Natalie's mother and Natalie's mother would give her *hail Columbia* for helping her daughter make her escape from safe suburban New Jersey to her new and exciting life in decadent New York. Naturally, my sister was already on the phone when I came skulking back in.

"So," she said when she finally hung up, "what brings you back?"

"I didn't mean it, and I shouldn't have said it. And I'm sorry."

"And I'm sorry too. Just remember, in Pop's book we are all that's important. So now do I get to read your poem?"

"I personally didn't think it was that great."

"I see. So maybe you'll show me the next one then. But what I think is we should think up something to do today, now that you're here. Just the two of us."

"Okay with me. Just don't call Natalie at her parents' house. You know how Mrs. Kizer is."

"On the warpath again?"

"She is as far as you're concerned."

Of course, I'd always had this huge crush on Natalie Kizer, even if with four years on me she was more mature. I'd always been sure she liked me too, and not just because we're both artists with so much in common, but because we believe in each other. Without her I never could have written "The Saga of Eddie LeVan", my play about the last of the manual pin-setters over in duckpin bowling country. And without me, how would she even know the day would come when nothing would be the same anymore, and it will happen that fast and she won't be able to stop it.

But for the time being I had more work to do on the birthday present I'd been making for Pop — some charcoal sketches mostly from memory of special places like the old library at the teacher's college where he went on the GI bill. And a couple more of Mom's family home in Amsterdam, N.Y., and of the family *camp* on the lake in the Adirondacks. And the one of our house that was giving me so much trouble, since each time I'd go out for another look, Pop would come trundling up the hill with his briefcase and his pint of hot cabbage soup fresh from Tabachnik's. Three times, this happened three times, and even now it could happen again.

I hated admitting his birthday was the one time each year I had any hope for the two of us. Even last year, the year he turned fifty, things looked promising only for a while. That time when I came home from school, it was snowing like it can snow in the middle of November here, and the door was already unlocked and there he was with a fire already blazing in the fireplace. "Today I'm fifty years old," he said. "I never expected to live this long."

He was standing with his hands behind him, his back to the fire. "When you're sixteen," he went on, "you don't give a lot of thought to what's coming. You should, but you don't. Besides I always had the idea I'd skipper some kind of party boat that I'd pick up on the cheap. But, of course, along came the war, and the war changed everything."

And that was it, the total conversation. He turned around and poked up the fire, sat down in his chair and opened his newspaper. It was as if he'd never said the first word. I wasn't sure he even realized he'd been speaking to me or knew I was there. All I knew was I'd never heard the party boat story before, and when I asked Sondra about it, she was as clueless as I was.

After Pop's fiftieth birthday, I decided I'd be ready the next time. I'd be the one to get the fire going; it was usually colder than heck on his birthday. I would already have put the folder of sketches on his chair so he could say, "What's this?" as if he didn't already know, and I could wish him happy birthday. I expected it to go well. And I was optimistic because I truly did believe he could get used to talking to me, if he tried, and if he'd just practice a little, like with anything in life.

Well, you know what they say about the best laid plans oft going astray. He apparently had a plan of his own, because he drove to the station and got on a train the morning of his fifty-first birthday. I had heard him call in sick. But even before that, his whistling said he was pleased about something. Still, I must have chalked it up to some kind of birthday thing. So when he came home, did he ever have a surprise in store. I mean he might have gone into the city by himself, but when he came home he came home with a boy named Orlando, age seven years and two months, who talked a blue streak and dragged in two big May Company shopping bags bulging with jerseys and jeans. I mean here comes Pop with this kid Orlando, and then gets the kid to charge up the steps and ring the doorbell like he's a delivery man delivering a C.O.D. package or something.

Only Orlando *is* the package. It turned out Orlando and his grandmother were tenants in Auntie Esther's house in Brooklyn. Apparently his grandmother asked Auntie Esther if she minded taking charge of her little grandson while she went into the hospital for her operation. Except, Auntie Esther said she wouldn't have the time and asked Pop, and Pop said yes, he'd be glad to, I guess. I'd have to say Orlando's been working out okay, now that I'm used to this one bad habit he has of leaning against my chair and resting his head on my arm. I mean he'll do this for half an hour and sometimes longer. I'll be trying to draw, or maybe I'll be doing my homework.

Thanksgiving was just around the corner, and Ruth was due in from Holland the day before. Natalie would be coming too, rather than going home to face the third degree about the terrible unsanitary conditions in the city. I mean, to hear Mrs. Kizer talk, you would never guess Natalie was enrolled at the Art Students League and boarded at the YWCA. And Nat didn't run with the beatniks, because she didn't know any.

Sometime over Thanksgiving I still plan to sit down with Ruth and get the skinny on my sister's Frenchman, because even now Sondra gets a couple of letters a week from a D. Macomb from some town beginning in 'S' in France. I have a pretty good idea Sondra is serious about this mysterious D. Macomb from the French town beginning in 'S', because I know my sister.

The next time Sondra went away for any length of time came six years later. By then I had a car of my own and two days left of spring break to drive her up to Albany. I was a sophomore in college, happily ensconced in the airy third floor room facing the garden of Auntie Esther's house on Bergen Street. Once in Brooklyn though, I had to admit my old stomping ground in New Jersey was the last thing on my mind. I was busy leading not one, but two, lives — my official daytime one at City College, and my night-time one at a nearby tech school. Meanwhile, it never occurred to me that the wheels might be coming off at home, not with Orlando, but with my sister.

Exactly when the trouble started, I couldn't say. Maybe Sondra was on the sad side before and we just never noticed, or maybe she got sad when Pop moved out. Pop moved into Auntie Esther's other vacant third floor room at the end of January. All I know was Sondra didn't sound like herself. Then one day Orlando came home from school and found her in a closet trying on Mom's clothes, apparently some of Mom's favorite outfits. Orlando told her she looked pretty, but afterwards called me to say he thought she'd been making some kind of shrine there in the closet.

The day I went out to see her, I found her in her old bathrobe listening to the same old programs on the same old radio, absently watching old Mr. Giddings next door toss bread ends to the same old birds. To me, even her usually glossy hair looked dull. Besides that, she hardly seemed to notice I was there. Possibly I tormented Orlando just to get a rise out of her. Still, all

I said was something about him being up to his old tricks again. It was a joke. He was one kid who never skipped school.

"Orlando sweetie, go on, and go now," she told him, sending a warning look in my direction.

"All right. I'm going. And don't forget my game today."

"I won't. Give me a kiss."

I followed him out the door and apologized. Once he'd been like a round-eyed little spaniel pup always wanting more attention. Now he was much too sober. I should have thought to tell him not to worry. I'd still be around when he got home.

"Same goofy kid," I said when I was back inside.

"Orlando is just the most wonderful little guy. You going to tell me what's eating you? Is it being here when you could be doing better things with your time?"

"It so happens I'm on spring break. Anyhow, now that I'm here, maybe you can fill me in."

"Last I heard everything here is hunky dory."

"Orlando called me. He said I should come. He said he was worried."

She sighed, pulling at a loose thread on her sleeve. "Do you know that kid does the laundry and runs the vacuum? When I come home from work, he'll say I look tired. Or I look happy or I look pretty. I mean he notices. He's so grown up."

"He said you were sad about Mom. Why don't we talk about her? Pop doesn't talk about her either. No one does. I mean did she do something terrible?"

"Of course not!"

"Because whenever I bring her up, Pop always changes the subject."

"You sure all this is really about Mom? Natalie tells me you're about to drop out of school."

"All I said to Nat was I didn't think history was my thing either, not engineering, not history, maybe just time to go in the army. You know, time to go waste a few Viet Cong for my country."

"That bad, huh? Well, I quit my job yesterday, so it's not like I can't understand. I'm not Auntie Esther you know."

"I think by now I know that," I assured her. But exactly what were we talking about? Wasn't the whole point of my coming to say I missed Mom too? And I appreciated my sister's many efforts on my behalf. And nobody else could have done what she did after we lost our mother. But that said, I did still have those days when I'd wonder what in my make-up made me so serious. Why wasn't I more like my friends who could just kick back and take things in stride?

That's when she asked me to drive her to Albany to Cousin Brooksie's. On the way up, she seemed her old self again, cheerily mentioning the Papagallos and the Capezios, who I took to be neighbors until for some reason I began to think breeds, only to learn the reference was to brands of ladies' footwear. My sister loved fashion in general and shoes in particular, and our cousin owned a ladies' accessory shop where Sondra could work in sales, probably no better medicine. Besides Mom and Brooksie grew up together, and over a whole summer there'd be time for everything never quite squeezed into our single week at the lake.

My moving back to the house on Hill Street was another matter. It brought Viet Nam home in a way that just didn't happen in the city. More often than not, soldiers listed as KIA and MIA were guys I knew — first the Briscoe boys, then Lonnie Denlea, most recently Joey Perlaw. And with the next lottery it could be anybody at any time. It could be me or Casey or Haskell, or all three of us. Only the year before, our birthdays had become our destiny. Student deferments were gone with the wind and Canada no longer was just a cold country to our north.

I can't remember exactly who said it, but I remember someone saying the lottery might well ring the death knell on the anti-war movement. It was only logical, wasn't it? With winners and losers, would the winners still man the barricades? And cynical too. From our perspective, there could be no more calculated a way to dismantle a movement.

We'd been knocking back beers — me, Casey, Haskell, a few others, the usual scene. But this one night we were juiced. First we divided the year into seven circles — five circles with fifty-one lottery numbers in them, two with fifty-five, a grand total of 365 birthdays.

Circle # 1 (1-51)—Say bye-bye, you're in the army now!

Circle # 2 (52-103)—Not too late to enlist! Even better, cross into Canada!

Circle # 3 (104-155)—You're not out of the woods yet, Private!

Circle # 4 (156-207)—Don't get cocky, asshole!

Circle # 5 (208-259)—Hallelujah, I'm a bum!

Circle # 6 (260-315)—Hallelujah, we're all bums!

Circle # 7 (316-365)—Only the worst SOBs ever luck out like this!

That was the summer we had jobs with the Recreation Department. That same night we put together a whole Canada plan before reporting for work the next day. We settled on New Brunswick, because it was closest to home and we liked the idea of boats and water. After our usual regular courses, we'd take night classes in drafting and welding and the Canadians would hire us because we'd have the skills.

I remember briefly hoping we would get the bad-ass, low-ball draws. If old man Hershey wanted us in his army, then by God he'd just have to come up to Canada to get us. But most amazing of all was that I was in on this, a kid who got homesick at summer camp, who pictured bloodsucking leeches patrolling a swampy borderland between his own country and that great unpopulated wasteland to the north, in whose mind lingered the tragic lesson of eighth grade English, the lesson of poor Philip Nolan sentenced to remain forever a man without a country.

But that was last summer. This summer, Casey and Haskell found lifeguard jobs at a resort over in duckpin bowling country, and we hardly ever saw them. Still, having Orlando back in my life was a lucky break. After supper, we'd stake out places in front of the big rotating floor fan for friendly games of dominoes. On really suffocating nights, we'd strap bedrolls onto a pair of rusty Schwinns and pedal out into the countryside. We'd lie on our backs and talk to the stars about things people don't talk about, about his mom sniffing glue and either jumping or being pushed off their 6th Street roof, about the morning in the Shop-Rite parking lot when my mom's heart stopped beating forever, about last December when Pop quit his teaching career over a freedom of speech difference with his school board.

Tough luck for me. All this ruminating wasn't getting me a summer job. Just maybe it was the reason every place in town seemed to have all the warm bodies they needed already, meaning I registered as rebel just by the way I walked in the door. I'd have to lose the beard and get the haircut and press the creases back in my trousers, because I did have to pass GO to get a job. Then, what luck! My sister's old newspaper decided to take me on. I felt so great I didn't want to go home at night, even before Laela Price-Pruitt came on board. She had to be thirty, or maybe even thirty-five, and it wasn't her looks so much, at least not in any usual way.

It wasn't just Laela. I loved running against deadline. I loved hitting our marks. And I will probably always regret my first newspaper job being as brief as it was, just for that summer. The lottery for draft eligible men born in 1951 was only a day away. I reminded the editor I'd need some time off, and he reminded me every private doesn't serve in the front lines. "If they call your number," he advised, "tell them you can type and type your way through it."

All along I'd been keeping my own counsel. I knew I wasn't as high-minded as the war objectors serving time in prison or the soldiers serving overseas. Still, I knew I loved my country. My mother's forbears had come when New York was still New Amsterdam, my father's people three centuries later. We were Protestant and Jew. We stitched gloves and swept streets, laid track, and taught school. But we weren't just our country's muscle, not just its brains. We were its conscience as well.

When I got home from work, Orlando was hard at work writing his autobiography. Ever since I got him the second-hand typewriter, he'd been writing steadily on "The Very Good Life of Vicente Orlando Ortiz". While eating supper, I turned on the evening news. A forty-four-year-old woman had given birth to her third set of twins, a new fire chief was fifth in a long line of fire chiefs, and the longest heat wave all summer was expected to break by Thursday. There was no mention of the lottery. Strange when the lottery was the one thing keeping me up nights choosing what I'd take with me and what would stay behind should the time come to leave one life and begin another in Canada.

I had started down to the basement when I heard a noise, like a branch brushing up against the house. When I looked out, there was old Mr. Giddings. "My Willie," he said through the screen door, "my lovely Willie. She won't come 'round."

"You want me to call an ambulance for you, Mr. Giddings?"

"If you would, please, if you wouldn't mind."

Mr. Giddings' wife lay curled on the love seat and looked to be napping. He told me how he had just gone to the kitchen to put the kettle on for their tea. "Always have our tea and our biscuit," he said, stroking her hair. "Her never made a peep."

When I called Sondra after the ambulance left with Mrs. Giddings' body, she was asleep. "I can be on the first bus in the morning. I'll call and give you the time. Go on over and sit with him now, Ray. He'll need someone with him."

I'd always known them. I'd known Mr. Giddings played football as a young man in England and worked here as head gardener at one of our local estates. Before I was old enough for school, I was left in Mrs. Giddings' care. Together we'd paste stamps in savings stamp books and put groceries away.

What I hadn't known about were Mrs. Giddings' birthday teas before I was born, teas to which my sister and mother wore hats with gloves tinted to match and counted among Mrs. Giddings greatest satisfactions in life. "Her never wanted to come here," Mr. Giddings confided, his pale eyes brimming as I picked up the photograph of the Giddings' son Reg in paratrooper harness facing a photograph of his mother pinning a corsage to my mother's lapel. Much later, and I may have imagined this, a floral scent seemed to stir in the corner where we pulled up our chairs, as if the roses twining the wallpaper had commenced a final memorial bloom.

At some time I dozed off, but not before hearing another story I'd never heard before that night. It was when the war had come to the Giddings' doorstep, just a month before their son Reg was shot down. Mr. Giddings knees were not an inch from mine, his old man's tremolo barely a whisper. It was past three when he laced his fingers across his stomach. Eventually I must have slept too, awakened only when the sun streamed through the east windows pooling at our feet.

My sister's bus wasn't due to arrive for another two hours, but the results of the lottery were already here. My draw, #154 (in the "don't get cocky, asshole!" circle), could be the last number my draft board called up. Still, in all likelihood, I was home free, as was Haskell with #169. Only Casey was unlucky, drawing #62. Casey's predicament brought back something Pop said a long time ago, one of the few times in my life I could recall him saying much of anything to me at all. Even so, he hadn't been talking as much to me as to himself. I'd been fourteen, maybe not yet fourteen. He'd been speaking of the plans he had before the war. And then along came the war, he'd said, and the war changed everything.

Down in my room I put my socks and underwear back in the drawer, my shirts and trousers back in the closet. I arranged my shoes in a row under my bed and took my portable typewriter out of its zipper case. The limbo of the past two years was over, and it had happened fast. As cynically as I'd viewed the lottery system in the past, very likely I would never have to flee and risk a life in exile. I would likely never be called.

I went out in the yard to where Mr. Giddings weeded his flower bed on the far side of our fence. He wore his customary sweater vest, even as the mercury stood on eighty, giving me only a nod when I told him my news. Back in the house I tried thinking up what I could say to Casey. I'd want to sound positive, not sound as if the worst had happened. I was debating whether the worst had happened when the phone rang.

"Poor old Casey," Haskell said.

"It stinks," I agreed.

"But at least the two of us made out all right."

"All I can think about is what if he enlists. What if Casey just decides to get the whole war thing over with?"

"He won't. He'll go to Canada. Canada's not Siberia, you know."

"It will feel like Siberia," I insisted. "If it was me, I'd go in the fucking army before I'd go someplace and never be able to come home again."

"But then you don't have to go in the fucking army, Ray. You don't have to do anything and neither do I."

"That's what I mean. We're out of the soup, and like you said, we don't have to do anything."

A half hour later I got in the car to go downtown to pick up my sister. At the bottom of our hill, Orlando flagged me down, his trunks still dripping from his swim. I had him sit on a pile of old newspapers in the back seat. He was in a good mood, possibly as good a mood as I'd seen him in since Sondra left for Albany. He was a terrific kid for all he'd been through in his life. At his age, I'd always worried about losing more of my people and still do. But at the moment I'd have to say that what had me more worried were all the changes coming between me and my friends and between us and our country. It worried me that nothing felt solid anymore and we were already spinning permanently away from anything familiar.

Of Love
and History

THE SUMMER OF 1975 WAS ONE OF THOSE TIMES that can feel almost like your due. Finally, staff changes at the newspaper had opened up a path for me. From beat reporter/drudge I'd been moved up to assistant night editor. Two years before, I'd lucked out in the lottery and beat the draft. Romance-wise I was in love with Natalie, the feeling more than mutual; I was the one stalling on the move to her place in the city.

As for the family, my sister Sondra had married and moved to Canada. Auntie Esther made her peace with a pensioner's lot and the pivot from lesson plans to itineraries. Only our ward Orlando remained at loose ends, and he was a week away from orientation and his freshman year in college. Lately, even my pop had a girlfriend.

What could possibly happen to make me think all this well-being might not last? With nothing obvious to point to, I traced my unease to a trunk I had opened in Auntie Esther's basement. True enough, she had asked me to address the mess down *in steerage* while she was away on her trip. But I had better things to do with my time and Auntie Esther's trunk was heavy. Under the circumstances, I'm sure most people would do what I did. They'd look inside.

For the first few minutes all I did was look. After that I remember getting down on my knees, not believing my eyes and wiping my hands before I touched anything. I remember trembling when I picked up the November 24, 1847 edition of *The New York Herald* to read the Honorable Henry Clay's November 13 address to a mass meeting in Lexington, Kentucky, on the Mexican War then in progress. I remember two more such papers: one, *The Weekly Herald* Christmas Day Edition of the same year, an illustrated newspaper showing Santa Ana and General Zachary Taylor's opposing armies engaged in battle; the other, the May 11, 1846 edition of *The New York Daily Tribune* edited by Horace Greeley. Another from the same period covered the final interment of John Quincy Adams.

There was little chronological or any other order to the contents. A single-sheet *Balance Advertiser* from Hudson, New York, dated February 16, 1808; a *Columbian Centinel* dated May 31, 1809 out of Boston giving news of the 11th Congress; a *Daily Evening Transcript*, also from Boston designated Vol. 1, No.1 providing shipping news of 1830.

A line in a *Protestant Churchman* will always stick in my mind: "A lull of warlike commotion is now so absolute in the city that it is difficult to realize a large army encompasses the capital". The city? Washington City. The day? Saturday, August 24, 1861. I let the phone ring as I poured over a letter to the editor in a second *Protestant Churchman* giving an eyewitness account of the Union Army's ragged retreat following the rout at Bull Run.

After that I went upstairs and phoned Natalie, my voice betraying my emotions. "I was anticipating bed linens or clothing, not newspapers dating back to Henry Clay and John Quincy Adams."

"What are you talking about? What newspapers?"

"I went down to sweep out my aunt's basement, and what do I find but all these old newspapers inside a trunk. You're still coming over, aren't you? That was you calling?"

"It's a hundred degrees inside my ice box. You bet I'm coming over."

That was it, the last time I ever saw them. One hurried, over-heated and sensational peek. All I had were the notes I scribbled on the lid of a shoebox, the names of those ten or twelve newspapers on top, the dates and the few quotes about chaos in Washington City. Of course, I was thinking there would be time. And if not for the extreme heat, I know I would have read them, read every last one of them, read every word. Still, it was my mistake leaving Auntie Esther's trunk open like I did and not taking more care.

A week later though, I had yet to return to the basement. First my aunt called to say to expect her on Saturday, that she was done-in after a month in Saskatchewan with my sister and *Sgt. Preston*, as she called Sondra's husband, who was a Mountie after all. She made a request for a serene homecoming *this time*. I'll admit I do recall the incident, not the bash she described, but some friends of mine sleeping over the night before Casey was due to report to his draft board. Now we talk of amnesty, but nobody talked of amnesty then. Nor did anyone speak of living in exile. Only Casey, his girlfriend, Haskell and I knew just where in Canada Casey would be going to live in exile for the rest of his life.

Before I could finish policing up for Auntie Esther, a postcard came from Pop the next day. "Expect me Tuesday," he wrote, adding it would be very nice if I could have a room ready for his friend Dominique. It seems his friend Dominique's apartment was sublet for the rest of the week. As far as I knew, they shared a room if not a bed on their trips south to New Orleans and north to Maine and New Brunswick. I had to think even Auntie Esther would have a snicker at that.

I was welcoming when Pop and his friend Dominique arrived mid-afternoon Tuesday. Before I left for work, we chatted on about their trip and my new job. In reply to a question concerning my friend Natalie, I said only she was keeping busy; more than two could play the game. Still, with all the chit-chat, I got into my car to leave before I remembered. "Say Pop," I called from the street, "you might be interested in some newspapers I found. Take a look in Auntie Esther's trunk in the basement."

I know it wasn't that same night he called me at work, or even the next night. So it had to be the night before Auntie Esther was due back from her trip. "Everyone's fine," he began as he always did. "Will you be finishing up there anytime soon?"

"Not for another hour," I told him.

"Then can we talk now?"

"Talk? Talk about what?"

"Talk about your aunt's trunk. I finished sweeping out her basement. As far as we're concerned, her old newspapers don't exist. We wouldn't want her to think we've been prying into her private affairs. She has her own way of going about things, and we must respect that. I know I can depend on you not to mention anything about those newspapers to her or anyone else."

He could depend on me. Still, if Natalie had asked what Pop called about, I wouldn't have hesitated, because she knew about the trunk and its contents already. What threw me had nothing to do with my aunt's newspapers or anything to do with Pop being so conscientious. What threw me was him trying to reach me at my girlfriend's. I didn't think he had that one figured out yet and wasn't so sure I wanted it figured out.

"He really tried to get me here?"

"Um-hmm. Sometime round about midnight."

"What exactly did he say?"

"He said 'Hello, this is Mr. Simonds, Raymond Simonds' father. Would my son Raymond happen to be there with you?'"

"And you said?"

"I said you weren't here yet, he'd have to try you at the newspaper. Why? Is this a problem?"

"Whether it is or not depends. You're making crepes again?"

"Yes, I'm making crepes again. And I could care less who knows we sleep together. The whole world can know. John Foster Dulles can know and the emperor of Japan. Of course, Uncle Laszlo knows already. What, I didn't tell you? Uncle's zonked out in my bed. But surely we can behave ourselves this once. After you finish your crepes, we'll go on a nice long ramble and wait for the sun to rise."

That was fine, though I could have done without Uncle Laszlo. He had a bad habit of showing up Friday nights. But still, what could I do about it? He was the one person in Nat's family she got along with. Still, why was it always poor Uncle Laszlo? He had a job, and not too shabby of a job either. Taking tolls for the turnpike was a heck of a deal for a newcomer like him. In fact, I'd heard one of the linotype guys in back say they made as good money as he made, though I kind of doubt that somehow.

My attitude was what got me in Dutch with Natalie. Or maybe Nat and I were just never meant to be. Even she said it, had been saying it since the day she got me to take my clothes off and model for her one-woman life drawing class. After that it wasn't even civilized the things we'd say, not that there was anything quite like making up with Natalie. One minute she was raving, the next, good as gold. So, of course, we had a problem, because naturally I'd say things, provocative things.

Somehow though, we kept this up all summer. One particularly steamy Saturday, I had to change a flat, fortunately on a country road with a good place to pull over. Flat tires depressed me just looking at them and all the more because I was the one cranking the jack and balancing on my ass to get the damn thing fitted on the lugs, while all she had to do was stand there and chew gum when it was her art show we were going to.

Luckily, the judges were moved by her still life that time and we could make the drive back in peace for a change, her best-of-show ribbon pinned to the heel-at-the-wheel's breast pocket. Later on that summer though, there was no more denying what a mismatch we were, too different and too alike at the same time, one of us always drowning, the other performing heroic blocks and parries and labored cross-chest carries back to shore, any chance for a happy life together never getting closer.

I didn't plan it, but one overcast afternoon late in August I just stopped seeing her. I drove into the city and parked on her street. I opened the door to get out and walk the block and a half to her building. Somehow though I never quite made it out of my car and instead sat there, feet propped on the curb, watching as her super went by with his youngest boy, Angel I think was his name, a kid of about five, and as Mrs. Borrone from across the hall rounded the corner with her bags of groceries. Mrs. Borrone, whose toilet had yet to be *incorporated*. Then a customer hurried up the steps from the hand laundry next door, and two girls from a life study Nat did of them came out to skip rope on the sidewalk. It was nearly four when I turned onto Avenue B to test my resolve one last time. *If I don't see her here...* I told myself again. And I didn't see her, and so I drove uptown to the tunnel and home.

I was aware of close friends running roughly this same gauntlet, maneuvering between stark certainty and back to featureless gray again. She was pure gold; she was pure poison. True, I was anti-Hungarian where Uncle Laszlo was concerned, but anti-woman? Fortunately, I had my work. And I had Orlando coming home from time to time with diversions of one kind or another. It would have been Columbus Day weekend when we went to Hudson's, Orlando in his country squire phase trying on lumberjack shirts while I checked out the shoe department. However, it was more a way I was looking for than something to put on my feet. Still, I purchased a compass that day and a pair of heavy-duty socks.

A month later I finished *The Compleat Walker* by Colin Fletcher. I began walking to work, a distance of 1.8 miles each way. I looked over the Schwinns and Rudges at Pep Boys before springing for a second-hand Raleigh listed in our Classifieds. Memorial Day weekend I went on my first long-distance bike ride to Gettysburg and back, after which I wrote a check for $575 payable to my friend Casey's sister for a 1963 Nova wagon with 80,000 miles on it. Soon, maybe as soon as my summer vacation, I'd head west to the Mississippi and on to the Rockies.

But at the moment I was due down at Conklin's Radio & TV Repair. Casey's dad would be holding court on the usual Saturday topics — the Mets bullpen, the abomination to be known as the World Trade Center still rising down where Radio Row used to be, lefty-liberal politics, labor unions, the long wait for amnesty. To hear Mr. Conklin tell it, he had yet to live down the fact his son once shook the hand of teacher's union boss, Albert Shanker, in my aunt's living room. But somehow this same man had been able to justify his son fleeing to Canada. He'd been able to see how warring with a people one knew nothing about half a world away made little sense.

Likely, that was when I started thinking in a different way about which group I belonged to as a natural member in a world intent on partitioning us into opposing groups. Likely, it was when I began to understand that should I live to be old, I'd look back on our times and see what we shared was our times, and this would include all of us and all of our good and bad behavior, because we were here when certain things came to pass, and we alone would know what the pressures were. That those who came before or after us and who would judge us could not know our times; they could only know their own, and would be judged by those who both preceded and followed them. That it was a ledger without end.

Still, I had to count myself among the lucky ones. I loved my nights in the newsroom with the teletypes chunking out copy, the squawk boxes squawking out code. I loved running against deadline — the copy in, the copy out, the jargon, the jokes, the dependable irreverence in the press room, the hand-off at shift change. I loved how heroic it all felt, as if each time we put the paper to bed we did a job as important as launching a space capsule or saving a species.

Better yet, I loved the certainty of knowing we in the newsroom would always have jobs. Knowing those jobs would remain should the bean counters in the front office ever figure out a way around paying the so-called profit-killing union wages demanded by the guys in the press room. Knowing as long as there was news there'd be newspapers. And the news of my children's day would follow the news of my day as mine followed the news of Henry Clay's day and Horace Greeley's — the daily newspaper: the best and often only dependable record of what really happens. Even with change all around, like every thinking scribbler I had no doubt my country's life blood did then and ever would rely on the free flow of ideas circulated in a free press.

Next week we'll start Orlando taking calls on the day shift. Then we'll send him out on a story. My first story was a house fire in which the only survivor lost his wife of a dozen years, lost his two sleeping children and his dream house on the hill. In the morning all that was left standing was the skeleton of the house, and the man of the house left fighting for his life in a hospital bed. That's the kind of school where we have to make the grade. Either we get the job done and make our deadlines or we get the axe. A tough business this business of getting the news out, as tough as any, as tough or tougher than love or history.

Scull on! Toes to Greenland

THE ENVELOPE WAS ADDRESSED TO BARE'S FRESH MARKET, Groomtown, New Jersey, postmarked Blue Toe, Tennessee. Robbie Bare, sole proprietor of Bare's Fresh Market, read the tribute through, cleaned his glasses and read it again. Lately, it seemed he sat down to a regular diet of page-filling, small weekly prose remembering the lives of local worthies from here and there. But the scriveners of Blue Toe had outdone themselves, serving up a history lesson on the failed State of Franklin while providing precious little of interest on Mrs. Marander Mumpower herself. Had they never heard of Anna Middleton, the brave English girl that Mrs. Mumpower saved in the war? Were they even acquainted with the six-foot-tall East Tennessee woman who walked in seven league boots?

This sad, not unexpected news had come in June. Soon after, Robbie had his sister Penny compose a note to Marander's one surviving kinswoman, also of Blue Toe. She wrote movingly of the mind over matter practicality that Marander brought to their New Jersey inlet for the duration of the war and beyond, of the late Anna Middleton's gratitude for the many years of care so willingly bestowed. Then, he added a few lines of his own recalling his one journey to Blue Toe as a very young boy.

Meanwhile, the time had come to put his produce market up for sale. After all the years of building up his business, the prospect of turning it over to a stranger was hard. He had begun to think too hard when a stranger made an offer he couldn't refuse. She would retain not only Bare's Fresh Market name, but his life-sized cast-iron grizzly on a braided leather leash at the entrance, his loyal long-time assistant, and three hard- striving part-timers. She would possibly add a barista to her payroll, some tables and chairs and new awnings out front.

With Labor Day close at hand, Robbie was over his retirement blues. Up at the break of day for his usual coffee and toast, he took care to match socks and drop in on The Scientific Barber for a monthly chat and trim. He called old friends to join him for lunch. This particular morning, he had plans out for the skiff he intended to build, up to this point little more than over-priced marine materials stacked in his barn. He was on the way there, plans in hand, when Penny called to say she and Magnus would be down on the twelve-ten. Could he meet them at the club to make a day of it? He assured her nothing would suit him better than a day with his sister and his nephew at the beach.

If he got moving, there was time for a vigorous over-arm crawl to the jetty and for a leisurely side-stroke back again. He'd been nine when a boy his age drowned in an undertow; he was a lifeguard in his teens joined at the hip to Anna, the brave English orphan yet on his side of the Atlantic; and close to thirty when solitary ocean plunges became his routine. He drove the limit, relieved that no safety gates were down at the crossings. The tide was out when he waded in and swam in the direction of Montauk and the Maritimes on swells so benign they barely breached. Halfway there, he turned on his back and sculled on, toes to Greenland, still going strong a month before his sixty-sixth birthday.

"I knew that would have to be you out there," said Penny, patting the canvas beach chair beside hers. "The bus made it down on time for a change, but Magnus couldn't make it down after all. His thesis, of course, what else? We'll be in our winding sheets and he'll still be tap-tap-tapping away on it."

He leaned down to plant a saltwater kiss on her cheek. "What thesis would this be?"

"His master's thesis for his master's degree, and don't say you didn't know," she said sending him a pained look. "Something about Jay Cooke, the financier, and financing the first transcontinental railroad. And speaking of writing, Marander's sister-in-law finally wrote back. She says Marander just went to sleep and didn't wake up."

Robbie shook out a towel and spread it half under the umbrella, half in sun, hoping for more on the one person who brought belief to their worried inlet in those tough early war years. He watched his sister rub in sun block and flop belly down on the towel next to his.

Just past fifty, her first President had been Eisenhower during post-war plenty; his FDR, over the decade-long, world-wide bloodbath never witnessed before or since. He dug his toes down in warm sand, the play-by-play voice of the Mets giving the 3-1 count on the Mets' shortstop on a radio nearby. At some point he tuned out the game, trying to recapture the night-rending wail of the southbound train to Blue Toe waking the hill folk of upper East Tennessee.

"It was wartime when Marander and I went down," he began. "Her father had been badly injured in a sawmill accident and wasn't expected to live. Then he died before we could get there. I can still picture the mourners streaming out of the hills, the wagon carrying the casket mired down to its axles in mud." He described a cabin with a long slick foot path, one with a cold water creek running through, set back in the laurel fortress of the Blue Toe hills. "Now I wonder if there even was a town. All I recall is deep river valleys carving through the state Marander always claimed was the one true state of mind over matter."

"The state of Tennessee?"

"The State of Franklin. Anna arrived November 1942," he went on, "which would make our trip to Blue Toe the spring before that — before I was school age and Mother was leaving me in Marander's care next door while she went to work at the fort."

"Poor Anna, still in Coventry," Penny said mournfully, as if Anna were still in Coventry.

"Yes," he agreed, "poor Anna."

"And Mr. Mumpower?"

"Everyone said he was lost at sea. All I ever saw of him though was a grainy photo of merchant ships off in the distance."

"Mother doubts there even was a mister. But when I spoke to Marander's sister-in-law, she gave me to understand Mr. Mumpower was in the corn trade and never in the merchant marine at all. And she insisted Marander wrote the newspaper account herself. She said all that State of Franklin business was Marander's idea. What's more, the sister-in-law had never heard of Anna Middleton. She didn't believe a word I said about Anna. At any rate, with Marander gone, this sister-in-law will have to go into some kind of retirement home they have just for cotton mill ladies down that way. And Mother says she wants her royal-blue summer-weight blazer, as if her sky-blue summer-weight blazer won't fill the bill. How I hate being sent on these wardrobe missions of hers."

He passed on correcting Penny's cotton mill ladies reference, as ever since she saw the movie "Norma Rae", his sister would not be convinced otherwise of opportunity down that way. As for Marander writing the State of Franklin tribute, of course, as long as she lived, so did her family's proud charter role in an important early chapter of the history of Tennessee. The bit about Mr. Mumpower's line of work came as no surprise. And now that he thought about it, when had Marander ever said more than need be said. Indeed, as long as the girl she rescued from the ruins of

Coventry knew she was cared for, who else need know? Should anyone have pressed her as to why she never mentioned Anna Middleton to anyone in Tennessee, she would have said Anna was a child in need, not a feather for her hat.

The horseshoe crab was making its slow progress past the second of the town's three remaining ocean-front mansions when they overtook it. He gave his sister the benefit of Stan-the-scientific-barber's tutorial on the primitive species: not a crab at all really, more like a giant member of the lowly tick family. He added a bit about the color of its blood — blue and not red — blue as Gus Snyder's, were they to credit their former stepfather's claim to royal descent. Lastly, he explained certain curative capacities inherent in the blood of *Limulus Polyphemus*. Up to a third of an individual horseshoe crab's blood supply could be drained and it still would survive.

Later, after one last dip, Robbie drove Penny out to their mother's mostly vacated house on the Point. No rush; he'd find a game on the radio. In the end though, with the sun nearly down and the Yankee lead holding in the bottom of the eighth, he switched off the game and went inside.

"It's not like I haven't been in every closet," she said. "Mother tells me what it looks like — like I won't know a royal-blue summer-weight blazer when I meet one? Besides, I really do think she does this to plague me."

"You think she'd ask you to look for something she knows isn't here?"

"I just think this whole miserable chapter of my life should be over with."

He shrugged. Who knew better than he how the hard part was being in Gus Snyder's flood-lit monument to himself even for a minute — the home from which Penny and their sister Paula had been sent away to boarding school following their mother's brief second widowhood and hasty third marriage to Gus the next year.

"Let's go," she said finally, still fuming as she re-zipped the last wardrobe bag. "If I don't make my bus, I'll have an hour's wait."

Her bus, due at the corner of Ocean Avenue and Beach Street at ten minutes past the hour, never came, or else came and went in the two minutes they had been late. "No problem," she insisted, out of his car and on the sidewalk before he could think to object, her expensive suede totes parked smartly on the curb, one at each foot. In the end though, he prevailed. In the morning he'd gladly drive her into the city, he assured her, returning her totes to the back seat.

The next morning he was up first, or thought he was before glimpsing his sister's cropped new boy-cut disappearing from view down the path to the barn. His habit was to turn in when the sun went down. But with the bottle of wine uncorked, he might have known that her nostalgia for the good years in their grandfather's storied house on the inlet would find a way into their conversation. Count on Penny to reminisce about sleepovers at Marander's tiny Groomtown farm, the site where seeds for his fresh produce business first were sown. Still anything to bring up old times it seemed, as how fond she had always been of Anna and Marander, as they had been of her.

"Sorry, no cream," he told Penny as she plopped down beside him on the porch glider, "but there's two-percent in the fridge."

"No per cent is my limit, but thanks. Was there not a cat somewhere growing up?"

"Not at our house," he said, thinking *not the cat again*, when it was never a real cat, but a puppet, a rowdy tom that Anna named Marco Polo. "And not at Marander's. Marander had Babs."

"Right, Babs the tortoise. So the cat was over at Martinelli's, because I distinctly remember a cat, a gray tom. Magdalena and Mario were the tap-dancing Martinelli twins, the same age as you. Daddy sold them their tap shoes at our shoe store. Then Angelina was born in 1954, the same year I was, the year Hurricane Carol aimed for New Jersey and hit New England instead. Between the twins and Angelina were four more boys, all with brown eyes and double-jointed thumbs. Daddy always said, 'Such a lot of twaddle in such a pretty head,' and mean it as a compliment. Not that our adorable sister Paula wasn't always his favorite."

"My impression was that *you* were."

"I just tried the hardest. Mrs. Martinelli did alterations, which put Anna's puppets first in line for discarded shoulder pads and busted zippers, for buttons, buckram, rickrack, wooden spools, embroidery yarns, and all available shoe leather. Remember Anna's show 'School for Puppets' and her bristle-browed, pointer-waving, Methodist deaconess e-nun-ci-a-ting her diph-thongs?"

"As if I've ever been allowed to forget."

"Remembering people you've loved isn't a sin, Robbie. Why not remember them? I mean as long as you were at Grandfather's, life was good. You had Marander and Anna right next door to keep up your spirits. And all those war jobs flushing out good honest folks from the hinterlands like bunnies from the brush. So many good people around back then! If you count Marander, you even had a spare mom. Sure, eventually Mother would have Daddy and the shoe store, but Paula and I, we came this close to being born a bigamist's kids."

That he remembered. He'd been a boy of ten when it all came out in the wash. "Let's not," he objected, as if one mention of the two-timing, side-winder from the west could still turn his ears red, a yarn-spinner who knew just what to say to a boy. Things like *critters* and *riding the circuit* and *bagging my limit*. What if Marander had been less astute and not pegged Sarge for the spoiled goods he was? Or worse, what if his mother's lonely heart had ruled?

"Mind soft-boiling me an egg while I shower? I have to get back."

"One egg... soft for the little lady in the wrinkled shirt."

This sister's view of the world, he'd had to conclude, was probably not so different from anyone else's, bright-side-up when not-so-good things were happening to others or before her time. By her reckoning, his father's premature death was a setback. Their mother's long train commutes and six-day work weeks at Depression's end, the brass ring; close calls in the mating game — no real harm done. From his perspective, saddest of all, was her blithe prediction they should look for Anna on the next plane, when in 1961 Marander had bought Anna's one-way ticket home to England. As if Penny could even begin to understand how homesick their poor Anna was by then.

"Hope you don't mind," Penny said as she hiked his men's large terry cloth robe up off the floor, her hair still damp from the shower. "I have a feeling we all got these last Christmas. Lately when Mother goes shopping, she goes shopping in catalogs. And she talks on and on about Bare's Shoes for Boys and Girls. She says these days that we don't fit shoes. We buy shoes that don't fit and throw them away."

"And she's right too. Muffin or toast?"

"Just the egg for me."

"I was twelve when your father adopted me, five years yet till you'd be along. He taught me the ABCs of getting a customer in the door, how a high wheel c.1889 Columbia bicycle prominently displayed by the entrance could save your business a bundle on ads. Good old Roy, always thinking. All those envelope flaps of his covered in doodles. Remember his doodles, Pen?"

"Of course, I remember. Daddy died three weeks after President Kennedy died, two weeks before I turned ten. When I woke from mourning, my childhood was done. Where were you? Because all I remember is everyone was gone — Anna, you, Marander, the President, then Daddy. Nobody was left but Mother and Paula. And I never knew Grandfather. All I knew was his house."

For reasons Robbie could never divine, Penny would always blank on her own brother in uniform. He'd enlisted in the army when Anna left for England. When Roy died, he was en route to Asmara. "You obviously don't remember this, but I was ready to ship out when Kennedy was killed. And when Marander returned from getting Anna settled in England, she went on back home to Tennessee."

"Sorry, I remember now. But you'll always be my touchstone, Robbie. You're why I *scull on, toes to Greenland*. I do, because you do. I may even wish I was you. All I know is I have to pay through the nose for this new boy-cut. What do you think? Am I improving with age?"

"I've always thought you were the funniest," he said, but if he'd had his eyes shut, his impression might have been of lips turned down at the corners, an over-sized tear sliding down a mime's chalk-white cheek, an effect she might have been trying for. With Penny, he never knew what to think, though it was true what she said; she'd known only Grandfather's house, never the man himself. Now their mother was up in years, the only house left was the house on the Point still doing its best imitation of the Taj Mahal.

"Thanks," she said. "I feel fine too, except sometimes I can't quite picture the important things anymore. Once I could conjure our inlet complete with rotting bulkhead and leaking rowboats, Grandfather's shabby old Victorian there behind the bulkhead, hiding its poverty in horse chestnut shade, Anna and you in the swing, Marander singeing pin feathers off our Sunday dinner, Daddy bushed after long days of fitting shoes, all those lively Martinellis in their house built for the ages next door… Mrs. M flirting with Daddy, dreamy Mr. M undressing Mother with his eyes…"

They didn't talk much on the way in, too many phone calls. If high tech was her cup of tea, fine with him. And in the end, naturally she changed her mind. They were on the bridge heading inland, the white-capped Atlantic, historic Spermacetti lifesaving station, and the wild blue yonder behind them. Somehow, he'd sensed the change in plans coming. "I'll just take the bus back in," she said, assembling her totes as he drove down the far side of the bridge to the bus stop. "No need to spoil another day. I have my ticket. This way you don't give up your swim." He didn't argue. He loved a drive, but hated an argument, especially an argument with her.

He didn't go for his swim in the ocean though, or even go for a walk. By eleven, the club parking lot had begun to fill with freshly liberated young mothers, their children delivered to school desks and someone else's supervision. From the boardwalk, he heard some of them ask the beach boy to arrange their umbrellas in a half circle against the wind, the ash blond he thought of as *the misfit* not among them. They'd had a friendly exchange just after the club opened for the season in May. She'd lost her charm bracelet, by the lifeboat, she thought. She looked to be older than the others, maybe even approaching his age, though taking some pains to look young. He looked familiar too, she told him, but didn't think from here, meaning the club. He'd seen her only one or two times since.

It surprised him somehow that the old stone church was still standing, the one he nearly drove by, the same one first his grandfather and then Marander had walked him to, taking the long way around. And the two blocks of squat summer cottages set in swamp willow shade were unchanged, as was the ripe vegetable smell of the salt marsh with the tide going out. There were many more cars on the street, not as many women pushing strollers or children on tricycles, no yards crisscrossed with clotheslines weighed down with heavy beach towels and terry beach robes and wet bathing suits.

His grandfather's house was still in need of fresh paint. The wine grapes on what looked like their old arbor were ripe, possibly past ripe, and the porch swing was there where he and Anna at thirteen had sat holding hands an entire love-smitten summer. The Martinelli's stucco house built for the ages was gone, along with attending concrete angels and a cast-iron church bell. The bulkhead in front of Marander's bungalow looked sturdier now. Two new fiber-glass versions of their ancient rowboats — one the Albertina, the other the Seabird, named for the big commuters making the New Jersey to New York run in his mother's youth — rocked in the shallows side by side.

In childhood, the bridge had been a place for games of conkers with Anna when the horse chestnuts ripened and fell to the ground, for dropping bait cans tied to the rail over the side, for meeting the doctor when Anna's chronic lung condition caused her lungs to collapse. Anna, who was never strong... or tall, who when she went home to England at twenty-three was only half the weight of the big woman from Tennessee — a woman who could win every foot race and every boat race who could stand shoulder to shoulder with his grandfather tossing back rounds at Kirk's and still get them on their pins and back home again.

Now Kirk's was gone and the bridge gone and, since that day in June, Marander was gone too, making those times seem but a distant interlude, a time when people from different walks of life came together for a moment, and afterwards went their separate ways again. Now at the mid-point of the seventh decade of life, he was himself no longer a man in the thick of things, but a man often sidelined by a changed world. Perhaps, the time had come to reflect on long ingrained hierarchies and habits of mind laid down in his youth, to consider what lost State of Franklin he would rise to defend. Though, to the end he hoped to hear the age-old confabulations, ones like *Scull on! Toes to Greenland*, so instilled they might have heard them as they rocked and sloshed in the womb. Not that anyone knew the origin or the exact meaning of them, just that there was much comfort in them.

He was in luck for a change; only one customer at The Scientific Barber's, an older man of eighty or so with a hearing aid in each ear. He had to be a new customer or someone from out-of-town. Something about him though had caught Robbie's attention, not an accent, but a way of putting things — calling a *whirl pool* a "sucky hole", something Marander would say.

"The fellow just leaving was signal corps," Stan said by way of explanation, starting to sweep up after the man left. "He's been coming for half a century, but this is his last reunion. Not that many WWII vets left anymore. He was telling me about his work for the Geological Survey. He had a job with them when they discovered it was a meteorite that opened up Cumberland Gap 300 million years ago. Daniel Boone's destiny writ large by a falling star. Here, take a look."

"Scatter cones? Never heard of them. Shocked quartz?"

"The clues tipping them off. I'll see what else I can find out. You in for a trim or just for a chat?"

"Just a chat."

"Your sister Paula's youngest was in day before yesterday."

"That'd be Roy."

"He was telling me you lived with your grandfather by the river growing up. I told him I didn't know that part of your history. I just know you from here. The same way you know me."

"All I hope is this Roy turns into half the man his grandfather was, because the first Roy was really somebody. Not that there weren't lots of others just as fine back then. But these days I'm not so sure. Sometimes I think what it all comes down to is sorting out what's important and finding the guts to take things on. Like this woman I once knew who came up from Tennessee to do her part for the war effort."

"One of those 'Rosie the Riveter' types?"

"No, not that she couldn't have been. She didn't go in the service either, but by some means she did manage to get herself shipped overseas on a merchant ship in the middle of the Blitz. I have a picture of that ship somewhere. Then she came home with a little war orphan she was nursing back to health. You've possibly heard of Anna Middleton."

"The same Anna your sister Paula speaks of so fondly?"

"The same."

"Whatever became of her?"

"Eventually she went back to England." He would have gone on to say the woman who went over to help when Anna turned so ill at the end was that same woman from Tennessee. But then the two youngest Crosley boys had come in, followed by Cristela Ruiz and her son Rafael. Cristela had been one of the regulars at his market, one of two or three who still kept in touch, calling Mr. Robbie quite often with her news. A native of the Dominican Republic, she wired money home each month. He wired money too, receiving snapshots of smiling strangers in return.

Groomtown was that kind of town, the kind where people know each other by first and last names, where the fruit stand man holds the spare door keys to a dozen private homes and the key to the kind of secrets only the few are privy to. And not just the 300-million-year-old geological kind finally traceable to anomalous forms found in Cumberland Gap. Very important was this durable mortar that bound the parts of the whole together, securing all that will rise on the foundation.

Back when he was a boy cared for by Marander, she usually was prompt calling for him after his Sunday school class let out, arriving with ruddy cheeks and giving off whiffs of Lucky Strike cigarettes, salt air, and plain old-fashioned satisfaction. But there was that one extraordinary Sunday when she arrived late, her cheeks pleated and pale as she told of a young feller standing guard in the guard tower erected for the coastal defense. Marander always said it "feller", as if "fellow" came with an "r" at the end. She said this boy was by then eleven years of age, not yet seven when he'd been made a ward of the state at a time when many folks were poor. Such a sad young man she described, one with long shaggy hair hanging down over his eyes, the same troubled green-brown as the churning surf they gazed out on.

For years after the black-outs were over and the coast secure again, after the victory gardens had long since been reseeded to lawns, he would imagine a young boy climbing the concrete steps to his watch. And for years after that, he imagined he'd see him coming in past the big cast-iron grizzly for his fresh Jersey tomatoes and his fresh ears of corn, looking as if he too had prospered and was aging nicely into an older version of that shaggy-haired youth.

Over the years, Robbie had pondered starting with the one small plot and adding another and another, gradually building up a people's garden in the field lying fallow just down the end of his road, a garden lush and fruitful renewed over long frozen winters to green up come the spring. Each time he'd pause to consider if by his time in life he was already too late, if the season for sowing was already gone. Now recalling Marander and her one true state of mind over matter, he was reminded that "too late" was never more than a poor excuse for not even trying. And he'd have plenty of time now. Now he'd have all the time he'd need and maybe even time to spare.

*NOTE:

[The State of Franklin existed in a transitional period at the end of the American Revolution when the Continental Congress found itself heavily in debt and in need of assets. It consisted of four remote northwestern North Carolina counties that the state legislature voted to include in a 29-million-acre cession to the federal government. Two years later those same counties would form the State of Franklin (1784) with both a constitution and a governor (Sevier) before collapsing in 1789 and being returned once again to the control of North Carolina. Soon after, these independent, hard-to govern trans-mountain counties were ceded to the federal government to form the Southwest Territory, the precursor of Tennessee.]

The Ballad of
Ashe-lee Wilkes

MY WHOLE LIFE I HAVE WANTED A STORY OF MY OWN, but now that I've got one, I am almost too pained to tell it. From the very first I could see the light shining, a glow given off from deep down on the inside of only truly good people. And my friend wasn't one little bit proud or important, lest maybe a wee tiny bit proud on the beauty side of things. She did have those two round-as-a-hoe handle plaits down to her brisket that could get a person to wondering where she was from. Where she was from was right here in the good old U. S. of A., as American as we are.

Why I would ask her up on my porch was because she had a way about her. Naturally it suited me having some grown-up company. In those days I'd get lonesome, tied down with two babies and Marion mostly gone on his route. It didn't hurt either passing off a whole entire afternoon swapping tales, mine all about how these old blood stains would come back up through the porch floor in the same exact spot on the same exact day of the year when this traveling man took a knife and cut up the neighbor woman. It happened yonder, past the Free Will Church and the last low water bridge before the little fork joins up with the big fork. That's how I'd tell it. Lord, how I did love that tale.

This girl Hana stayed here at the house with me all the rest of that week. She carried me to the A & P and to pay my electric, and to look after our graves where Old 16 takes off down the mountain. This one day she carried me clear to Yadkinville and then on over to Daddy Hob's Curb Market in Stokesdale. She'd have took me just anywhere and surely taught me to drive her straight shift car, except what would be the use in that, seeing as Marion didn't want me running around the countryside.

Like I said, this girl was a single girl. All the kin she had in the world was her brother, and he lived out in Utah or Idaho. Once I could call up the exact place because Wade would forget sometimes and leave her mail off here by mistake. Wade could be careless that way. But this Hana was a good hand to get work done for being so slight of stature. Over the years, she patched up our leaks and pulled oil pans and stuck calves and laid out row on row of queer little vegetables and cooked up the best tasting dinners we ever did sit down to.

But I'm getting ahead of myself here, and if I have any hope of getting this right, I surely do need to keep to the order of things. The times we were a-living in back then weren't like now. Then we still visited over our party lines. We traded help with our haying and with hanging and grading our tobacco. We flagged our neighbors down in the road to pass off the time. We praised alongside kinfolks of a Sunday and lay down next to them finally in the same graveyards as the ancestors before us. It's how we were then, us kin, every which way you can be kin and her with no kin at all.

Then about the third night she stayed here, my husband's brother Hamp took a notion to come meet who was riding me around. And I reckon Hamp's courage came out of a quart jar, for he busted in just a-singing and got the babies woke up and next I know she's woke up, too. Because in he come and flopped down in her bed, and me not being a drinking person or ever once seeing Hamp or Marion or any Howell take the first swallow of whiskey, I had to call in the Rescue.

By rights that shoulda ended it, but then Marion turned up a day ahead, on a Thursday night and not a Friday night. And setting outside his house in the moonlight was this strange car with the strange plates on it, though to his credit he did keep his head and stay outside in the barn till I went out to milk come morning. Still, what you have to wonder is would I be calling any of this up had this Hana gone on like she planned? If not for me hunting a way to keep her here, would all the trouble not have passed us by?

Of course I was set on her staying. In my mind we'd hire her to help out Hamp with his chores. He needed help and we wouldn't be so out of pocket with some room and board thrown in. But I'm here to tell you, Hana woulda done anything for him, and he was like a new wet colt each time she'd come back from Utah or Idaho or from wherever it was she went. For Hamp, it was like the sun had went to rising in the east again. Lord, you never saw a man so gone on a woman as poor Hamp was on her.

I need to mention now about the polio he'd had as a child, because it was why he dragged his one leg so bad. But his misfortune maybe kept him humble too, since Hamp was the one looker of the whole Howell line. The girls all have those pug muzzles and little pig eyes, and Marion and the two other boys just shot up and never did fill out. But their sister Cora was who in the end did him in with something she fixed him for his dinner. Hamp and my husband and a whole truckload of Howells sat up making music the entire night just before Cora came down. I mean to tell you, there wasn't a thing the matter with Hamp Howell, not then. I was there.

But after Cora came down, Hamp never was the same again. First his head was a-paining him and then he wouldn't eat his supper nor anything the next morning either. The third day, he commenced telling his mommy it was past time he took a wife;

this when his mommy already was gone to Jesus. Naturally, we called Doc Elhart out and stayed all night with him, then two nights more till he fell back on his pillow and died. He was forty-eight years old and, by then Hana had been with him for over a dozen years.

I mean to tell you this is some hard remembering calling up all this long-ago story. For a good while, I was too sorry to speak her name for we didn't do right by her. I told Marion I'd never forgive him if he did what he was about to, which was break that will. And, of course, he did break it, and I didn't forgive him, not that our book of troubles opened or closed with that chapter. He was always high and mighty about his Howell name, when all we owned in this world was land the creeks rode up and scrubbed clean of all our hard work. Lord, and even our best land a clean shot straight down to the valley.

I truly did believe Hamp making out his will the way he did was only fair. For after all was said and done, was it not still just an old cold country house? What was Marion going to do with that pitiful place anyway? What would it hurt? And why not show some gratitude for all the good help she gave us? But then before I could get up my courage, my friend Hana slicked out of here whilst we slept. The day after we laid Hamp in his grave, Hana was gone.

The phone call that got all this revved up again came from Hana's niece. By that time though, I'd had some twenty-five or more years to disremember most all of it, so when she said she was Hana Niko's niece Junko, it didn't mean a thing to me. But according to my least daughter Dinah, I went white as a bed sheet. And after that I hardly could sleep for what would come into my mind of a night, none of it good because even a run-of-the mill sinner at something past sixty can apply herself to Satan's book of temptations and get a passing grade. But Dinah said my imagination was working on overtime, and since when did our old friend Hana coming to see us mean bad news.

"Well," she said, "and then what about the night we went out to see the total eclipse of the moon with her and that woman from New York staying in her school bus down in our laurels?"

I told her I remembered it. I'm here to say it wasn't one of our good times. And maybe it *was* us Howells and Hana. But the woman from New York staying in her school bus down in our laurels wasn't with us that night, and we never did see the total eclipse of the moon either because of what went on. Dinah was only a little child, still too young yet to appreciate just how ugly certain people can turn, especially when the certain person was her own daddy — not that I'm excused in all this.

What I remember is Hana making the acquaintance with some woman from far off when she went to get gas down at the river bridge store. Hana was friendly with everyone, and as far as I knew, might of went and met the whole countryside while I was home folding my sheets. By some means, this woman she met had got her school bus moved down to our big laurels where, if quiet was what a person had in mind, it was quiet as it was likely to get. And no way would you even know her little bus was there, lest you stumbled upon it. And that was what Marion did when he shooed us out of the wind the night of the total eclipse of the moon.

Now I need to back up some and say I don't believe any of us ever knew just where this woman staying in her school bus was from. To us, New York was as foreign as Fiji back then. If we went anywhere, we went to Winston in the ambulance or to revival down in Wilkes. A big adventure was thrill-riding the back roads with only the moonlight and a blanket of fresh snow to light the way. We only said she was from New York because she didn't much care what anyone thought of her, and mostly didn't wear shoes in a time when some could remember the Episcopals from up North coming down to mend our barefoot ways.

Still, that school bus of hers was just like a jewel box inside. Where we'd sit she'd have these big old velvet pillows, and she'd give us hot tea in little tea cups and tell us about her life and where all she'd been. Evenings after the sun went down, she'd tie a silk shawl around her shoulders and then one around her waist. She looked like a gypsy must look, and I always had it in my mind I might be a gypsy too, as much as I was anything. I can remember her telling about some far-away place and how it turned a golden green come springtime and the scent of apple blooms lay so heavy and sweet upon the land. But I couldn't say how many summers she came and stayed down in our laurels, because I cannot truthfully remember anymore, only how good it was her being with us each time she was here.

Now something you have to understand about is how some Howell men will fly out at you. It's why I say the night of the eclipse was not a good night for us Howells. And why it would turn out to be the beginning of the end is because, in Marion's book, Howell loyalty was what counted. When Marion found out his own brother knew about the school bus being parked on our Howell land and knew about the woman living down there and never once said, and even worse went and took up for Hana and me on that dark and terrible night... well, like I said, it was the beginning of the end. And when the end would come was only a matter of time.

So now I'll say who I was before I married a Howell, because before that I was a Meadows, and before that even, I was a woods colt till somebody dropped me at the Children's Home. I stayed there till 1950 and I left when I was eight. My lawful name was Ashe-lee Wilkes and everybody thought I was named after the man Leslie Howard played in "Gone with the Wind", but how I see it is, they put the dash in for the simple reason they wanted me to know I came from Ashe or Wilkes county up here by the Virginia line.

My best memory of the Children's Home was of sleeping porches and watching a family over across the way out my window. There was a mother and a father and a girl about my age. I remember the girl riding a little red bicycle up and down the street, waiting for her daddy to come home. He wore a necktie to work every day, and so I told myself he had a good job in one of those cigarette plants downtown. Other than that, all I remember is busloads of children in Sunday clothes coming to see how us orphans lived and BJ bragging her folks were murdered by Indians and Faith telling about her famous circus family getting killed in a high wire accident and going all around the country living in a Pullman car. And me, I didn't have a story of my own, not then.

But Mother Meadows always did have the stories. She'd tell people she picked me because I was pretty and pink, even though we all knew it was all because I behaved. She did truly like pink, and I did have color in my cheeks and my chest, and my shoulders would go a bright shade of pink any time I played hard. It wasn't the sun either. It was just how I was. Before she came and picked me because I was pink and had light hair and eyes, I always wanted to be cocoa colored like the girl riding her little red bicycle across the way from the Children's Home.

But there can be important things missing in your make-up even when you do get adopted. It's just you don't always understand what makes you so quick to latch on. I know I latched on tight to Mother Meadows, but not out of love. I let her train me up like a little puppy dog and never did raise a fuss over any part of it. She broke me of my whistling. She dressed me. She took me out of school when it suited her, picked where I worked summers and said who all I could date. I wouldn't call them boyfriends exactly. And long before I ever became a Howell, I was already the state champ for going along.

As for Daddy Hob though, I always did worship the ground he walked on. By the time Daddy Hob took me to his deMolay picnic and we met Marion for the first time, I was ripe for any young man with a nose for opportunity. I just didn't know it. I didn't know it because I didn't know anything. I had my head up in the clouds. But was it love? I told myself it was, and then let Mother Meadows pick my bridesmaids and let Daddy Hob give me away and Marion take over from there.

It would have been the next day after the eclipse of the moon talk I had with Dinah when I woke up feeling so out of sorts. I won't deny I was dreading Hana coming. Some things in life you'd sooner not face up to. That's when I went to pulling up my flowers and my bean plants and got out my bristle broom and went to sweeping, and then I pulled my hose around and washed down everything in sight. After that, I went and lay down in Marion's old Dodge truck for I couldn't say how long, an hour maybe or two hours, or it may have been a day or even a week.

I can tell you about the dream I was dreaming whilst I was lying there. I can tell you it was in the month of May, for our apple trees were blooming and, in this dream I was about to pin apple blossoms to Hana's bosom, and the spring air was so thick and sweet that day we could have poured it from a pitcher. And besides, the bride looked happy and the groom looked handsome, and even the preacher looked to be the same one as the one who saved Marion and me so very long ago.

Just let me say this. The last times I saw Hana before she left out of here, she was like always. Still no bigger than a minute, her long plaits shiny and dark as the day she came. A good old soul who liked everybody and everybody liked her back. But then Hamp died and you never saw a light go out so fast. I can't say it was the funeral for certain, but you know funerals. All the people coming, and the pews filling up, and still more people standing in the aisles. And everyone telling stories about different kin maybe you never did know because they maybe go back closer to the beginning of things, and then you think, *just who am I in all this?* I probably shouldn't be saying this, should I, because I don't know that's how she woulda felt.

I was expecting someone with some wear on her, a woman of sixty or sixty-five or even seventy. I never did know Hana's exact age. And I waited for her and her niece to get up on the porch before telling about Marion and me. I said we weren't still married, and said how it's better that way when two people are so opposite. That's about the time she said she never meant to cause trouble and did truly love Hamp, and that Marion always did have it all wrong about her. I said Marion was old-timey, and people like him try to stand off any changes coming, and even knowing Sprinkles his whole life wasn't enough when it came to Harley Sprinkle marrying one of his girls.

The hard part though was telling Hana there wasn't a house anymore. I told her Marion had the volunteer firemen out and they bulldozed it after they burned it down. We were standing just inside the door. I was looking behind her at the catalpa tree where the road branched to go to Hamp's, thinking I won't tell her the worst. I won't tell her where Hamp's house once stood is where now stands Cora's double-wide. And I won't tell her across the road is its twin for Marion. And alongside it is the old green school bus he keeps his Banties in. But then, bless their hearts, here come my girls, Mattie and Dinah, who hugged Hana and hugged her pretty dark-haired niece Junko too, acting like it was just another summer day.

I wish I could remember more of that day. I can picture Mattie at the foot of the table, Hana and her niece across from Dinah with her back to the kitchen. And I can hear Hana telling about this one hot June night. How we'd settled Mattie between us on the porch swing, but Dinah kept fighting sleep till Hamp got out his mouth harp and went to playing all those old blues tunes he'd learned back when he had polio and had to stay in the polio hospital down in Greensboro. For once, nobody bothered about color at all and for once, black and white could bunk side by side and play on their harmonicas. Now I surely know at least some little part of every one of us is not all that is known, if known at all. Otherwise why would I not have been told the story about Hamp and the little black boy down at the polio hospital? Why would Hamp think to tell it to Hana and not think to tell it to me? I would love to have known that story because I live for stories like that one, even if I can't say just why.

But still, I did know in my heart what she'd come back to tell me after all those years. I'd seen at least the one letter Wade left here by mistake with all those strange numbers on the envelope. And I knew she'd come up hard, her and her brother both, because she'd told me how their daddy died in the war and their mother died young and being locked up like traitors broke her Japanese-American grandparents' spirit. And I surely knew when you come up hard, you need to be more than just good to get on.

More than that, I knew just how much Hana loved keeping Hamp's old house for him. And how much getting out of a cold winter morning to feed his cattle meant to her. How she looked forward to the end of summer and leaning our sticks of tobacco up in rows of golden tents to dry in the sun. I knew how she loved her life here, and all I had to say was, "I know, Hana. I know everything. I know about your brother being in the prison. And I know about you and Hamp. It's fine. Really. All of it's fine." I could have said it many times. I could have unlocked those words of love inside of me so many times.

These days I think about all that's gone before. About the little black girl riding her bike and about Daddy Hob. About my children and my home and how we don't grow our Burley anymore. I think about the stories, Hana's about Hamp and the boy at the polio hospital and the different stories the woman in the school bus told. I just told my sons-in-law the one about the truck farm Hana's family once owned free and clear out by a big white snowy mountain away in the west somewhere. And the story about after Pearl Harbor and how President Roosevelt rounded up all the people who looked like Hana and the story I'm just now telling for the first time — how I turned my back on my friend and didn't lift a finger when I could of done.

Now we've got these new people moving into the old Speas place across the way. I can hear them over there; Dinah tells me the wife of the house works at our bank. One day I'll go over and meet them all; now I'm myself again. Just yesterday I went to whistling a tune that brought back the name of the woman in the little green school bus. I think of her out sunning, down where the old grinding mill got washed away in the flood. I do truly believe she was a gypsy, and believe a part of me could be a gypsy too in a world so upside down as this one is.

About the Author

JOANNE JOHNSTON FRANCIS rarely thinks of herself as a writer, rather as a person in search of the meaning of "home". Unlike her character Sparrow, whose constant uprooting leaves her uncertain as to where home is, regular uprooting over a lifetime has left this author believing almost anywhere is home.

In finding her "way into" very different lives, she sees the challenge as a matter of growing accustomed to the local rhythm of a day's work, whether hanging burley leaves to cure in a Blue Ridge Mountain tobacco barn, carving a Salish journey canoe from western red cedar using adze and crooked knife, or learning how to rhyme couplets from her eighth-grade students in Harlem, before rap.

On display here in this memorable collection are lives lived off the beaten track. The author begins with the premise that no one person is average and no single culture wholly unique. Her stories celebrate our small individual moments of courage and the fact that those moments of courage are more common than we think.

Acknowledgments

My geography keeps me connected with those making this story collection possible. It begins in Monmouth Beach, New Jersey in 1943. Happily, my mother Christine Johnston at 100 will see her name in print here and read my book. The 1950s took our family west to El Paso, Texas, then south to locations in North Carolina's Piedmont. With so much continual uprooting, old friends have given me a gift of roots I would never have without them. My dear high school friend Iris Anderson White and college friends Karen Parker, Beth Fineberg, Mary Ann Fitzgerald, Stephanie Wilbur-Danhi, Bonnie Mayerson, Sondra Wilson, Perry Young, Charles and Pat Thompson, and Gary Poe, have given me continuity and a sense of belonging.

In 1969 my geography turned me westward once again, this time from New York City to the State of Washington. My many Washington homes include island, mountain, urban and quite remote rustic ones. My supporting cast here includes so many, among them Mark Runions, Reni Moriarity, Susan Sailer, Linda Finkas, Sarah Morgan, Bob Ness, Wendy Firth, Jill Kinney, Therese Grant, Jennifer Fox, Mona Davies, Pam Ryker, and Bryce Cornatzer.

An inspired return to North Carolina in the late 1970s brought me friendship with Joanie Bell, my cover artist and longtime friend. Not so long ago a twist of fate sent me to a closet in search of old letters. So much of life and living is accidental; so much of what makes life rich and worthwhile, complex. Over the years the stories and experiences of each of your lives have enriched my life. Through all, Dale Francis, my husband of 33 years, has steered a steady course. For his support and for that given me by all of you I stand forever in your debt.

And finally, this collection stood in need of one last leg-up. My intrepid editor, Val Dumond, brought belief in both my storytelling and in the opportunity offered by independent publishing. With Val as my ever-cheerful navigator through this process, these fifteen stories have now become a book.

Made in the USA
Lexington, KY
17 September 2017